The Siege of Eternity
Book 2 of The Eschaton Sequence

The Other End of Time
Book 1 of the Eschaton Sequence

O Pioneer!

BOOKS BY FREDERIK POHL

THE HEECHEE SAGA
  Gateway
  *Beyond the Blue Event
    Horizon*
  Heechee Rendezvous
  The Annals of the Heechee
  The Gateway Trip

THE ESCHATON SEQUENCE
  The Other End of Time
  The Siege of Eternity
  The Far Shore of Time

  The Age of the Pussyfoot
  Drunkard's Walk
  Black Star Rising
  The Cool War
  Homegoing
  Mining the Oort
  Narabedla Ltd.
  Pohlstars
  Starburst
  The Way the Future Was
    (memoir)
  *The World at the End of
    Time*
  Jem
  Midas World
  Merchant's War
  *The Coming of the
  Quantum Cats*

Man Plus
Chernobyl
The Day the Martians Came
Stopping at Slowyear
The Voices of Heaven
O Pioneer!
The Best of Frederik Pohl
  (edited by Lester del Rey)

With Jack Williamson:
  The Starchild Trilogy
  Undersea City
  Undersea Quest
  Undersea Fleet
  Wall Around a Star
  The Farthest Star
  Land's End
  The Singer's of Time

With Lester del Rey
  Preferred Risk

With C. M. Kornbluth:
  The Space Merchants

The Best of Frederik Pohl
  (edited by Lester del Rey)
The Best of C. M. Kornbluth
  (editor)

*denotes a Tor book

FREDERIK POHL

THE FAR SHORE OF TIME

A TOM DOHERTY ASSOCIATES BOOK
NEW YORK

This is a work of fiction. All the characters and events portrayed in this book are either products of the author's imagination or are used fictitiously.

THE FAR SHORE OF TIME

Copyright © 1996 by Frederik Pohl

Edited by James Frenkel

A Tor Book
Published by Tom Doherty Associates, LLC
175 Fifth Avenue
New York, NY 10010

www.tor.com

Tor® is a registered trademark of Tom Doherty Associates, LLC.

ISBN: 0-812-57783-3

First edition: July 1999
First mass market edition: March 2000

Printed in the United States of America

0 9 8 7 6 5 4 3 2 1

For Betty Anne,
as always

PART ONE

Before

We were actually on our way home when it happened. We didn't have any doubt that that was where we were going, and we were, boy, *ready*. We had been months and months in the captivity of a weird alien creature from another world, the one we called Dopey. He was alien, all right. He looked sort of like a large chicken with a kitten's face and a peacock's tail, and he had kidnapped the lot of us—snatched us right out of the old Starlab astronomical satellite and thrown us into some kind of space-traveling machine that whisked us from *here* to some unbelievably distant *there* in no time at all. And *there* was where Dopey kept us, in one damn miserably uncomfortable prison or another, on this unpleasant planet we had never heard of before.

That was a truly nasty experience, but, the way it looked to us at the time, it was *over!* Against the odds, we had escaped! Our chance to get away came when some rival gang of nonhumans, these ones called the "Horch," invaded our prison planet. In the confusion we fought our way to the matter-transmitter thing, and jumped in, and were on our way home. I was the last to climb into the machine. . . .

And I saw the pale lavender flash that meant it was working. . . .

And I came out again. . . .

But I wasn't home at all. The place I was in didn't look at all like Starlab. A pair of those silvery-spidery Horch wheeled fighting machines that had been trying to kill us were standing there, not half a dozen meters away. This time they weren't shooting at me, though. If they had been, I couldn't have shot back, because something I couldn't see grabbed me from behind—no, *enveloped* me, in an all-points hug that didn't let me move a muscle—as I heard the machine's door open again.

Dopey spilled out on top of me, plume all ruffled, little cat eyes glaring around in terror. He took one look at the machines and began to shake. Something hard and painful was pressing behind my right ear. I managed to yell a question at Dopey; and just before the lights went out he sobbed an answer: "Agent Dannerman, we are in the hands of the Horch."

And that was the nastiest, the very nastiest, moment of all.

PART TWO

Interrogation

CHAPTER TWO

When I woke up I was lying on a hard, glassy floor. My head felt as though someone had taken a baseball bat to it.

I kept my eyes prudently closed for a moment. I listened, trying to figure out where I was and what I was doing there. All I heard was an occasional skritchy-tinkly sound, like an incomplete set of cheap wind chimes, and now and then a faint whir that sounded a little like skate wheels on a hard floor.

That told me nothing useful, so I took the plunge. I opened my eyes and scrambled to my feet. That made my headache worse, but was the least of my immediate worries. I was in serious trouble.

The room I found myself in was smallish and square, with shiny walls that looked as though they were made of some sort of pale yellow porcelain. There was nothing on the walls—no windows, no decorations—only a couple of doors, both securely closed.

I was not alone in the room.

Two bizarre machines were hovering over a small chest, made out of the same primrose chinaware as the walls. They weren't the spidery Horch fighting machines I'd seen before. What they looked like, more than anything else, was a pair of squat, crystalline Christmas trees. They had spiky glass branches coming off a central trunk, and twigs off the branches, and needles off the twigs—yes, and littler needles coming off the needles, too. For all I knew there were still littler needles than those as well, but I didn't see them. Each of the machines was topped off by a sort of glassy globe, where the angel should have been on a proper Christmas tree, and these were faceted and glittery, like the rotating mirror spheres people rent to cast little spangles of light around a dance floor. One of the things was a pale green, the other a rosy pink. It seemed to me—that was hope speaking, not wisdom—that they looked pretty fragile. Whatever they were up to, I thought, I would have something to say about, because one swift kick would shatter a quorum of their glassy needles.

I was quite wrong about that, of course.

They evidently took notice of the fact that I was awake. The green one did something queer with some of its needles. Clusters of them rearranged themselves, fusing into colorless, faintly glowing lenses pointing in my direction, while the other extended a branch toward something I couldn't see inside the porcelain box.

I must have made a sudden move, because there was a quick, new pang from my head. I reached up to touch the part that hurt and made an unpleasant discovery. Something that didn't belong there was just behind my ear. It was ribbed and hard-surfaced, and faintly warm to the touch, like my own flesh. It seemed to be embedded in my skin. It hadn't been there before, and I didn't like it.

That was when the littler one—its needles were like slivers of shell-pink glass—rolled up close to my face, waving its nearest sprig of needles under my nose.

Then it really surprised me. It spoke to me. It said, "You will be asked questions. Answer them quickly and accurately."

That put a different face on things.

I know it sounds peculiar, but when the machine said that to me it actually made me feel a bit better. Interrogation was something I understood, having done plenty of it myself. I spoke right up. I said, "My name is James Daniel Dannerman. I am a citizen of the United States of America and a senior agent of the American National Bureau of Investigation. I have been a captive of the Beloved Leaders, who are your enemies as well as my own—"

That was as far as I got.

The Christmas tree unhurriedly stuffed a fist of needles into my mouth to shut me up, and the needles weren't fragile at all. They were curiously warm. They didn't hurt, but it was like being gagged with a mouthful of steel wool. It said, "You have not been asked those questions. Answer only the questions you have been asked."

I'm not sure what I tried to say in response. With that glassy bird's nest stuffed in my mouth it only came out as *"wumf,"* but it made the thing remove the needles from my mouth and speak again.

"You will now supply information," the machine said, "concerning the conspecific persons you identify as 'Scuzzhawks.' Did their poor personal hygiene and use of psychoactive materials adversely affect their mortality and reproduction rates?"

CHAPTER THREE

Of all the things I could have expected to be interrogated about by a Horch machine, that one was about at the bottom of the list.

I did know all about the Scuzzhawks, of course. They were an ultralight plane gang that roamed the American Southwest, scandalizing law-abiding citizens. The Scuzz were more or less based in Orange County, California, but they rallied anywhere from Bakersfield to Tijuana. They didn't bathe much. They didn't wear much, either—there was a limit to how much load their frail little craft could lift, and they reserved most of their carrying capacity for beer and shotgun shells. They painted the wings of their ultralights with obscene slogans; they relieved themselves wherever they felt a need, which was frequently—even while they were airborne, and often enough over the clean, well-kept patios of respectable homeowners. The Scuzzhawks were not nice people. They earned their fuel and food and beer and dope by drugdealing and petty crime, and sometimes crimes that were not so petty; and early in my career with the Bureau I had been assigned to infiltrate them. That mission hadn't been my choice. When it was over I felt lucky to get out of it alive and generally disease-free.

Why this pink-glassy Christmas tree was asking about them, I could not guess, but the reason didn't matter. The important thing was that it did want to know about them.

That gave me bargaining room. Information is a valuable commodity, worth trading for. I said, "Let's be reasonable here. I'll tell you all you want to know about the Scuzzhawks, but first I have a couple of questions of my own. What's this thing behind my ear?"

The rose-pink one didn't answer that. It simply rolled away on its little wheels to the chinaware chest, where it extruded enough twiglets to open the chest and take something out, while Greenie rolled forward and grabbed me again.

It was strong, too. It held me tightly, but not painfully. I would have guessed that some of those glassy needles would have punctured my skin where they touched. They didn't. Retracted, I supposed, like a playful kitten's claws.

Then I saw what the pink one was carrying toward me, and I felt better right away.

The thing it had taken out of the chest was a helmet of a kind I had seen before. Dopey had given us one when he was our jailer, and it was a truly wonderful little gadget. When I wore it I could tap into the mind of that other Dan Dannerman, the copy of me who had been sent back to Earth, in a marvelous kind of virtual reality. (I'm not talking about the Dan Dannerman who escaped with the others. This was a different one. I'm sorry about that. I know all these copies are confusing . . . especially to me.) With the helmet on I could see what that other Dan was seeing, feel what he was feeling, hear everything he heard. To all intents and purposes I was *there*—not counting that I couldn't *do* anything, just observe.

It had not occurred to me that the same kind of helmet could be used to give me a sort of briefing lecture instead, but if that was what Pinkie had in mind, I was all for it. I said chattily, "That's better. There's no reason for us to argue, is there? We're both on the same side. You work for the Horch. I was taken prisoner by the Beloved Leaders. And the enemy of my enemy is my friend, right?"

Pinkie wasn't listening. It was fitting the helmet over my head, and I didn't resist. I waited complacently until it had flipped the earflaps into position, expecting some sort of lecture with diagrams, or—well, I didn't know exactly what to expect, but I was pretty sure it was going to be helpful in some way.

It wasn't.

It not only wasn't helpful at all, it was bloody awful.

As soon as everything was snapped down I found myself indeed in another place, but it was not any place I would have chosen. I was lying flat on my back, and I was looking up at a couple of the Christmas trees. And I was yelling. The one standing over me was an unfamiliar golden color, and it was methodically ripping my clothes off. I was struggling to stop it, but there wasn't any use to that. I was tightly fettered to a kind of operating table. I couldn't move a muscle.

Not even when Gold-glass began to operate.

It started by pulling out my toenails, one by one.

Then, as my yells of protest turned to agonized screams of pain, it did even worse. With one set of its twiglets it grasped me by my private parts, and with others it began to hack away.

See, the virtual reality those helmets provided didn't feel at all virtual. It felt bloody damn *real*. The pain was real. My screaming was real. I was fully aware that I was, for no reason I could understand, being slowly and painfully tortured to death, and I was bellowing with agony accordingly.

Gold-glass didn't seem to care about my screaming one way or another. It went right on with what it was doing. And then, as it gouged a slit in the skin of my belly from breastbone to the beginnings of my pubic hair, and then began methodically flaying the skin off my body, the pain passed the point of being endurable.

I endured it, though. I kept on enduring it, for much longer than I would have thought possible, until the machine's rummagings in my belly seemed to hit something crucial. Then, I think, I died.

And then the other Christmas tree, the real, pink-colored one, lifted the helmet off my head, and I was once again cowering on that chinaware floor, still screaming, but intact.

I had my clothes on again. I was alive again, and—not counting the headache that still persisted—as far as I could tell, in as good shape as I had ever been, toenails, balls, bowels and all.

That is, *physically* I was all right, though the memory of the pain was nearly as bad as the pain itself. And Pinkie said, "Now you will answer our questions about those conspecific persons called 'Scuzzhawks.' "

CHAPTER FOUR

From then on I answered all its questions, all right. I had learned that that was a good idea. When I hesitated, all it had to do was gesture toward the box with the helmet. Then I stopped hesitating right away.

See, no matter what you've heard, nobody ever holds out against serious, protracted physical torture. The body doesn't allow it. When real agony starts, the body cuts the volitional part of the brain right out of the circuit. It doesn't matter what your intentions are. First you suffer, then you scream, then you do whatever the person inflicting the pain wants you to do, including giving away every secret you ever knew.

Bureau doctrine told us there were things we could sometimes do about it, provided you had a chance to do them—including, as a last resort, biting down on a capsule of one of the Bureau drugs that turn off all physical sensations, so the guy who's interrogating you can do any horrible thing he likes and you just don't feel a thing. Provided, that is, that you've had a chance to get the capsule into your mouth ahead of time. Even that doesn't really solve the problem. You know exactly what is happening when the guy starts inflicting major and irreversible damage on the only body you own. Then you almost certainly talk anyway.

I didn't have to go the way of irreparable body damage. The pain was enough. I talked, and kept on talking, for a very long while.

I don't know how long, exactly. The only way I had of measuring time was by the internal clocks of my belly, bladder and bowels. By their count, that first round of questioning went on forever. I told the glass machines everything there was to tell about the Scuzzhawks, Green-glass taking it all down with his microphones and lenses. That wasn't the end of it. Then Pinkie switched without a pause to questions about the precise nature of their smuggling operation, and what "smuggling" meant in the context of Earth's more or less independent political entities called "nations," each with its own laws about what was forbidden or taxed. And then it wanted a detailed catalogue of all the sorts of things that were smuggled—dope, money for laundering, weapons—and then what the weapons were used for. Which led to many more questions on some large subjects. Crime. Terrorism. Why such aberrations were permitted to continue when they obviously interfered with the orderly workings of government and commerce.

Then, without warning, the lights went out in the camera lenses. The green-glass machine that had been operating them turned to the wall and a door opened. And the pink one said, "Go through there and attend to your biological needs. We will resume when you have finished."

I hesitated. Perhaps I hesitated a moment too long, because my headache was still slowing my reflexes, but the machine wasn't patient. It reached out toward me in a way I didn't like. I turned and hurried to the doorway.

CHAPTER FIVE

The biological-needs room was a twin of the one I'd just left: bare walls of the same yellow chinaware, no windows, no pictures. The big difference was that there were three doors instead of two—all securely locked against my immediate attempts to open them—and in addition to the chinaware chest against the wall (also unopenable by me), there was a pile of food on a low chinaware table.

The food at least was familiar. I had seen it all before. In fact, I had seen a lot of it. We had been living on identically that same grub for months, me and Pat, in all her copies, and Rosaleen Artzybachova and Jimmy Lin and Martín Delasquez. Apart from a few unfamiliar and unappetizing ropy twists of something smelly and purplish, it was the food Dopey had copied for us when we were his prisoners, duplicated from the stores on the Starlab orbiter we had been snatched from. Apples. Corn chips. Heaps of dried or irradiated meals in cans and jars and cartons, every one of which I was totally sick of. When I first saw that pile of rations it made me suddenly aware that I was, as a matter of fact, pretty hungry. When I realized it was the same boring stuff I'd eaten much too much of already, a lot less so.

There were a couple of jugs of water beside the stack of rations. I took a swig out of one of them—it tasted flat, as though it had been distilled—but while that relieved one biological need, it just made another one worse.

I had to pee.

I looked doubtfully at the floor. When we were captives of Dopey and his Beloved Leaders, our cell had this trick floor that doubled as a sewage-removal system. Any waste that hit the floor was absorbed and carried away without leaving even a stain. Even human waste.

This canary-yellow porcelain stuff was something else again. It didn't look promising. However, nature was not to be denied. I selected a corner of the room and let fly; and when I was through I watched, without much optimism, to see if the urine would seep away.

It didn't.

I said, "Shit." All right, that's a trivial thing. But it was one more damn blow, on top of a lot of others. You have to remember that, just hours before, my future had seemed really bright: home, safe, with the dear Pat Adcock I had just discovered I loved.

But I wasn't home. I wasn't safe. Pat was God knew where, and I was worse off than ever. Literally, now I didn't even have a pot to piss in.

So I did the only thing I could do. I fell back on my Bureau training.

I took a deep breath. I crammed some corn chips into my mouth, popped open a random jar (chicken à la king, it was, and really unpleasant in its cold and slimy state). I looked around the room to see if any curious eyes were observing me—didn't matter if they were, of course—and I began to tap systematically at the walls and chest and doors.

Now, why did I do that?

It wasn't out of any real hope. I didn't see that I had an ice cube's chance in Hell of ever getting back to NBI headquarters in Arlington with whatever odd bits of information I might learn through all this poking and prying. I did it anyway, because it was my job.

Back in basic training, the meanest of my drill instructors had explained that to us, while we were lined up, as sweating and stinking and sodden as we were, right after the obstacle course and just before the five-kilometer run. DIs rarely show sympathy.

This one had none at all. "What are you, tired? You don't know what tired is yet. You assholes are gonna be a lot worse off than this before you've put your twenty years in! Times you're gonna be exhausted and shitting your pants, but that don't let you off *nothing*. Whatever happens, whatever the bad guys do to you, you do your job. If they beat the piss out of you, if they cut off your balls and gouge out your fuckin' eyes, you don't forget what I'm saying. You ain't paid to give up. You're paid to keep on doing what you're missioned to do, so, if there's a miracle and you get out alive, you can report on every goddam thing you see and hear. Any questions?"

I was stupider in those days. I said, "Sir! How are we going to see anything if they've gouged out our eyes?"

She had an answer for that. She said, "You! Fall down and gimme thirty!"

So—having nothing promising to do—I did what I *could* do.

I knew what I wanted to do. I wanted to get out of this place, and find some way to get back to the transit machine, and zap myself back home. I didn't quite see how I was going to arrange that, but the first step was to gather information.

So I tapped the walls and tried the doors every way I could think of. The doors stayed locked. They were perfectly ordinary doors that swung open on hinges the way a door should do—nothing exotic or super high-tech, except that they didn't seem to have any handles. However I pushed or kicked them, they didn't move. Neither did the lid of the chest, when I went back to that. I didn't give up. I rummaged through the pile of food to see if there was anything hidden under it, and I even took one fairly nauseating taste of the purplish stuff, and I pulled and tugged at the unknown object behind my right ear, trying to figure out what that was all about. I could tell a few things about it. It was about the size of a pigeon's egg. It was smooth-surfaced, either metal or ceramic—when I tapped my fingernail against it, it sounded more ceramic than metal, but I couldn't be sure. It was ribbed, and the skin of my scalp seemed to have grown right around it as though it belonged there, the way your gums surround your teeth.

But that was all I could tell about the thing. So I went back to my tapping and probing, because, even if there wasn't any drill sergeant around to make me do push-ups if I didn't, that was my job. And while I was hard at it, nibbling at some kind of dried fruit bar while I did, one of the doors opened. It let in another couple of those glassy robots—one bronze, one cherry red; I didn't think I had seen either of them before—along with my former captor and present traveling companion, the little alien creature with a body like a peacock and a face like a nasty-minded cat, Dopey.

The robots stood silently communing for a moment, but I didn't see what they were up to. I was looking at Dopey. It was clear that the ugly little creature had been having at least as hard a time as I. His decorous little muumuu was stained and, where it opened for his peacock plume, it was shredded. The plume itself was muddily dark, with none of its usual shifting iridescent colors. Dopey's fur had stains of its own, his belly bag was missing and he was wearing a decoration I hadn't seen before. It was ribbed like my patch and gold in color, which my own might well have been since I couldn't see the thing. The only difference was that his patch was on top of his head instead of behind one ear. He gazed at me blearily out of those kitten eyes and groaned.

"We are in terrible trouble, Agent Dannerman," he informed me. Then he waddled over to the food and began attacking the purplish stuff without another word.

I didn't need to be told that we were in trouble, but there was a good side to it. Now I had someone I could talk to without penalty.

What stopped me was the presence of the Christmas trees. I eyed them warily, but they were ignoring me. They had busied themselves with domestic chores. The cherry-colored one was mopping my little pool of urine from the floor, while the other did something to the porcelain chest that opened it up. Inside the chest was a heap of something that looked like oatmeal. The bronze one tapped the side of the chest with a thrust of branches and pointed another cluster at me. "This is to contain your excrements," it said. "Do not continue to soil the floor." And then the two of them left.

            I had been a captive before, but this was the first time I had been given a litter box, like some old lady's pet cat. The place was full of humbling experiences.

But we were alone, and it was my chance to talk to Dopey. I followed him to the food stacks and said, "All right, as you say, we're in trouble. But *where* are we in trouble? And how did we get here?"

He chewed greedily for a moment before he answered. Or didn't answer, actually. He said, still chewing, "If you have eaten all you wish, Agent Dannerman, you would be well advised to sleep now. You may not get many opportunities."

Well, I knew that, but what he said sounded odd to me. I couldn't quite think why. Then I realized that Dopey had spoken to me in English.

That was when I became aware that I hadn't been speaking English with the Christmas-tree machines. I had been talking to them in their own chirpy language, of which, I could have sworn, I had never known a single word.

CHAPTER SIX

Well, I was exhausted and I still had the residual headache, but I figured out the explanation for that fast enough. It had to be the thing they'd stuck on my head that accounted for my sudden fluency in Horch. The important thing was that, in whatever language, I now had someone who might answer some questions for me.

"Just tell me what happened," I coaxed.

He looked at me, and then at the remainder of his meal. Then he made the body-wriggle that was his version of a shrug. "Very well, but you should have deduced it for yourself, Agent Dannerman. When we entered the transit machine we were transmitted to your Starlab, you and I along with the others. But, of course, once a pattern has been constructed in the machine for transmission, it remains available, so that from that pattern copies may be made at any time. As, you will recall, I had previously made copies of your Dr. Adcock for you."

I didn't have to be reminded of that. I remembered everything there was to remember about Pat Adcock.

"Therefore it should not surprise you that the Horch made copies of us so that we could be questioned."

"But where are we? I certainly don't recognize this place—is it some kind of Horch base?"

"It is now," he said sourly. "Nevertheless it is the same base, on the same planet in the same globular cluster that we were in before. I do not know by what treachery the Horch were able to break into our transmission channels, but it enabled them to surprise and occupy this base—at great cost in lives and matériel, of course, but the Horch do not care about such things. Of course, the Horch have obviously made some changes in the structures to suit their own purposes. I assume from the changes that some time has elapsed since we were transmitted."

"How much time?" I demanded. He just did that body-twitching shrug again. I tried another tack. "About the questioning, Dopey. They're asking some pretty funny questions. Wouldn't you think they'd want to know the important stuff about Earth, like our technology, what kind of weapons we have, like that?"

"But they surely know all those things already, Agent Dannerman," he said, looking surprised. "They are simply filling in gaps in the knowledge obtained from the others of us whom they have already copied and questioned. Did you think we were the first?"

As a matter of fact, that was exactly what I had thought. I wished I could go on thinking it, because if they had questioned other copies of Dopey and of me, it was unpleasantly likely that they had also done the same thing, with the same brutal tactics, to Rosaleen and Jimmy and Martín . . . and to Pat.

To my own Pat.

My own Pat, whom I knew to be a pretty self-willed person when she chose to be. She wouldn't have taken any more guff from the Christmas trees than I had, at first. And then they would have done to her what they did to me.

That was not something I could bear thinking about. While I was thinking about it anyway, because I couldn't help myself, Dopey was going about his own business. He didn't speak to me again. He finished his meal, decorously relieved himself in the litter box, then selected a spot on the floor and crouched down, tucking his head under his plume for a nap.

I couldn't let that happen, because I needed to get the image of Pat being ripped open by a robot out of my mind. I said, "Wait a minute, Dopey."

He pulled his head back out again and regarded me crossly. "You are willful, Agent Dannerman," he complained. "Did you not understand what I said about sleeping when we could?"

"I did, but I wanted to ask you something. Why do they have to torture us?"

That made him wrinkle up his little cat mouth in annoyance. "Because they want truthful answers, of course."

"But can't they just *make* us do whatever they want?" I touched the ribbed thing behind my ear. "By putting some kind of controller in with this language thing?"

He blinked the cat eyes at me. "Controller?"

"Like the one the Beloved Leaders implanted in you," I explained. "So you would have to do whatever they wanted."

He made an indignant noise and stood up straight on his tiny legs, glaring at me. "You are so stupid, Agent Dannerman! Why do you think I have a controller implanted in me by the Beloved Leaders?"

I looked at him in surprise. "Don't you?"

"Of course not! There is no need for that! I am a rational being, as are all of my people, and so we know where our interests lie." His pursy little mouth was twitching and his plume was an angry red, but then he calmed down enough to explain. "The bearers which you call Docs do require such devices to be of value to the Beloved Leaders, because they are very willful beings. The warriors also need to be controlled. The reason for this is that in the course of their duties many of them must inevitably be dispatched to the Eschaton. Although they have been informed that this 'death' is actually a boon, not a tragedy, their natures prevail. They are not able to rid themselves of their instinct for self-preservation which would interfere with their duties. For the rest of us servants of the Beloved Leaders, my people included, self-interest takes a different form. We are glad to obey the Beloved

Leaders, because we know what they can do to us if we fail them."

He didn't seem sleepy anymore, just scared. His plume faded to a bilious green as he said, "You do not know the Beloved Leaders, Agent Dannerman. You have never even seen one. I have been more fortunate—not once, but three times. One even spoke to me, though not in person, of course. It was while I was monitoring your planet from the orbiter Starlab, and a Beloved Leader addressed me on a screen to give me an order. I was very frightened, Agent Dannerman. If you are not also frightened, it is because you do not understand the immensity of their power, or the consequences of their wrath. Do you really think your pitiful little planet can withstand the Beloved Leaders? It cannot. As I have told you, you are a fool. Their scout vessels found your Earth once. They will find it again, if indeed they have not already done so.

"It is true that these evil Horch and their machines are also extremely powerful. I do not think they will prevail against the Beloved Leaders, though. When the Eschaton comes, I believe it is the Beloved Leaders who will rule. Rule all of us. For eternity. And oh, Agent Dannerman, I have failed them, and so I am very, very frightened of what that eternity will be."

CHAPTER SEVEN

That was the end of Dopey's conversation. He put his head under his plume again and kept it there. I thought I heard him sobbing for a few moments, but then he was quiet.

I fell asleep then, too, not because I wanted to but because I couldn't help it. When the green-glass machine woke me up Dopey was still in his corner, making the faint, muffled snickering sound that did him for snoring, and an idea was forming in my mind.

I didn't have much time to think it out, because Greenie was already snaking one branch of its twiglets under my right arm to get me up, then hustling me back to the interrogation room. But on the way I remembered doctrine.

Basic Bureau tradecraft said that if you couldn't get your interrogators to give you the information you wanted, perhaps you could at least lead the questioning in such a way that even the questions were informative. In practice sessions, back in my training days, it had seemed like something that might work. I'd never tried it in the field, but it was worth a shot. It was something to do, when the only alternative was simply to give up.

It seemed that the machines had heard all they wanted to hear about the Scuzzhawks. Now the topic of the day was sex. What did sexual intercourse feel like? If it was pleasurable, why did some human beings deprive themselves of it? How often had I had sexual intercourse, and under what circumstances, and with what persons, and why? Why was sexual intercourse with another person preferable to masturbation? What forms of sexual experience other than direct stimulation existed, and what did I mean by "fetishism" and "masochism"? How was it possible that some of my conspecifics could achieve sexual gratification just by inflicting pain on others?

I did what I could. I answered every question, and tacked on a little question to each answer. Masturbation: didn't the Horch masturbate? Hugging and kissing: I supposed the Horch had their equivalents. And didn't some Horch get a charge out of hurting other Horch? Without exception, none of my questions got an answer. Mostly they were ignored. Sometimes Greenie cautioned me to stick to straight responses. Twice it gestured toward the porcelain box that held the helmet, which was enough.

And the questioning went on and on. When it stopped at last it was only long enough for me to relieve myself and cram down a few bites of food, and then it started again.

CHAPTER EIGHT

I don't know how long the interrogation sessions went on. I tried to keep count of them, but there wasn't much point to that. The number didn't tell me much, because I had no good measure of how many hours each lasted, or how long I was allowed to sleep when I did. I didn't know, either, whether it really mattered for me to keep on sounding the walls, trying to peer past the doors when they were opened, even, once, deliberately falling against one of the Christmas trees to see how they felt. (They didn't feel like anything I had expected. No needle stabs, no feeling of chill glass spikes against my skin; the thing caught me and cradled me as though in an instantly created form-fitting basket of its twigs and set me back on my feet, and I had learned nothing at all.)

I wished for Dopey's presence so I could ask him more questions. That didn't happen often. We seemed to be on different schedules; once when Green-glass woke me up I caught a glimpse of him, sound asleep. But when I was allowed back in the biological-needs room he was gone.

And the questions didn't stop. Sports: how were players selected for football teams, and why would any sentient being risk life and limb in so violent an activity? Currency: What determined how many Japanese yen were given for one American dollar? What caused "inflation"? Why did humans play board games? How was "ownership" of land areas determined? What was the role of the stock market?

And I was reaching the ragged edge of fatigue.

I wasn't getting very far with trying to slip questions in, either. I was pretty sure that the robots were very familiar with that little stratagem, and I thought I knew why: they had dealt with Dan Dannermans before, and they knew our tricks.

Then I thought I saw an opening.

The questioning turned to religion. What was the nature of the religious experience? What evidence did the priests and preachers have for the existence of a "God" or a "Heaven"? Or, for that matter, of a "Hell," or some other form of postlife reward or punishment for transgressions?

And all of a sudden, I saw what I had been waiting for. I had something to tell them that I was pretty sure would dislodge some data for me. "Excuse me," I wheedled, the very model of a prisoner beaten down past the point of resistance, trying to curry favor with his captors, "but if you permit, I can tell you a story from my personal experience that might illuminate some of these questions for you."

Green-glass paused, its needles stirring in silence, apparently thinking that over. Then it spoke.

"Do so," it said.

What I wanted to tell the machine about was a memory of my grandmother, from when I was six or seven years old. That was when my parents began to make me spend a few weeks each summer at Uncle Cubby's place on the Jersey shore.

Uncle Chubby was J. Cuthbert Dannerman, the one with the money. I didn't specially want to be spending summers in his house. Uncle Cubby wanted it, because he liked having kids around now and then, possessing none of his own. And my father, who hadn't done nearly as well with his career as his older brother, wanted me to be there, too, because he was well aware that when Uncle Chubby died there would be a considerable estate for someone to inherit.

Well, that part didn't work out for me, for one reason or another, but those summers in New Jersey turned out not to be so bad. After I had cried myself to sleep for a week or so I began to enjoy myself. My cousin Pat came along most summers, for the same reasons. Unfortunately she was a girl, but at least she was someone to play with, and after a while her gender turned out to be an asset. That was when we discovered some interesting new games, like I'll Show You Mine If You Show Me Yours.

The bad part of the summers was that Grandmother Dannerman was there, too.

Grandmother Dannerman was a dying old woman, but she was taking her time about it. She was bedridden, feeble and incontinent. There was always a faint smell of old-lady pee in her bedroom, although the big windows that looked down to the river were generally open wide. After her fifth or sixth major operation she had got religion, and she wanted me and Pat to have it, too. She explained that when she died she was going to go to Heaven, because she had been a good Christian woman. She fully intended to see us there with her, so once a day, after our naps and before we were allowed to go swim in the river, she taught us Bible stories in her tiny, wheezy voice.

That was a drag. It did make playing Doctor under the boat deck half an hour later a little more exciting, but it never had the effect on us that Grandmother Dannerman intended. She didn't make us want to go to Heaven. She told us there was no sin there, and what was the fun of someplace where you weren't allowed to sin a little?

That was then. This was now, and I thought I had finally found a good use for Grandmother Dannerman's sermons. I told them to the green-glass Christmas tree and, obedient to my training, I did my best to put a little spin on them. The angels in the old lady's Heaven: Were they sort of like the way the Horch would be at the Eschaton? Did the bright, angelic swords of fire correspond to the weapons of the Horch? When we all got there, would we spend our time singing and playing music and never, ever doing anything the Horch might consider a sin?

That's what I tried.

It didn't work very well. Green-glass didn't want questions from me. Green-glass wanted only facts. The first couple of times I tried throwing in a question it simply ignored what I asked. Then it instructed me to stop doing that. And then it got worse.

See, I couldn't stop. I was convinced that I had no other way of gaining information, and I kept on doing it, and so the Christmas tree took its inevitable next step.

That was the second time I got the helmet. It was just as agonizing as before; but it had a surprising result.

I expect I screamed a lot. When Green-glass at last took the helmet off my head and I lay there, shaken and miserable, I saw that something had changed. One of the room's doors had opened. Something I had never seen before was looking in at us.

It was a pretty hideous specimen.

What it looked like, more than anything else, was a scaled-down model of one of the dinosaurs I'd seen in the museums when I was a kid—an apatosaurus, they called that kind—only this one was standing on its hind legs and wearing a kind of lavishly embroidered jogging suit. Its arms weren't like a dinosaur's, though. They were lightly furred and as sinuous as an elephant's trunk, and so was its long, long neck, with a little snaky head at the end of it that darted around inquisitively. It had a round little belly that was covered by a circular patch of embroidered gold—it almost looked like a particularly fancy maternity dress—and I recognized it at once from the pictures Dopey had shown us when we were his captives.

It was the Enemy. I guess my screaming had attracted it, and so I was in the presence of a living, breathing Horch.

When the Horch entered the room the Christmas trees stopped what they were doing, their twiglets turning deferentially toward it. It did not speak to them. It came toward me, arms and neck swaying, and it darted its little head at my face, sniffing and staring into my eyes. Then the long neck whipped the head away and the creature turned toward the door to the biological-needs room. The door opened at once and the Horch passed through, followed by the rosy-pink robot.

What they were doing there, I could not see, though I could hear sounds from inside the room. The Horch and the Christmas tree were twittering to each other, though I couldn't make out the words. There was something else going on, too: squeaking, gasping noises I couldn't identify. Then the Horch came back into the interrogation room, didn't speak, simply left it again through one of the other doors, with that long neck curved back and the snaky little eyes peering at me.

Rosy-pink buzzed back on its little roller-skate wheels to where I lay. It didn't comment on the visit from the living Horch. It didn't resume the questioning, either. "Attend now to your biological needs," it said, and that was the end of that session.

The mystery sounds had come from Dopey. He wasn't alone, either. A bronze-colored Christmas tree was holding him down while a pale yellow one was doing some obviously painful things to him.

It looked like a torture session to me, and that was both surprising and *wrong*. I mean sinfully wrong, a violation of order and propriety. Interrogations didn't take place in the biological-needs room! No prisoner likes to see changes in the rules, because changes are almost always bad, so I squawked a feeble sort of protest. It didn't go any further than that. The pale yellow one extended a clutch of branches menacingly in my direction, and I took the hint. I shut up. I couldn't help watching, though. Every time the machine touched Dopey he twitched and squeaked in pain, though they weren't asking him any questions. Then, abruptly, they released him and rolled out of the room.

As soon as they were gone I knelt beside Dopey. He was breathing hoarsely, obviously hurting. "Are you all right?" I asked.

He turned the kitten eyes on me. "No, Agent Dannerman, I am not all right," he gasped. "Leave me alone."

I couldn't do that. "Did you see that thing? It was a living Horch, wasn't it?"

Dopey gave me a look of disdain. "Of course," he said, pulling himself together. He stood up uncertainly, then limped toward the water jug.

I followed. "You weren't surprised to see him?"

He took his time about answering, drinking from his little cupped hands. It seemed to revive him. "The Horch rule here," he said, licking his lips. "What is surprising if one looks in on our interrogation? Did you expect it to be kinder than its machines?"

As a matter of fact, I had, sort of. "He looked like he was inspecting the way we were treated," I said, unwilling to give up what little hope I could find. "I thought he might do something to help us, maybe."

He gave me a look of contempt and said his favorite thing: "You are a fool, Agent Dannerman. Kindness from a *Horch!*"

"Not kindness," I said stubbornly. "Common sense. If we get sick, we won't be any good to them."

"In which case," he said, "they will simply scrap us and make new copies. Now I wish to sleep."

He looked as though he needed it. "All right," I said reluctantly. "I forgot they'd been torturing you."

He gazed at me with an expression of blended contempt and woe. "Torturing me? No, Agent Dannerman, they were not torturing me. They were doing worse. They were giving me medical treatment to keep me alive. Now let me sleep!"

CHAPTER NINE

Day followed day, and the pointless, endless questioning went on, on the robots' capricious choice of subjects. Childhood games: How many players were necessary for hide-and-seek? Were Little League baseball players paid like their adult colleagues? Theater: What had Christopher Marlowe written besides *Dr. Faustus* and *The Jew of Malta*? What was the function of the chorus in Greek drama?

Those questions puzzled me at first. I certainly knew a lot about theater, because that's what I had majored in in college, but why did they ask me about the parts I didn't know instead of the early-twentieth-century playwrights I had studied?

It took me several days to figure it out, and when I did the answer gave me no pleasure. The robots had asked all the obvious questions already, but they had asked them of some other Dan Dannerman. As Dopey had said, now they were simply filling in the gaps that remained.

Along about then that living Horch dropped in again on my interrogation. This time he didn't come alone.

The Horch who came with him was female. There was no doubt about that. The evidence was clear, because she was suckling an infant Horch with one pendulous breast, though otherwise the two adults were hard to tell apart. They both wore the colorful jerkins, with soft, flexible half-sleeves over their snaky arms. The only difference in their costumes was that her belly was covered not by embroidered fabric but by a shiny metal dome, almost like a medieval knight's helmet if it hadn't been on the wrong part of her anatomy. When the infant released her breast it dangled over the metal dome until she tucked the breast away and slung the infant under one ropy arm, the baby's little neck swinging foolishly around.

The interrogation had stopped, the robots standing silent and immobile. The two adult Horch paid them no attention. They conferred for a moment, snaky necks almost intertwined and the little rattlesnake heads so close together that I couldn't hear anything. Then the female darted her head in my face. "The least grandson of the Two Eights, Djabeertapritch," she said—I thought that was the name she used, as close as I could make it out—"is of the opinion that your physical state is deteriorating. Is that the case?"

I goggled at her. The last thing I had expected was that a Horch would concern itself with my physical state. While I was puzzling over that, the other Horch took a hand. "It is to your advantage to answer her, Bureau Agent James Daniel Dannerman," he said. "Please respond."

The most startling part of that was the "please," but the other thing that struck me was that, although there was no doubt they were speaking the same language, the male's accent was markedly different. The female's was identical with that of the robots. His was throatier and more drawn out.

I managed to answer. "Yes. They're really giving me a hard time."

"Djabeertapritch is also of the opinion that if you were allowed to rest, however, you might survive indefinitely," the female stated.

I didn't much care for the way that was put, but I managed to answer. "I hope so," I said cautiously, and that was the end of the interview. The two of them marched out without another word, the baby flailing about under its mother's arm, and at once my interrogators returned to life.

"Tell us," Green-glass said, as though there had been no interruption, "why you consider craps a game of skill while roulette is merely chance." And we went right on with the interrogation.

I decided that what the female Horch had said was a good thing, however unattractively it had been put. I almost believed that the Horch were beginning to take an interest in my future. That was encouraging; it suggested that I might actually have one.

But when I saw Dopey again he cackled humorlessly at me. "Do not attribute kindness to the Horch, Agent Dannerman," he advised. "Their motives are their own."

I could see that he hadn't been receiving much kindness from them. His breathing was fast and shallow, and he was clearly in pain. I don't think of myself as a person without compassion. Treacherous little freak that he was, Dopey was still the closest thing I had to a friend anywhere within some distance measured in light-years, and I didn't really want to cause him more suffering.

On the other hand, the thought that I might somehow survive all this had revived my desire to learn whatever might be advantageous to the human race. I said, doing my best to sound sympathetic, "I guess they're forcing you to tell them all kinds of things, Dopey."

"That is a correct assumption, Agent Dannerman."

"Including the things that you wouldn't tell us when we were your prisoners?"

"Including everything. Why do you ask?"

"Because," I said, "if you've been spilling your guts to the Horch robots already, what's the point in keeping secrets from me anymore?"

He considered that grayly for a moment, then gave his wriggly sort of shrug. "Very well, Agent Dannerman. What is it you wish to know?"

I said, "Everything."

*   *   *

Everything" turned out to include more information than I could grasp in a single session. Since those sessions occurred only at the convenience of the robots, they didn't come very often, either, and they didn't last long when they did. Worse than that, a lot of what Dopey admitted to having told the Christmas trees did nothing for me. I had no particular interest in the dietary needs of the other species who worked for the Beloved Leaders—Docs, fighters, half a dozen other serving races—and when I asked him what part those other weirdos played in the grand Beloved Leaders scheme, his answers made little sense to me.

But the Christmas trees had also asked him in detail about the way he had come to Earth, and that might be worth knowing. It was radio that had done us in. One of the random scouting ships of the Beloved Leaders had detected some early terrestrial broadcasts, and that was the signal they had been looking for. At once the ship changed course, homing in on the radio signals, and we had become targets.

All that took time. How much time, Dopey couldn't tell me with any precision, but from the nature of those first broadcasts—sports events, political speeches, random news programs, and all in AM sound radio only—I figured out that the scout ship had had to be more than a hundred light-years away at the time of detection. Which meant something over a hundred years of travel time for the ship. And sometime along the way, as the ship sniffed its way down the electronic scent trail of humanity, Dopey was dispatched to the ship to begin the task of deciphering what those broadcasts were all about.

"Not just one of me," Dopey clarified. "It is what I am trained for, but the volume of data was too great for a single person to handle. Many broadcasts, from many parts of your planet, and ultimately with vision as well as sound. We eavesdropped on every scrap of voice and picture. Altogether there were seven copies of me, to share the work of deciphering your preposterous number of languages. I do not know what happened to the other six. But I was the one who was tasked to remain on your Starlab orbiter, until you and your party came to investigate."

That was as far as we got in that session, and I was burning with impatience to learn more. When the next chance came, Dopey was looking frailer and closer to his Eschaton than ever. He didn't really want to go on talking to me, but I wasn't willing to let him stop. He told me how the scouting ship had dropped off the pod that attached itself to Starlab, and how they had filled the old satellite with recording and transmission devices. He described the scout ship itself to me—a vessel much larger than Starlab, with a crew of dozens of beings of several different races. And then he became obstinate. "This is all foolishness, Agent Dannerman," he complained. "What is the use of telling you all this, when there is no chance that you can pass it on to your conspecifics?"

I said staunchly, "I'm still alive, Dopey. So there is always a chance."

"But," he said reasonably, "you do not know if your planet still exists. We have no way of knowing how long it has been before these copies of us were made."

I had an answer for that. "It can't be very long," I told him. If it was all over on Earth, they wouldn't still be asking me all those questions."

He looked at me in surprise. "That is not so. You are forgetting, Agent Dannerman, that the Horch and the Beloved Leaders wish to know everything possible about all intelligent species. Even the extinct ones. It will make them easier to rule at the Eschaton."

CHAPTER TEN

I wasn't willing to believe that. I couldn't afford to. But it stayed in my mind.

I stripped down and used my wretched underwear for a washcloth, while Dopey watched me with lackluster curiosity. While I was wringing out my shorts and draping them on the edge of the table to dry, I said, "If I only had some clean clothes, I'd almost feel human."

That wasn't entirely true, but I was trying to cheer Dopey up. It didn't work very well. He didn't respond. He just sat there, perched on the far edge of the table, with his eyes half closed and his great peacock fan the color of mud. He had been taking punishment, all right. There were rips in the periphery of his fan that hadn't been there before, and new stains on the jumper he wore. I tried again, encouragingly. "We don't have to give up, you know. There's always a chance to escape."

He didn't answer that, either, just sat there, breathing raggedly. He wasn't asleep. His eyes were more or less open, and he hadn't pulled his fan over his head to shut me out, but he wasn't listening.

I gave up. I spooned some water out of the drinking jug into one of the cups of dehydrated stew, and ate one of the apples while the stew was soaking. I tugged at the lid to the litter box, thinking it might be some kind of weapon if I could get it off. I couldn't.

Then I saw that Dopey had begun to move. He levered himself painfully off the table and waddled slowly over to the water jugs. He drank some, then splashed some over himself.

I took him by his frail little arm and said clearly, "I intend to escape. I need you to help me make a plan."

He grunted without actually answering. I squeezed harder on the arm. "Talk to me!" I demanded.

He wrenched himself free. "If you make a plan," he said, "you are telling the Horch what to expect. Are you an even greater fool than I thought?"

"But—but that was why I asked in English!"

He sighed. "They listen in, no matter what language we speak. Whether we see them or not, they are observing us at all times."

I said, "Hell." Of course it was only an illusion, but I had believed we had at least that much privacy. I shouldn't have. That was a Bureau trick, too. I'd done it myself: after you've interrogated a couple of suspects for a while, you put them together and listen to what they say to each other.

He was talking again. "In any case," he said gloomily, "there is no hope of escape. We will die here, Agent Dannerman, and the next time I see you we will be at the Eschaton."

His certainty was bringing out all the stubbornness in me. "If there's really going to be an Eschaton," I said.

"But of course there will!"

I shook my head at him. "Pat didn't think so, and she's an expert in that subject—"

"An Earth-human expert!" he sneered.

"All the same. Pat said it had been conclusively shown that there wasn't enough mass in the universe to make it contract again. It will go on expanding forever and never shrink down again to the Big Crunch. So no Eschaton. She said there was no doubt about that at all."

Dopey made the gagging rattle in his throat that was his version of a contemptuous laugh. "Your primitive beliefs! Both the Beloved Leaders and the Horch are far, far wiser than Dr. Pat Adcock. There is no question."

He turned his back on me and limped over to gaze without much interest at his purple food. "You don't seem real happy about it," I offered.

He put a small chunk of the stuff in his mouth, chewing unenthusiastically—and sloppily; crumbs were falling to the floor. Then, with his mouth full, he said, "You do not understand, Agent Dannerman. I have betrayed the Beloved Leaders. Their judgment will be sure."

"Oh, maybe not," I said. "It might go the other way, you know. Maybe the Horch will win, and then you won't have to face your Beloved Leaders."

He turned the cat eyes on me mournfully. "Do you think that would be better for me? Or for you, either?" He swallowed the rest of what was in his mouth, then put the remainder of the stuff down. "In any case, Agent Dannerman," he said, "I think I will find out which it is quite soon."

Well, he was right about that.

A few sessions later, when the Christmas trees released me for my pee-and-chow break, I discovered Dopey lying next to the table. His plume dragged limply on the floor. One of his kitten eyes was closed to a slit, and the other queerly distended. Neither was looking at me. And his body was cold.

I shouted, but no one came. When one of the crystal robots did eventually appear, it paid no attention to my dead companion. It only hustled me off to my next interrogation, and when I came back to the room his body was gone.

CHAPTER ELEVEN

Never mind about the next while. The easy way to describe it is that it was more of the same, but that's not accurate. It was worse. Not only was I now alone, more alone than I had ever been in my life, but too little sleep for too long was doing me in. My thinking was getting fuzzy. Every time I got to the biological-needs room I fell asleep at once, without bothering to eat, and that was not improving my state.

I can't say that I was giving up hope, because I hadn't had all that much hope to begin with, but I was getting too bleary even to think about a future.

And then something did come along.

The Christmas trees' questions had been getting sillier and more erratic than ever. Sometimes both machines stood silent for a few moments, apparently deep in thought, before coming up with some new asininity.

Then, after a particularly lengthy period of cogitation, Pinkie rolled away from me and stood silently beside Green-glass, whose lenses began to disappear. Both machines seemed to shrink into themselves, retracting whole hordes of their finer needles.

Remember, I was staggeringly weary. By the time it registered with me that the robots were in some sort of standby state, and thus in good condition to be attacked, it was too late to do anything about it. The door opened. Three living Horch came in— the one with the funny accent, the female I had seen before and an unfamiliar male, who wore the same gleaming metal belly helmet as the female.

The female darted her head toward Green-glass, I suppose giving it an order I couldn't hear. I didn't have any trouble seeing the results, though. Both Christmas trees sprang into action. They advanced on me and grabbed me, but not as they had done before. This time not all their needles were retracted. They pricked me in a hundred places, and they hurt. I yelped in pain and surprise. That didn't stop them. They investigated most of the parts of my body with their sharp little spikes. Then, without a word, they dropped me to the floor and rolled back to the Horch at the door. There was a low-toned conversation while I was picking myself up, and then the two Horch with the metal belly plates left, the Christmas trees went into standby mode and the one with the embroidered fabric stomacher came toward me. "Bureau Agent James Daniel Dannerman," he said, "the interrogation is terminated. You have been given to me for disposal."

It was the first time I had ever been close enough to a live Horch to touch, so I summoned all the energy I had and grabbed him by the throat. "Tell those robots not to interfere! You're going to take me out of here," I croaked, as menacingly as I could make it.

He didn't seem worried. He didn't need to be. He was a lot stronger than I was. Both of the Christmas trees snapped out of their down mode and sprang forward, but he waved them away. Those ropy arms of his pulled my fingers from his throat without effort.

"Yes, of course," he said. "Transportation has been arranged."

He turned and left through the open door; and, carrying me, the green-glass Christmas tree rolled after him.

PART THREE

The Compound

Outside the interrogation room the Christmas tree waited for a moment while the Horch climbed onto a funny-looking kind of three-wheeled velocipede. He flopped onto it on his back, belly up, with his long neck twisting around so he could see where he was going. Then he whizzed away and we followed.

As before, it wasn't a sight-seeing trip. The machine carried me hugged to its bristly needles, my face pressed so that I could get only gimpses of the scenery, but I recognized it. Dopey was right. The last time I'd seen any of this, it had been shattered and smoking junk, but it was definitely the old Beloved Leaders base, the fires out now and here and there a Christmas tree diligently taking the ruined machinery apart.

The Horch made better time on his tricycle than we did. He was waiting beside it when we arrived and the Christmas tree set me down.

We were at the edge of the built-up base, with that vast, empty, ocher-colored desert in front of us. A different kind of vehicle was parked there, with an alien standing next to it. I recognized the creature as one of the huge, pale, multiarmed ones we called "Docs," but there was something odd about it. It took me a moment to realize what it was; all the Docs I had seen before wore nothing but a kind of jockstrap, while this one was fully clothed.

I turned as I heard a skitter of wheels on pavement behind me—the Christmas tree was skating away, its work here evidently finished—and when I turned back the Horch was looking me over. He sniffed at me with the little nostril slits in his pointy snake nose, then drew his head back to stare into my eyes. "You will be all right, I think," he said. "This medical sapient will take you to a safe place and care for you."

He signaled to the Doc, who picked me up, more gently than the machine, and held me as the Horch came over for a last word. I could feel the breath from its mouth as his head stretched toward me. "Perhaps you will want a name for me. You can call me Beert—" trilling the *r*, clipping the final *t*. "It is the short form of my name, as yours is Dan. Another one called me that before he died."

I was practicing saying the name for myself when he got to the last part. Then I opened my mouth to ask about this "other one," but Beert wasn't listening. "Yes, you say my name quite well. No questions now, please. I have duties to attend to, but I will come to you when I can. In any case, everything will be explained to you, if you survive."

If you survive. These creatures from other planets were great at dropping conversation-stoppers on me.

Helping me to survive appeared to be the Doc's job. He didn't speak, but he laid me down on a bench in the vehicle and began to palp my throat, belly, groin, skull. I didn't see him do anything to make the vehicle start, but while he was poking at me the door closed, the car lurched and, evidently on autopilot, we began to glide away on its air cushion.

The Doc rolled me over and began doing something radical to the small of my back. It didn't hurt, but it felt unwelcome. Then it began to feel a little better.

If I had been a little less bone-weary-frazzled, I might have tried to see where we were going. I didn't. There were no windows operating in the car, and besides, the Doc's ministrations were making me feel a little bit relaxed, for the first time in quite a while.

So I suppose I fell asleep. At least I was surprised when the door opened and I realized the car had stopped.

Another Doc peered in. The two of them, my medic and the new one, mewed at each other in a high-pitched language I had never heard before. Then they helped me out of the car.

I was standing in bright sunshine, with half a dozen of the Docs gathered around to stare at me. The new one spoke. "You are Dannerman," he informed me—well, more accurately, she informed me; it wasn't until a little later that I got the genders straight. "My name is . . ."

Was something I had a lot of trouble pronouncing, much less writing down; it started with a kind of baritone purring sound, then something like clearing the throat, and at the end finishing with a deep-toned hiss; the closest I can come is "Pirraghiz." "You are safe here," she went on. "Do you know what this place is?"

I frowned at her. She was rapidly making my pleasant languor evaporate, and that struck me as a stupid question. How would I know what it was?

Then I looked around more carefully, and I did.

There were a couple of strange-looking buildings that I knew I had never seen before. Shiny. Yellow, like the chinaware walls of the interrogation room. Five or six meters high and sort of elliptical in plan, with sides that tapered up from the ground. What they reminded me of mostly was pictures I had seen of the ancient Civil War ironclad, the *Merrimac,* and they were not in the least familiar.

However, that wasn't all that was in sight. There was a little stream not far away, crossed by stepping-stones. There were trees in the distance. There was something that looked like a primitive stone fireplace. And there was a tepeelike thing that wasn't exactly a tepee. The last time I'd seen any of those, Jimmy Lin had given them a name. He called them "yurts."

"Oh, my God," I said, because, yes, it was a very familiar place. "I lived in those yurts when I was a captive of the Beloved Leaders."

"That is correct," Pirraghiz told me gently. "You lived here before. Now you will stay here again while we feed you and try to make you well."

CHAPTER THIRTEEN

I spent most of the next few days sleeping. As far as I could tell, Pirraghiz never slept at all. Every time I woke up she was there, carrying me to a toilet, spoon-feeding me more of the foods I had been eating for so long, rubbing the small of my back with that special little touch of hers that seemed to be meant to put me back to sleep, and always did.

So for the next forty-eight hours at least, it could have been more, I was pretty much out of it. I was hazily aware that sometimes she was doing other things to me—massaging, poking, cupping my head in her two largest hands—but I didn't know why, except that it felt good. Now and then I know others came into the room to look at me, mostly other Docs, but once or twice, I think, the Horch. Those fuzzy periods of nearly waking didn't last. When Pirraghiz saw that I was wakeful she touched me with one gentle talon and I was gone again.

When the time came that I was very nearly wide-awake, for very nearly an hour or so at a time, I took a closer look at my surroundings.

The bed I was in was comfortable enough, except for being maybe a little firmer than I would have preferred. However, it was built to Doc dimensions, nearly four meters long and more than half that in width. The room was in the same statuesque scale. On the walls there were a couple of mural-like paintings— or still photographs, I couldn't decide which. One was a group of Doc infants at play, the other a misty, idealized scene of a seashore with gentle waves breaking on a pink-sand beach. Elsewhere along the walls were shelves that contained clothes and things—Pirraghiz's, I supposed—and others with spools of a glassy sort of ribbon (the Horch equivalent of books, I found out later). A squat cylindrical thing by the window blew air at me, I supposed for comfort. In recesses in the walls there was a thing like a chromium soup bowl a meter across that was standing on one edge—for what purpose, I did not know—and a couple of smaller bowls of a different kind that were filled with a kind of peat moss. Unfamiliar blue-green buds poked out of the moss. The whole place had a lived-in look. Naturally enough. It was Pirraghiz's own room. She had given it up for me.

When she came to check up on me she was astonished to find me standing up. Before she said anything she carefully felt me all over. Then, more or less satisfied, she allowed me to walk to the toilet on my own.

I haven't said what the toilet was like. There were three of them lined up, huge, Doc-sized things that looked like Chic Sale outhouses on pilings. They were built right over the flowing stream and you got to them by a small bridge. I must have said something that Pirraghiz hadn't expected, because she looked at me curiously. "Are you dissatisfied with the sanitary arrangements?"

"No, of course not. Well, a little surprised, anyway. It's just that the sanitary arrangements don't seem very sanitary. On Earth a lot of people get very upset if they find anyone using the streams for toilets, because of the risk of spreading infection."

That stopped her cold. The snowy, mossy eyebrows went up in astonishment. "Are you telling me," she asked, sounding scandalized, "that your excrement may contain live pathogens?"

"Doesn't everybody's?"

The great bland face was wearing an expression of revulsion. "That is a disgusting concept, Dannerman. No. We will have to provide you with other facilities, for the protection of other species who are downstream from us . . . and you must not excrete into the river anymore."

* * *

By the time Pirraghiz was finally letting me feed myself, and did not immediately put me back to sleep as soon as I was finished, I was remembering the lessons my old DI had beaten into me. I had a duty. It was time for me to start scoping this place out, so I insisted on being allowed to go outside.

Physically I was feeling pretty good—no, more than that; I was feeling better than I had in a long time. I was still weak, though. When we came to a short flight of stairs I wasn't really ready for—tall, Doc-sized stairs, they were—Pirraghiz didn't stop to ask permission. She just picked me up and carried me to the outside door, and I was glad she had.

I had not expected it to be night outside.

If I had had any uncertainty about where we were, the sight of that night sky removed it. My dearly beloved astronomy expert, Pat, had suspected that the prison planet we were on was in the middle of a globular cluster which, she said, was a collection of maybe thousands of stars crowded so close together that the whole clutter of them was bound by each other's gravity, sailing around in complex orbits and all very, very near all the rest. There were certainly hundreds in that overhead night sky that were very near to us: giant brilliant lightbulbs hanging in the heavens, blue and red and yellow and white and all the shades in between. At least a dozen of them were as bright as the Moon from Earth, and a couple so incredibly bright that I squinted when I looked at them. In one corner of the sky there was a cobwebby film of white, brighter than the Milky Way. It wasn't anything like the Milky Way, though, according to Pat. The Milky Way was made up of millions and billions of individual stars, so distant that their light smeared together into a luminous blur. This stuff, she thought, was masses of gas and plasma that some of the stars were stealing from each other.

Pat had had something else to say about this display. According to her, in a globular cluster novas and supernovas might be relatively common, and when a star exploded in one of those ways it was likely to release floods of seriously damaging radiation, with very bad results for any living thing nearby.

When I said something about that to Pirraghiz, she said, "Of course that is so, Dannerman. Showers of deadly radiation are quite frequent. That is why the Horch restored the protective shield over this planet as soon as they finished occupying the base. It was down for only a few days, but in that time many persons of many species died from it." Then she touched my throat with one of her lesser arms and frowned. "You are being too active for your first time out. Come back. You can eat, and then you should rest some more. There will be plenty of time to explore."

I didn't actually need to do a lot of exploring. I already knew this place very well.

Before we escaped back to Earth—I mean, before the ones of us that did successfully escape did—we had spent a lot of time here. It was a prison, or zoo, where the Beloved Leaders kept a few samples of the sentient races they had met—and, often, exterminated. We lived in the yurts, but we didn't build them. Some others had lived here before us and, we guessed, died here too, because all that remained of them was their works.

Now the compound belonged to the liberated Docs, or at least to the thirty or so surviving ones that had managed to escape being killed in the fighting. The Docs looked a lot different now. The ones I had been used to seeing were silent; they obeyed orders, and when no orders were given they stood frozen, waiting for the next command. These present Docs were never still, as they worked around the compound, chattering back and forth in their high, chirpy voices. And they were fully clothed. They wore decorous trousers over their lower parts, and above the waist a sort of loose, gaily colored blouse, with sleeves for all six of their arms. Each wore a huge, floppy hat to keep the sun away.

As I peered inside the surviving yurt—it looked like the one we had kept our food in, but it was empty now—I felt that gentle touch on my neck. I turned. It was Pirraghiz, of course, once more taking my pulse or whatever it was she did when she touched me there. "Are you getting tired?" she asked anxiously.

I assured her I wasn't, though I was pretty certain she knew my condition better than I did. I pointed to the yurt. "How come you left this one standing?"

She looked faintly embarrassed, or as much so as a creature with a great, moss-covered moon of a face could look. "It did not seem right to remove them all. The people who built them are gone, and there was no other way to remember them. I know this is not a sensible thing, Dannerman." Then she patted my shoulder with a lesser hand. It wasn't a medicinal touch, this one, or even a particularly affectionate one. It was the way your mother might put her hand on your shoulder when she wants your full attention. "I have a question for you, Dannerman. You have been all over this area, looking at everything. Yet you have seen almost everything here before, so what is it that you are looking for?"

The truthful answer was, a way to get out of here and go home. I was pretty sure she suspected as much. But I didn't want to confirm it for her, and anyway there was something else I'd been hoping to find.

So I told her the other thing: "A grave. A friend of mine died here. Her name was Patsy, and she was killed by some electric amphibians. We buried her around here."

She bought it without question. She patted me again, consolingly this time, and said, "I will lead you to it."

The plot was farther away from the yurts than I'd remembered, but I recognized it at once. The ground had settled a little—which suggested to me that some time had elapsed before the Horch whipped up this present copy of me—but you could see where it was. Touchingly, someone—I was willing to bet it had been Pirraghiz—had put one of those flower bowls on it.

However, it wasn't alone. There was another plot beside it, a little less sunken, with its own little bowl of pale buds.

When I asked Pirraghiz she looked at me mournfully. "He was another copy of you, Dannerman. Djabeertapritch begged for him when the machines decided it was better to abandon him and make a fresh one. They let Djabeertapritch have him, but he was too far gone for us to make well. He died; and we buried him next to your friend."

Pirraghiz was about as tactful a nonhuman as I'd ever met. Well, that doesn't say much, considering who the other nonhumans were, but she was a good scout. She ambled away, leaving me to mourn for my dead other self.

I don't think that is exactly what I was doing, though. I was thinking about funerals of Bureau agents.

When an agent is buried he's entitled to a military ceremony, complete with the rifle volley from the honor guard and the bugler playing Taps and all. He usually gets it, too, except when they haven't found enough of him to bury.

I couldn't provide any of that for this other me, but Taps kept running through my mind. There are words to the melody, a fact that most people don't seem to know, and the last line of the song says, "All is well. Safely rest. God is nigh."

I guess a little of Grandmother Dannerman's Bible lessons had rubbed off on me after all, because I was certainly hoping that was true.

CHAPTER FOURTEEN

As my strength began to come back I got serious about my duties as an agent of the NBI. I would need to be in the best possible physical shape if an opportunity to escape ever turned up, so I began systematic exercises. That worried Pirraghiz a little at first because she wasn't sure doing jump-squats was good for me, but she finally stopped objecting. And I got more diligent about spying again.

Pirraghiz had the right of it when she said I'd seen about as much of the compound grounds as there was to see. The inside of their two-story longhouses was a different matter. There might well be some kinds of technology there that were worth knowing about, so I spent some time pondering over them.

I figured out what some of the domestic appliances were for easily enough. The desk was a desk—probably. Its surface was a mosaic of squares the size of my palm, but it had nothing on it except some stacks of my food rations, and no drawers to open. The bowl-shaped object that stood on its rim in the wall turned out to be a kind of TV, though I didn't know how to turn it on. The stubby, purring cylinder on the floor was, as I had guessed, a kind of air conditioner. It had some unfamilar features: It not only wafted warm air into the room when the night grew chilly, and cool air in the heat of the day, but the scents that came out of it varied with the temperature of the air. They smelled meaty and almost sweaty at night and like fresh-cut greenery during daylight.

That was interesting, but not the kind of thing the Bureau would be wild to hear about—assuming I ever got the chance to see Arlington again. The real puzzle about all this machinery was where the power came from. There weren't any wall outlets, or cables going to them; but they kept on going anyway.

I found Pirraghiz outside and asked her about it. She didn't seem to object to my curiosity, but she wasn't much help, either. She seemed preoccupied, gazing toward the stream where two other Docs were standing. "I am only biomedical, Dannerman," she explained. "I know nothing of mechanical things. Mrrranthoghrow might know."

"And who is Mrr—Mrrran—"

"Mrrranthoghrow, Dannerman. He is a friend. He comes here sometimes, and you can ask him if you like. For now, would you like me to show how the picture bowl works?"

She was still gazing toward the creek. "Yes, please," I said, and then I saw what she and the other Docs were looking at. I thought at first that it was one of the flat rocks that were used as stepping-stones across the water, though this one was of an odd greenish color.

Then the rock moved. It erected stalked eyes to peer at the nearby Docs. Then it raised itself on short, splayed legs and walked away.

I turned to Pirraghiz. "What the hell was *that?*"

"Ah," she said, understanding. "You have never met a Shelled Person before, have you?" And when I asked what a Shelled Person was doing here among the Docs, she was amused. "Is that hard to understand, Dannerman? All we species were enslaved one way or another by the Others. Why should we not talk to one another now and then?"

That sounded interesting. "Can I talk with them, too?"

"Not in this case, no. She has no language you could understand. Some of the other species do, and if one comes here, I will tell you. Now I will show you how to work the picture bowl."

Turning the picture bowl on was easy, once you knew how. I had been looking for controls on the bowl itself, but there weren't any. They were in the desk. You moved a section of the top aside in the right way, and it uncovered a sort of clockface, tiny holes arranged in a circle with what might have been numbers inscribed over each. The numbers were meaningless to me. The little holes weren't much help at first, either. Pirraghiz showed me how they worked by delicately extruding a claw to poke into them, but I didn't have a claw.

The first thing Pirraghiz showed me in the bowl was the planet we were on. It appeared like a globe, in three dimensions, in the bowl, and she showed that it could be rotated or zoomed in. "This is where we are," she announced, pointing with a lesser arm.

It looked like a park, seen from above. I recognized the familiar hexagonal patterns that had been enforced by the Beloved Leaders' energy walls, imprisoning each group of us in our own little space. Now those walls were vanished, but lines of abrupt discontinuities in the kinds of vegetation showed where they had stood.

Some of the plants looked to be in bad shape, and when I said as much to Pirraghiz, she said, "Of course, Dannerman. When the shield was down the radiation killed many things, and not simply plants." There had been nine captive species in the zoo of the Beloved Leaders. Some of them had come from worlds with a higher concentration of oxygen than this place, and so extra allotments had been routinely pumped into their enclaves. When everything broke down the oxygen stopped, and one whole species—Pirraghiz called them Tree-Livers—had gasped and died. Two others had needed extra humidity for their health, which had been supplied in the same way. Most of those species had survived. "But they are not comfortable away from their own areas," Pirraghiz informed me. "So you will not see them here."

I stared at the picture of the planet. Outside of the enclaves everything around was the rust-colored, arid rock and sand. It was not an attractive planet. "Why do you suppose the Horch bothered to take this place over?" I asked.

Pirraghiz sighed. "I do not know. The Horch do not tell us everything. Simply because the Others had it, perhaps."

"And why did the Beloved Leaders have it in the first place?" I asked, covering a yawn.

"Perhaps because it is so hostile to living things. Apart from their preserves, there was no place on it for the captive species to escape to," she said, but she hadn't missed the yawn. "Are you overtired again?" she asked fretfully. And then, "Hold still."

She pinched a fold of my belly flesh in her surprisingly gentle paws, the claws considerably retracted. The results made her give a disapproving lip-smack. "You must gain more body fat, Dannerman. You must eat more."

"I'm getting pretty tired of corn chips and spaghetti bolognese," I complained.

She said defensively, "I added water and heated it, precisely following the instructions on the container." I shrugged. She looked thoughtful for a moment, then turned off the picture bowl. She opened some of the food containers that had come from the Starlab store and, one by one, fished out a tiny crumb from each. She tasted them experimentally.

"I see," she said at last. "Wait for a moment, Dannerman."

She was gone for a lot more than a moment, and when she came back all six arms were carrying packets and clumps of strange-looking vegetable things. "Taste this," she ordered, holding out an object that looked like a small, sky-blue corncob with the kernels removed.

I looked at it with skepticism. "How do I know it won't poison me?" I demanded.

She gave me a surprised stare. "But did you not see me analyzing your food? These are quite compatible with your dietary needs. Also I am right here, in case there is any unexpected adverse effect."

Actually, it wasn't bad, tasting a little like a very mild onion. She opened up a pot of thick stuff the consistency of honey and advised me to dip the cob into it; it was peppery and rather good.

Becoming adventurous, I reached for a fruit she had split open, spiky on the outside, round and reddish within, but she snatched it out of my hands. "One moment, Dannerman. Wait."

Then I saw another way in which those little retractable talons were useful. The fruit was full of tiny greenish seeds. She quickly coaxed them out with her claws, one after another. Then she handed the fruit to me. It was moist and cool, and it tasted vaguely of roasted chestnuts. Pirraghiz looked approving. "Now it is safe, Dannerman, but you must never eat the seeds. The other one of you did, by accident. Perhaps he would have lived if he had not. Now try this—" handing me a sort of lemon-colored potato. "it will make you sleepy, and so you will rest."

The new food was an improvement, and so was the picture bowl. That looked like a spy's dream of a bonanza: I figured I could roam around the channels and learn everything there was to know about the Horch. That was borrowing a page from Dopey's book; it was just what he had done about the Earth when he was monitoring all of our broadcasts from Starlab.

That had worked out for Dopey. It didn't for me. I managed to work the controls with a toothpick-sized scrap of ceramic Pirraghiz found for me. I picked channels more or less at random, not knowing any other way to do it. Most of them were incomprehensible to me. There were a lot of what I supposed were the entertainments of the Horch, something like choir singing, something like No plays. They didn't entertain me. There were scenes of what probably were a number of different planets, or different parts of the same planet. Those had voice-over commentaries, all right, and those might have given me a lot of information if I could have understood them. I couldn't. They were in the high-pitched and totally incomprehensible language of the Docs.

There was certainly data to be got from the bowl. I just didn't know how to go about getting it. And then, while I was scowling at a particularly uninformative view—a pair of Horch were silently playing some sort of board game—the picture bowl beeped at me. The game-players disappeared, and another Horch was staring out of the bowl at me. "Hello, Dan," he said, and I realized it was my friend—or my captor—or, actually, my savior—the one named Djabeertapritch.

Evidently the picture bowl doubled as some kind of communications device. I said guardedly, "Hello, Beert."

If he detected anything in my tone, he didn't show it. He said, "I am sorry I have not been able to visit you in person, Dan. There is much I am trying to learn from our Horch cousins, so I must spend much time with them. Also with some projects of my own. We will have more time together when you come to our nest."

It was the first I had heard that he planned to move me again. "When will that be?"

"When you are fully recovered. Are you feeling better now, Dan?"

"Quite a lot," I admitted.

"That is good," he said, sounding as though his mind was elsewhere. "Now there is someone I wish you to meet," he added more briskly, getting to the point. "I have a reason for this. Go outside now. Pirraghiz is waiting to take you to him. Good-by."

That was the end of the conversation. Beert disappeared, and I was looking at the Horch game-players again.

When I had turned off the picture bowl and climbed down the stairs, Pirraghiz was hurrying toward me. "It is a Wet One, Dannerman," she told me, taking my arm to speed me along. "He has language, so you can speak to him. Come, he is in the creek."

Perhaps that should have warned me. It didn't. We were almost to the stream when I saw that someone was half submerged in the water.

Only it wasn't a someone. It was a slate-gray creature the size
of a hippopotamus. It had a writhing Medusa mustache of tentacles around its mouth, and it wore a collar. I knew it well. I
tugged myself free of Pirraghiz's arm and walked away, shaking.
I couldn't help it.

Pirraghiz came after me, put one hand worriedly on my
throat, bent to peer into my face. The great pale face was puzzled.
"You are upset, Dannerman. What is wrong?"

I pointed to the amphibian. "That's wrong. Those things
murdered a friend of mine. Her name was Patsy, and she's the
one who is buried next to the other one of me. She was bathing.
She didn't even know there were any of those things in the water,
but there was a scuffle and they electrocuted her."

She stood for a moment, looking from me to the amphibian.
"So you won't even talk to this Wet One?"

"I won't."

"Djabeertapritch wishes it," she wheedled.

"No."

She sighed. "This episode was certainly unfortunate," she said
reasonably, "but it is an event in the past. It is true that the Wet
Ones use an electric charge for defense, but only when they feel
threatened. This one will not attack you, Dannerman."

"I won't give it the chance."

She stood there, looking down at me. "You cannot forgive
that incident?"

I shook my head. "Forget it, never. Forgive it—maybe later.
But not now."

She was silent for a moment. Then she said sadly, "Then can
you forgive me, Dannerman?"

I stared at her. "For what?"

She seemed reluctant to speak, but she sighed again and went
on. "You know that there were other copies of yourself and your
comrades, and that they were examined physically?"

I did know. I knew what those physical examinations were
like, too, because Pat Five had gone through them and she told

me. I felt a flush of remembered rage. "You mean they were vivisected," I said.

"Yes, that is true," she said, her tone mournful. "What is also true is that I was one of the ones who did the vivisection, Dannerman."

CHAPTER FIFTEEN

Was I angry at Pirraghiz? You bet I was. In fact, "angry" wasn't a strong enough word; I was seething with rage. My nursemaid and pal was one of the torturers who had cut up the helpless bodies of my living, screaming friends. The first thing I thought of doing was to find the nearest rock and pound her head bloody with it.

I didn't exactly do that. I did pick up a rock, but I didn't attack Pirraghiz with it. I threw it as hard as I could at the nearest tree, and then I stalked away, leaving her gazing unhappily at my back.

I didn't look back. I kept right on walking, right out of the compound along one of the ancient trails that wound through the woods. It had rained during the night, and the footing was still a little slippery. I suspected Pirraghiz was trailing after me, but I didn't turn around. I didn't want to talk to one of the creatures who had carved up my friends—and me!—bit by bit, while they were wide-awake and screaming, just to see what made them tick. As you might do with an unfamiliar machine, and with no more regard for the machine's feelings. What I had gone through with the Christmas trees' helmet didn't compare to their ordeal. It didn't bear thinking about.

So I did my best not to think about it. It didn't matter. What mattered was getting out of there, and there was only one way to do that. The transit machine was obviously still working—the Horch machines had used it to make me. My job was to get back to it, and away.

But I couldn't do it without help. And the only help around was the person who was silently following along the trail, no more than eight or ten meters behind.

So I turned around and beckoned to Pirraghiz. "I'm sorry," I told her as she approached. "I overreacted. It was a shock to me, that's all. I understand that you couldn't help yourself."

She looked at me warily. "Do you understand, Dannerman?" she asked.

I patted her great upper arm. "I do, Pirraghiz. You had a control implanted in your brain, and you had to do whatever the Beloved Leaders wanted."

"Yes, but do you *understand?* Do you know what it is like to be *owned?*"

There was an expression on Pirraghiz's face that I had never seen there before; I couldn't tell whether it was sorrow or implacable anger. "Well—maybe not, exactly."

"But you should know, Dannerman," she told me sternly. "What happened to us may happen to your own people, in exactly the same way. We were not always slaves of the Beloved Leaders. We had our own lives, on our own planet—that was many eights of eights of generations ago, and we have only stories to remind us of what it was like. But it was a good life—I think—and then the Beloved Leaders came, and they saw a use for us. We were a clever people. We still are."

She paused to give me a challenging look. I said, "Of course you are. I know that."

"But do you also know what it is like to be clever, and to be *owned?* Under the Beloved Leaders we could do almost nothing they did not order us to do. Most of the time we could not even speak to each other, only when we were very young, or when we were permitted to breed."

That surprised me. "Breed? I didn't know—"

"No, Dannerman, you didn't know. I did once bear a litter of three after I was bred to the male, Perjowlsti, but I was allowed to keep them with me only until they were half grown. Then I watched while another Doc implanted them with controllers. They were very young and frightened. I had to lie to them. I said it would do them no harm. No harm! Do you hear me, Dannerman? I told them it would do them no harm! And I do not know what became of them. Since the Horch came I have not seen them, or Perjowlsti. Perhaps they were killed in the fighting."

She turned away from me and was silent for a moment. I thought she might be weeping, if Docs ever wept. I reached up and touched her shoulder. I hadn't forgotten about the vivisection, but I couldn't help feeling compassion. I said, "I'm sorry, Pirraghiz."

She said, "Yes," her voice muffled. When she turned around, the great cow eyes were dry, and her expression was less angry. "I too am sorry," she said, "for what will happen to your own species."

I straightened up. "My own species?"

She nodded with the great head, her hat flopping ludicrously. "You will serve them too, if they wish it."

Something was tasting very bad in the back of my throat. I did my best to repress it. "What would they want us for?"

"I do not know, Dannerman, but—" She thought for a moment, then sighed. "Have you ever seen the warriors of the Others?"

I remembered a half-dissolved corpse of a Bashful I'd seen in our escape. "No. Yes. I mean, I've seen a dead body, but—Wait a minute! Are you trying to tell me they'd make Bashfuls out of us?"

"I do not know what a 'Bashful' is"—I had used the English word—"but to use you to fight their battles for them when there is occasion for fighting, yes. I think so. It is known that your species is good at wars and violence. Was that not the reason for your own work before you were captured?"

I was aghast. "No! We won't let that happen! If we're going to fight, we'll fight them!"

"Of course you will, Dannerman," she agreed somberly. "As

I suppose we did, all those years ago. Even now, sometimes—you see, the control channels are very effective, but they are not perfect. If one of us finds himself surrounded by a kind of wall of metal mesh—I do not know the name for it—"

I guessed, "A Faraday cage?"

She shrugged. "Perhaps. In such a situation the controls are weakened. Then we have enough volition, sometimes, to try to fight back. But we do not succeed. As soon as that happens the others of our own kind who still belong to the Beloved Leaders come at once, and recapture us. Or kill us. They have no choice, just as I had none when the Beloved Leaders caused me to cut the flesh of your conspecifics."

She gazed down at me searchingly. "It is not only persons of your own species that have been vivisected in that way by us. You are only the most recent. The same has been done to members of every captive species—the Wet Ones, the Shelled Persons, the Tree-Livers, even the captive Horch. Even to my own people. And in every case—" She broke off, looking at me in a different way. "What is it, Dannerman?"

She had puzzled me. "What do you mean, 'captive Horch'?"

She looked at me with surprise. "But I thought you knew. What did you think Djabeertapritch was?"

I blinked at her. "A Horch, of course."

She sounded impatient. "Certainly he is a Horch, but until the other Horch captured this base, he was a prisoner, too. He and all his nest, Dannerman. Look, you can almost see the farms they cultivated, just past these trees. They were kept here since their ancestors were captured, long ago, for study and, yes, to be experimented on, just as your people were."

That was unexpected news. I had thought of the Horch simply as Horch. They were conquerors. I had not imagined that Beert himself had once been a conquered. I stared through the tangled vegetation toward where Pirraghiz had said Beert's people still lived. I couldn't see anything that looked like farms, but I knew what I had to do. I had to try my best to avert that horrible prospect of a subjugated Earth, and the place to do it was not here.

I turned to Pirraghiz. "You said Beert's village was out there?"

"The nest of the formerly captive Horch is, yes."

"All right. I'm as well as I need to be, and I want to see Beert. I'm going there now."

She did not seem surprised, only thoughtful. "I do not know if he will be at the nest. He may have called from the base."

"I'll wait for him."

"You do not know the way, Dannerman. You have never been there."

"I'll find it."

"It is a long walk. I am not sure you are yet strong enough for that—"

I didn't let her finish. "That's my problem," I said, but she finished anyway.

"—so I will carry you there myself." And she did. Hoisted me up into the crook of one of her great arms, and trotted away.

PART FOUR

The Nest

Dopey had always preferred being carried by a Doc to walking. I could see why. Pirraghiz held me comfortable and secure, and the ride, despite those elephant legs of hers, was rapid and just about jolt-free.

As we left the beaten path to cross over into Horch territory, she had to push her way through wet brush. Considerately she pushed the soggy branches away from me with one or another of her spare arms. Then, as we passed that invisible dividing line where weedy trees gave way to shrubs, we were in Horchland.

The difference between the two compounds was the difference between wilderness and civilization. Behind us was jungle. Ahead, neatly cultivated cropland. We came out onto a dirt road that bordered a couple of hectares of green stalks of grain, shoulder-high—I don't mean Pirraghiz's shoulder, of course. Between the rows two snaky heads popped up to stare at us in astonishment. Pirraghiz paid them no attention, but turned left on the road and loped along.

Although the road was dirt, it was smooth and almost rutless, even after the rain. Obviously the Horch were careful about keeping their place tidy. A kilometer or two ahead I could see something that looked like a huge, six-sided barn, but before we got there I heard a whirring noise from behind us. Pirraghiz didn't bother to look behind. She just moved courteously over to one side, allowing a vehicle to shoot past us. It was a three-wheeled cart, a little like the one Beert had used when he rescued me from the interrogation chambers. That one had had a motor, though; this one was pedal-driven by its occupant—one of the Horch who had gawked at us from the cropland, I supposed. He lay flat on his back, feet pumping at the pedals as fast as he could, while his neck swayed back and forth between staring at us and watching the road ahead.

As we got closer to the barnlike structure I could see that it was a kind of wickerwork tenement, four or five stories tall, with porches jutting out at every level. Some of the porches were enclosed in coarse screens, others open to the sky. I could see figures on some of them, perhaps taking the air. The whole thing looked like something some tribe of aborigines might have built for themselves out of willow withes and bamboo, in the days before the European colonizers came along with their whiskey, guns, row houses and syphilis.

It was the biggest structure in sight, but it wasn't the only one. I began to see sheds nearby, and a couple of peculiar trees, all circled by little clusters of flowering bushes for decoration. The trees were branchless until near the top, where they spread out in a crown like royal palms. The most peculiar thing about the trees was that they were all bent at a sharp angle from the ground up, and all at the same angle. There was something that looked like a wicker band shell—people were moving around it—and, as we moved toward one side, behind the main building a smaller structure appeared of a wholly other kind. This one wasn't wicker. It was made of the same glossy ceramic stuff as my former cell, though this was pinkish in color. A pair of the Horch Christmas trees were industriously unloading some sort of equipment to take inside it.

I wasn't pleased to see them there, but Pirraghiz paid them no attention. She set me down carefully. "Wait, Dannerman. I will see if Djabeertapritch is here."

She left me standing in a plot of damp, spiky grass, I suppose the Horch equivalent of a front lawn. There were low wicker benches scattered around—unoccupied—and a few smaller trees with buttercup-yellow blossoms. Although the robots weren't paying any attention to me, I was uncomfortable in their presence. I walked a little way around the great house to get out of their sight. When I looked up the woven-sapling side of the building, I discovered that someone was looking back at me. Three or four of those snaky heads were peering over the side of one of the porches. I waved, but the only response I got from them was to pull hastily back, some completely out of sight, one still staring at me with just the nose and eyes showing.

As long as I was here, I told myself, I should be keeping my eyes open for the kind of information the Bureau would want to hear when (I didn't let myself say "if") I got back. The trouble was, there didn't seem to be very much sensitive information lying around.

So I made do with what was available. To start, I heard shrill soprano singing coming from nearby. It was that band-shell thing, and it seemed to be functioning as a kind of Horch kindergarten. Eight or ten tiny Horch infants danced around as they sang, waving their sinuous arms and necks more or less gracefully. The two littlest ones weren't dancing. They lay on their backs in tiny wicker baskets, looking like some kind of musical calamari as they waved their limbs and piped along with the others. There was one adult with them to conduct the performance. By the swellings under her jumpsuit I judged she was female.

She moved quickly to interpose herself between me and her charges, thrusting her head toward me suspiciously. "What are you?" she demanded.

That wasn't an easy question to answer. Before I had figured out how to describe myself, she gave the neck-twist that was like a human nod. "Yes, now I remember. You are Djabeertapritch's new pet."

I didn't respond to that. I was digesting the implications of that word, "pet," and anyway, she was still talking. "Please go away. You are distracting the children and they must prepare to sing for the Greatmother." Her tone was commanding, and she gestured accordingly.

She was right. All the children had stopped what they were doing to goggle at me. I apologized. "I'm sorry if I interrupted you. I'm just waiting for Beert—for Djabeertapritch, I mean."

"You should not wait here," she said crossly. I might have argued, but then I saw two Horch ambling around the perimeter of the building toward us. They seemed in no hurry. They weren't looking in our direction at all; they were in animated conversation with each other, their necks winding close together except when they paused to examine some detail of the building's structure.

There was something about them that was different. It took me a moment to figure it out, and then I had it. It was the way they were dressed. All Horch seemed to like to ornament their round little bellies, but not all in the same way. Beert, as well as this teacher-Horch and the little ones in her class, sported a circle of colorfully embroidered fabric there. These two were dressed like the female I had seen with Beert in the interrogation room; their belly bowls were shallow domes of bright metal, as shiny as chrome.

I didn't have good feelings about the metal-wearing brand of Horch. The strollers didn't seem to have noticed me, and I preferred to keep it that way. I nodded politely to the teacher and left, as inconspicuously as I could.

When Pirraghiz found me I was in the middle of a sort of car park of those three-wheeled velocipedes; they were ingeniously put together out of four or five different kinds of wood, wheels, bearings and all. "There you are! You should have stayed where I left you," she scolded. "Now come. The Greatmother has summoned Beert. I will take you to a room that is available, where you can wait for him. And I will go back home to get food for you, and to pick up some of my own things so that I can stay with you here."

The wicker building was wicker all the way through, wicker walls, wicker floors, wicker stairs—and a lot of them—to take us to the upper levels. I marveled at the kind of engineering skills it had taken to create a five-story building out of withes woven together. "They must be pretty good designers," I offered to Pirraghiz, breathing hard.

She looked down at me with concern. "Of course. They are Horch. But are you all right? Should I carry you again?"

I shook my head. I wasn't willing to let her know how quickly I tired, not to mention that the steps sagged and protested Pirraghiz's weight with soft, squeaking sounds. I didn't think it was a good idea to add my weight to hers.

The stairs we were climbing circled an interior courtyard, like the atrium in a five-story Roman villa—if any Roman villa ever got five stories high. Balconies ran all around the inside of the structure at every level, and a few Horch paused in whatever they were doing on them to peer at us. We went up three flights, and I was panting in earnest by the time Pirraghiz reached the right level. She took me to a door—rather like a thick woven curtain—and flung it open. "This is where you will stay," she announced.

The room wasn't anything like the sterile chambers where the Horch machines had questioned me. It wasn't like any place I had ever been in before. I said politely, "It looks fine. I'm glad they had a spare room for me."

"They have very many spare rooms," she said somberly. "There are very few of this Greatmother's nest left. Will you be all right if I leave you alone for a while? It will only be for a little bit, then Djabeertapritch will be here. There is a place to sleep; perhaps you should do that. It will not be long until he arrives, I think," she said again, to reassure me. "You will be quite safe. If you need anything, you can call and someone will come, but do not eat anything until I return with proper food for you."

It had been a long time since anyone had fussed over me in that way. I couldn't help laughing. "Thank you, Mother," I said. "You can go. Honestly. Go!"

She went. But actually I had barely begun to investigate my new room when I felt the wicker floor vibrate again with her heavy tread. When I turned to the door, there she was again, carrying a large pottery bowl. "This is in case you need to relieve yourself while I am away, Dannerman," she said. "Now I will leave again." And she did.

The room the Horch had given me was a good size, maybe three meters by four. The walls were unadorned, except that on the interior ones the wickerwork had been woven together in strands of several varieties of withes, of different colors. The result was rather pretty, almost like an abstract tapestry. The outside walls were made of darker, more robust basketwork, and something like clay had been plastered into the wicker to seal the walls against the weather outside. The door to the balcony outside was made of accordion folds of the same material, and they were ajar. When I stepped out to look around I had a view of farm fields beyond the outbuildings and the curiously bent trees. A stream cut through them—the same stream that went through the old compound, I supposed. There were little rainbow-shaped Japanese-garden bridges over the stream here and there. Oddly, not all the fields appeared to be under cultivation. Some seemed to have been farmed once, but now bore only a scraggle of weeds.

That was all I saw from the balcony, because I didn't stay there long. Adult Horch weighed about as much as I did, and I suppose the builders had allowed some margin of safety. But it sagged disturbingly under my weight, so I stepped back inside. As I did I noticed something I hadn't seen before. Both the doorframe and the outer edges of the accordion doors were thick with some kind of pale purplish mildew.

It was the kind of thing any Earthly housekeeper would scrub away as soon as detected. Were the Horch as sloppy as that? I didn't think so. The stuff seemed to be there for a purpose. There were heavy cloth drapes attached to the lintel and doors. They were rolled back, but it looked as though they could be pulled out to cover the moldy purple stuff.

I put that aside for later thought. Inside the room were the chamber pot and the bed. Their purposes were unmistakable. I used them in turn.

Thankfully, this bed was a lot softer than Pirraghiz's. It was basically a sort of round mattress on the floor, maybe a hundred and fifty centimeters across—just about long enough for me to stretch out. The mattress was covered with something that felt like flannel, and stuffed with little round lumps like bolls of cotton. When I sprawled out on it I meant only to rest and think about what I was going to say to Beert when he arrived, but I think I dozed off.

What roused me was a sound from outside.

It was an airplane. When I got to the balcony to look out it was just landing in one of those untended fields, coming down slow and nearly vertically, like one of the Bureau's VTOLs. It rolled only a few meters, and as soon as it stopped a Horch got out, met by a couple of others who had been standing by.

Was the one who had just arrived Beert? I couldn't tell, but he was wearing the cloth belly patch, while the abdomens of the two who were meeting him glittered metallically in the sunlight. The three of them were having an animated conversation, snaky arms and necks swirling around. I couldn't hear, of course, but I wished I could; some of the flailing arms were pointing toward the building—in fact, to the balcony I was standing on.

I hastily stepped back, more or less out of sight, but it was too late to matter. The three had finished their conversation. One of the shiny-bellied ones climbed into the plane, still yammering at the other. And the one who had just arrived entered the building.

CHAPTER SEVENTEEN

The newcomer was Beert, all right. When I went to the door of my room and peered down the circular stairway, I saw him coming up, the ropy neck pointed straight at me. He called, "I did not think you would come here without authorization, Dan."

He sounded aggrieved. I didn't want him angry at me, but I stood my ground. I said, "I'm well now, Beert. I didn't see any reason to wait."

He came up and stood beside me, his pointy little face only centimeters from my own. "You do not know all the reasons for what I do, Dan," he said glumly, and waved me into the room. He closed the door behind us and sat on the edge of the bed, regarding me. "The Greatmother did not expect you yet," he sighed. "I will have to apologize to her."

Greatmother? That was the second or third time I'd heard her mentioned, and she sounded important. "I'm sorry if I got you in trouble," I apologized.

He waved the apology away with both sinuous arms. "I am not in trouble, Dan, but it is not appropriate for things to happen in the nest that the Greatmother doesn't know about. Where is Pirraghiz?"

"She went back to get some stuff. It isn't her fault, Beert. It was all my idea."

"Yes, I had supposed so," he said moodily. "It has been observed that your species is often unruly." He thought for a moment, long neck swaying, and then said, "You see, Dan, I am engaged in a number of discussions with the cousins. I had to leave them to come here, and I cannot stay very long. Perhaps we can spend a little time together, but first I must speak with the Greatmother about your presence here. Can you remain in this chamber while I make arrangements for you?"

"Sure I can, but I'd rather—"

He was waving both arms and the neck at me again. "Please, Dan. Do not be still unruly. It will not take me long. Stay here."

When he came back he looked less fussed. "The Greatmother extends you the courtesy of the nest," he told me, sounding pleased about it. "When she has time she wishes to meet you in person, but when that may be, I cannot say. Do you need to eat?"

Actually I had been beginning to think of food, but I shook my head. "Pirraghiz doesn't want me eating anything until she comes back to check it out."

"Yes, that's wise. Very well. I'm afraid everyone is quite busy, since we are so shorthanded now, but I think I have something that will occupy you until Pirraghiz shows up. Come, first I will show you the parts of the nest."

He did, too. From where we stood on the landing he showed me the door to something he called the Repository of the Nest—a sort of library, I gathered. We looked in on the children's dormitory, where a dozen or so little ones were taking their naps—the same ones I had seen at the band shell, I thought, because the female who was standing guard over them was familiar. Beert told me her name. He told me the names of all the five or six Horch we met along the way, but I didn't retain any of them. They all greeted Beert with friendly respect, sometimes intertwining necks. Even the teacher-guard. They seemed to be an affectionate bunch.

When we were on the ground floor Beert paused at the entrance. He slapped the accordion door with one arm and said, like any suburbanite with a new split-ranch, "What do you think of our nest then, Dan?" When I told him, as politely as I could, that it was very nice, but it struck me that wicker was a peculiar choice of materials for building a multistory habitat, he said in surprise, "But we could work only with what we had, Dan. The Others gave us nothing."

"The Others?"

"The ones you call the Beloved Leaders. When they dumped our ancestors here we had no tools, no machines, only our bare arms and teeth. Do you not think we did well? Every section of the nest reinforces every other. It has stood for many generations like this, and will for generations more."

"Unless there's a fire," I said.

That amused him. "But there is no fire in the nest, ever," he said, and led me to the shed that was used for cooking and eating. This one was made of clay bricks like adobe—and as likely to wash away in the first rain, I thought, but he showed me how the clay was covered with some sort of vegetable sap to protect it from the weather. A meal was being prepared. Though the smells were unfamiliar, they were definitely food, and I was beginning to wish that Pirraghiz would get back. The two Horch doing the cooking were friendly but busier than any two persons needed to be, chopping up vegetables, grinding tubers in a mortar, tending their cooking fires. When I asked Beert if everyone always worked so hard around here, the question seemed to disturb him.

"Not always," he said moodily. Then he sighed. "We do not have enough people for all the work," he admitted. "The farms to be tended, the children to be cared for, the nest to be kept in repair. Before we were—" He hesitated over the next words. "Before we were *set free*, it was different. Then there were enough of us to do all that needed to be done, and to have time enough to rest, and to study, and to do all the other things we enjoy. But now many of us have left the nest."

"To go where?"

His head darted around uneasily. "When the cousin Horch freed us they offered to take us out of here. Many nest-siblings went to the planets of the cousins. They wanted to see what a life of leisure was like, with machines to tend to all the drudgery.

This was natural enough, Dan. They had every right to do so, and the Greatmother did not object."

"But you didn't go?"

"It is my nest," he said simply, and then glanced at the shadow cast by one of those bent-over trees. "But look at the time! I must hurry."

The penny dropped. Of course. The trees had been coaxed to grow in that direction so that they could function as gnomons in vast sundials, the eight bushes planted around them marking the Horch equivalent of the hours of the day. I was so struck by the ingenuity of the system that I hardly heard the rest of what Beert said. Which was: "I have something to give you before I leave."

He wrapped one of those arms around my shoulders—it was warmer than I had expected—and led me to the pink structure. The two Christmas trees I had seen before were standing immobile not far away, but Beert ignored them. He seemed in good spirits, if rushed. "This is my personal laboratory," he said with pride.

I looked at it, and at him. "Does that mean you're some kind of a scientist?"

"Scientist? No, Dan. I am a student. All I hope to learn is what the cousins already know, and this is where I try to learn it. The thing I wish to give you is in the laboratory, but there are delicate machines here; it is better if you don't come inside until you know enough about them to take care. Wait just a moment."

He unlocked the door—at least, I guess that was what he did; he pressed both arms against the door in a complicated, sine-wavey pattern, something like an identification signature, I suppose; anyway, the door opened. Lights sprang up inside, and he went in.

I peered after him.

Beert had been right about the machines. The place was full

of them, in all stages of completion. It looked like the way he had been learning his cousins' science was by taking some of their gadgets apart and rebuilding them.

More important, it also looked like this was the place I had been looking for. If there were secrets of Horch technology for me to steal and take back to the Bureau, there was a whole treasure trove of them right here.

And he had implied that, sooner or later, I would be allowed to examine them more closely.

It was the most hopeful thing that had happened to me since Beert rescued me from the torturers. The only sour note was those two Horch robots. Most of their twigs were retracted, but I knew they could spring into action at any moment.

When Beert came back, carrying something in a wicker basket, he saw me watching them uneasily. "Do not worry about the robots, Dan," he reassured me. "You are here with the permission of the cousins, and there will be no problem. The cousins have been very kind. This laboratory could not have been built without their help. Now let us go back to your chamber."

CHAPTER EIGHTEEN

I never learned Beert's age, but there was something boyish about him. All the way up the steps he was hissing softly to himself—it was almost a chuckle—and darting his head, almost teasingly, toward mine. But he didn't speak until we were in my room and the door was closed. I was feeling pretty cheerful myself, partly contagion from Beert, partly the thought of all those Horch secrets waiting for me in his lab.

Then he lifted the lid of the wicker basket. "This is something you may use while Pirraghiz and I are gone," he said happily.

He took something out of the basket. I recognized it at once and suddenly was not happy at all. It was one of those Beloved Leader helmets. I jumped back, snarling, *"No!"*

That blew Beert's own cheerful mood. He darted his head at me incredulously. "You do not wish this? Oh, wait. Perhaps I understand. Are you thinking of the way the interrogation machines used this device? No, I am not giving you this for that purpose. I do not intend to cause you pain. Indeed, you can operate it for yourself. See, here are the selectors."

He flipped up the little tab on the side of the helmet, exposing its nest of colored grooves, as though he were revealing a great secret. It wasn't news to me, though. "I've seen this already," I told him. "Rosaleen Artzybachova was tinkering with one like it while we were captives."

That surprised him. "Did she so? I was not aware of this. Was she able to operate the helmet satisfactorily?"

"Well, no. Not very."

He wagged his long neck at me. "Indeed I think she would have had great trouble doing so. The selectors are designed for tinier digits than yours—the talons of your Dopey, or of one of Pirraghiz's people. Let me see if I can find some implement you can use—"

While he was scrabbling in the basket I took the little ceramic toothpick Pirraghiz had given me out of my pocket. "Like this, you mean?"

He swooped his head down almost to touch it, then peered up at me. "You astonish me sometimes, Dan. Yes, that will do." He took the little splinter out of my hand with the end of one arm—it split, like an elephant's trunk, to pick it up securely.

I said, "Isn't this a Beloved Leader device?"

"No longer," he said absently, tweaking the colored lines. "It is now ours." He had pressed the helmet against his belly, and seemed to be staring at nothing. Then, sounding satisfied, he said, "Yes, here it is. See, Dan—" holding up the helmet for me to look at. "I have accessed some of their records for you. You can change from one to another if you wish, but activate only the green selector, otherwise you will be in other files and it will be difficult for you to return to the ones of interest. Do you remember how to put the helmet on?"

I did. I held the thing warily, unable to forget what it had done to me with the Christmas trees.

But was Beert likely to be playing unpleasant tricks? I hoped not. I swallowed. I pulled it over my head, snapped the eyeshades in place—

And, just as before, I was instantly in another place.

I was on a familiar street in New York City. Vendors lined the sidewalk. I had stopped at one of the stalls. I was picking up bits and pieces of the kitschy merchandise this one had to offer, and I felt strange. I felt *female*. My body was not the one I had been born with; it was tightly bound at the breasts, and when I saw my hands the nails were bright orange and one finger bore a ring like a dragon, with wings out-spread. Female hands, all right. Certainly not my own. I—*she*—seemed to be interested in an old-fashioned wristwatch with the hands of Mickey Mouse pointing out the time, but when the vendor spoke to her she put it back and turned away.

As always with the helmet, I was *there*. I saw everything this body looked at, I felt everything she touched. I smelled a faint wisp of roasting lamb from a pita joint on the corner, and heard the scream of sirens from somewhere nearby—fire, ambulance, police car, I could not tell which, and the body I was occupying was not interested enough to look.

I pulled the helmet off my head, confused. "What am I looking at?" I demanded.

"Keep looking," Beert advised. "You will see someone you know well, so the other Dan said. These events are not happening now," he added. "These are recordings of transmissions which were received some time ago. See it for yourself."

Hesitantly I put the helmet back on. The body I was wearing glanced at her own watch and, now hurrying, crossed the street and turned a corner.

I recognized the entranceway. It belonged to the midtown office building that held the Dannerman Astrophysical Observatory, my grandfather's legacy to immortalize his name, where I had once gone to work for (and spy on!) my cousin Pat. The body announced herself—the name meant nothing to me—to the floor guard—new since my time—and while she waited for him to call her escort, she was covertly eyeing the man.

I realized that I was looking at a *man* through the eyes of a *woman*, and it was instructive to see where her eyes went: face, shoulders (he was pretty solidly built), with special attention to the region of the crotch, both front and back.

Then some other man I didn't recognize came down, passed her through the turnstiles, into the elevator, up into Pat's waiting room, and there I saw people I knew quite well. ◄

As I entered the room, Pat's receptionist, Janice DuPage, got up from her desk and greeted me with a quick hug. "Sorry I'm late," I—"I"—apologized, and Janice said:

"That's all right. Just let me sign out and then we can go."

Out of the corner of my eye I caught a glimpse of Pete Schneyman, just glancing at us as he passed through the reception room. And while Janice was picking up her purse and checking her makeup, the elevator door opened again. The person who came out was someone I knew very well indeed.

It was Dr. Patrice Adcock. My cousin. My Pat. The Pat I loved. The Pat I had lost.

My hostess's eyes were studying her, too, in her own way, while Janice said, "You remember my friend from the cruise? The one I didn't take?"

There was an edge to her voice, as of some remembered grievance, but Pat only said, "Of course." She shook hands. *I* shook her hand. I was actually touching the warm, firm hand of the woman I loved. And then she turned away and went into her own office and I tore the helmet off my head.

"What is this?" I demanded. "Whose body was I in? Was it Patrice?"

"It was not any one of your party," Beert said heavily, his neck hanging low. "Other humans were implanted with the transmitters."

I scowled at him. "How could that be?" Then a particularly nasty thought crossed my mind, and I said, "Unless—"

Beert's little snake head swung toward mine, looking into my eyes. "Yes, Dan," he said. "The Others have reached your planet now."

CHAPTER NINETEEN

I don't know when Beert left my room. I was under the helmet, obsessively eavesdropping on the many, many unwitting—or sometimes witting—human beings who were wearing the bugs implanted by the Others.

I knew of only six persons who had been bugged and returned to Earth, the five of us in the original batch from Starlab, plus Patrice from the ones who had been in captivity. Now there seemed to be hundreds of them.

So there was no question about it. I had to believe that what Beert said was true. The Others were on Earth—somehow—and going right ahead with their plans. And if I were ever to hope to get back and—somehow—help fight them off, it had to be done quickly.

All the same, I couldn't help peering out at my planet through the eyes of the bugged ones. They came in all varieties. There was a young woman in what I supposed was China, wearing the tracking collar of a house-arrest prisoner, sullenly trampling seedlings into mud with her bare toes, and seeing nothing but the other young women in the paddy and the old man who was dumping more baskets of seedlings at its rim. There was a store clerk in some hot and Spanish-speaking place; a blackjack dealer on what seemed to be a cruise ship, from the gentle rolling of the floor; a dozen or so in prisons. A *lot* of the bugged ones were in prisons, and a lot of those I took to be Chinese, from the uniforms they wore and the totally incomprehensible language they spoke.

I didn't spend much time with the ones who spoke languages I couldn't understand. There were a fair number of English-speaking ones, and a sizeable number of those were also in some kind of detention. Some, like that first Chinese girl, wore tracking collars as they went glumly about their business. Most were in a cell. Some were being interrogated, and the questioners were getting little joy from the answers they got. Uniformly the bugged ones claimed to have no knowledge of how the little gadgets had been implanted in their skulls.

Once, just once, I saw a face I recognized.

The face belonged to Nat Baumgartner, an NBI agent I had worked with once on the Michigan militia. What Nat was doing was standing in a hospital operating room, looking more worried than any Bureau agent should let himself look in the presence of a prisoner. I was his prisoner. I lay on my back, staring up at the operating-theater lights while someone I couldn't see was doing something with an IV in my arm. I supposed my host was about to undergo surgery, most likely to remove the bug from his brain, but I never found out for sure. Shortly after that, my carrier went unconscious, and that transmission stopped for good.

And all the time that I was looking through the eyes of other people, one part of my mind was scheming what to do about this situation. Make Pirraghiz take me to the transit machine and *go*. No, first take a quick snatch-and-grab run through Beert's laboratory and collect all the Horch technology I could carry to take back. No, before that, pump him for what he might know about the Horch plans for Earth, if any, and for any guidance he can give about what to do to resist the Beloved Leaders. No—

No, there were too many things to think out, and I couldn't think clearly about them while I was hunting frantically through the files of all those bugged humans. But I couldn't stop doing it, either. The person I was really looking for was Pat.

I was convinced there had to be other files in which she would appear. I picked frantically at the green line in the selectors, but I couldn't find them. Apart from that one glimpse in the Observatory office, she never turned up for me again. By dumb luck I did finally connect again with the woman who had gone to the Observatory to meet Janice DuPage, and watched it all over again for the sake of that one brief glimpse of Pat.

That brief glimpse was all there was. When I watched the file all the way through, all that happened was that the woman went to lunch with Janice DuPage. The good part was that I could taste the Caesar salad the woman ordered, but there was nothing else. What they talked about was the cruise Janet had missed, and how it had come to an end when something went wrong with the ship's engines. And after they had left the restaurant and were crossing a street, abruptly and strangely, the transmission ended. I mean, it just *stopped.* At one moment I was laughing and clutching Janice's arm as we dodged past a stopped truck; I heard Janice scream, and that was it. The next moment I was in total darkness, with no sight or sound or smell at all.

I took the helmet off to puzzle over that for a bit. Something like that had happened before, when the man in the operating room went to sleep. That was anesthesia, I had no doubt. But what kind of person went to sleep in the middle of crossing a New York street?

I had the helmet back on when I felt a touch on my shoulder—my *real* shoulder. When I took the helmet off it was Pirraghiz. She wasn't alone. Standing next to her was a male Doc, reaching out one of his arms in hospitable fashion to shake my hand. "This is my friend Mrrranthoghrow," she told me—as close as I can come to his name, which sounded like a voiceless purr, a coughing sneeze and a yowl at the end. "He came along to help me carry what I needed for you, but he cannot stay this time."

"I hope to see more of you soon," Mrrranthoghrow said politely. I mumbled something back. My mind was still full of what I had seen under the helmet; I hardly noticed when he left again.

Pirraghiz was looking at me curiously. "Are you all right, Dannerman?" she asked. "Are you hungry?"

Once reminded, I was. In fact, I was ravenous. I don't know how long I had been under the helmet, but while I was devouring the food Pirraghiz set before me, I discovered it was dark outside my window. Not inside the room, though; the whole chamber was illuminated with a soft glow, which, I saw, came from the mossy stuff around the doorframe.

I paid it only minimal attention, still thinking—worrying— about what the Others might be doing to my world. Pirraghiz watched in silence. It wasn't until I had swallowed the last of the berry-flavored tomatoish thing that was my dessert that she removed the dishes and said, "It is sleeping time. I will show you how to cover the light, Dannerman. Simply pull these drapes out, so, and cover the light like this, do you see?"

She left one little section uncovered, leaving the room dim. But there was enough light for me to see that she was regarding me with concern. "I will be in the next room, if needed," she said. "The Greatmother has given it to me for as long as you want me here." I grunted. Then she reached down and touched the helmet I had left on the table. "Did Djabeertapritch give you this so you could see what is happening in your home?"

"Oh, yes," I said, sitting on the edge of the bed. "He certainly did."

She sighed. "It is a sad thing, I know. All of you from your planet found it most unpleasant."

That got my attention. "You mean the copies you made of me?"

"Yes, often copies of yourself, Dannerman, but also of the others. Some copies of all of you were shown this material at the beginning of their interrogations."

"Copies of *Pat*?"

"Of course. But it was you who were most useful, since you had a broader experience of the world." She paused, looking down at me in the dimness. "This upsets you. But information was wanted, and so what happened was inevitable."

"Inevitable! Making a copy of Pat and killing her was *inevitable*?"

She looked defensive. "I am sorry. I know this troubles you. The fact that so many bad things are happening to your people troubles me, too." She stopped to consider for a moment, then sighed. "But honestly, Dannerman, it does not trouble me very much. You are not alone. How many sixty-fours of sixty-fours of sixty-fours of sixty-fours of persons have been sent early to the Eschaton in this struggle? And many of them died far more painfully than your Rosaleens and Pats. Here in this nest we have made ourselves look away from such horrors, Dannerman. We could not survive otherwise."

CHAPTER TWENTY

Those scenes in the helmet had put the fear of God into me—well, fear of the Others, anyway. They were definitely taking over my planet. Every last person I cared about—even Pat, even my other self!—was threatened with becoming a zombie servant of the Others, just like the Docs.

It was about the worst news I had ever had to face. I didn't see how I would be able to sleep with that haunting me. I was wrong about that, though. I dropped off as soon as Pirraghiz left the room, and I didn't even dream.

Maybe that was my own way of turning away, like Pirraghiz, from what was too hard to face. It didn't last. The minute I woke up, there it was. I didn't have any choice. I had to face it.

I stumbled across the dimly lit room to the balcony, my mind full of what I had seen. When I threw the accordion slides open it was bright daylight outside, and three or four Horch were getting into their tricycles to go to work in the fields. I stared at them without seeing them, thinking hard. What I wanted to do more than anything else was to escape from this place, back to Earth, to face whatever was still happening there.

What I had to do first, though, was something different. One additional warm body wouldn't be much help to the human race. To be of any use at all, I had to bring something useful back with me. What's more, I had to do it *now* . . . always assuming, that was to say, that what I had seen was what was still happening, and not ancient history.

When Pirraghiz heard me moving around she came in, bringing food. As soon as she was in the room she glanced at the drapes, shook that big head reprovingly and began to fuss with them without waiting to hear anything I might have to say. She scolded, "You mustn't cover the lights during the day, Dannerman. They have to charge up with sunlight so that you can use them after dark."

I wasn't in a mood to be instructed about housekeeping. I said to her back, "How long have I been here?"

She left off fussing with the drapes and turned around, peering at me. "What?"

"I want to know," I insisted. "Those scenes in the helmet, they come from all different times—some winter, some not. I can't tell anything from them, and I need to know how much time has passed."

"Do you mean since the Horch liberated this planet? Let me see." She stroked the mossy beard on her chin, counting to herself. "About four sixty-fours of days, I think. A little more."

I did the arithmetic in my head. Allowing for the fact that this planet's days were shorter than Earth's, it came out to about six months. A long time, and a lot could have happened. But it wasn't ancient history.

"All right," I said. "Now I want to know everything there is to know about the Horch and the Belov—I mean, the Others. Let's get started."

Pirraghiz was obliging, but she was puzzled, too, and she had a lot of questions. What exactly was it that I wanted to know? When all my answers kept adding up to that same single word—"everything"—she sighed. "I must have advice on this," she told me. "Wait for me. Eat. I will be back very soon."

She was, too. I was sipping from a ceramic bowl the last of something that tasted salty and faintly sour when she appeared at the door. She looked pleased. "Much of what you want to learn may be in the Repository of the Nest," she announced. "The Greatmother has given permission to take you there—as soon," she said, tidily beginning to pick up the dishes from my breakfast, "as I put these in my room."

I didn't want to wait for that, or for anything, but Pirraghiz was firm. Her room was about the same size as mine—pretty small, for a Doc—and she had fitted it with enough belongings to make me think she planned to stay for a while. Among the tiny potted flowers and the bric-a-brac I saw one of those great, cubical cookers Dopey had used. I thought of how much heat those things could produce, and wondered if Beert knew she had it in his fire-free nest. Pirraghiz caught my stare and asked, "Is something wrong?"

I didn't want to get into a discussion, so I lied. "I was wondering why the Horch have so many empty rooms like this," I said.

"Why," she said, closing the door and leading me down the steps, "the reason is simple. When the Horch liberated this planet, all of the captive Horch who wished it were returned home—well, taken to Horch planets, anyway; it has been so long since they were brought here that none of them really has a home anywhere else anymore."

That much I knew, more or less, but I kept her talking. "But not Djabeertapritch and these others."

She gave me one of those massive arms-and-shoulders shrugs. "The ones who stayed in this nest do not always agree with all the things about the cousin Horch."

That got my interest. If Beert and the "cousins" disagreed, there might be a place to drive a useful wedge between them. "What kind of things?"

But Pirraghiz was not willing to be drawn out on that. "You must ask Djabeertapritch himself," she said. "Now here is the Repository of the Nest."

The Repository of the Nest was a library, and it looked like one. It was a suite of three or four rooms,

all lined with ceiling-high shelves. In two rooms an assortment
of wooden boxes were shelved, most of them looking ancient
and worn. In the third some of the wooden boxes had been replaced with bright yellow cubes made of the Horch ceramic. In
that room a young Horch female was working at a high table, a
spread of documents in front of her. She gave us an unwelcom-
ing glance, but Pirraghiz paid no attention. Pirraghiz knew what
she was looking for. She went at once to a great, double-fronted
chest of drawers that sat in the middle of the room, and began
pulling out an assortment of those silvery spools I had seen in
her own room, back in the compound. As she picked each one
out she scanned the legend on its label before putting it back,
frowning.

I took one of the rejects from her hand to look it over. She
didn't resist. She only whispered, "Be careful with it." But it
wasn't helpful. Its label bore a string of curlicues and jagged
lines—identifying its contents, I supposed.

But the writing meant nothing to me. The gadget behind my
ear had its limitations. The Horch had given me their spoken
language, but hadn't bothered to make me literate.

I wasn't one of the Bureau's language wonks. Outside of English, the only one I knew well was German. But being unable
to read any language I could speak at all was new to me, and
depressing. I left Pirraghiz and wandered over to where the young
female was at work. She had one of the antique wooden boxes
open, carefully transferring its contents to a ceramic one. On the
floor next to her was a kind of balloon, almost a meter across,
with its valve gently hissing. She elevated her head warningly as
I came close.

"Do not breathe moisture on the records," she ordered.
"These are very old and very delicate."

I moved back a step, turning my head sharply away from her
as though about to be inspected for a hernia. Mollified, she explained what she was doing. The documents were the total records of the captive Horch colony, from their earliest beginnings.

Her job was to transfer them from their original containers to the new ones given by the Horch cousins. When she finished the box she would seal it and then purge the air out of it with an inert gas from the balloon at her feet. She was obviously proud of the responsibility the Greatmother had given her. She even pulled a few sheets out of their boxes for me to see. The earliest ones were very old, scratched on tough leaves; later the sheets were paper, somehow or other made by the colonists. But when the librarian read me a few lines, there was nothing there worth trying to remember; after their capture, the colonists had had a tough time, and their hardships were what they wrote about. Interesting. Even touching. But useless.

And so, it seemed, were the book spools Pirraghiz was sorting through. "I am sorry, Dannerman," she told me. "I do not think there is much here that will tell you what you want to know. These are gifts of the cousins to this nest, and they are all music and drama and such things."

"Nothing about the Others? Or technology?"

"No, Dannerman. Djabeertapritch may have some of that sort, but they are not in the Repository of the Nest." She hesitated. "There is one story which is very old and famous. It is about Horch who lived long ago, if you would like to see it? Yes? Very well, but let us do it in my room, so we will not disturb this female in her work."

So I viewed the thing, all the way through. It lasted for a couple of hours. In the first ten minutes I realized there was nothing useful here, but I stayed with it anyway—remember, I got my doctorate in drama and, in spite of everything, I was hooked.

The story took place in a Horch city, time not specified, and the plot was easy enough to follow. It was a kind of a love story. A female Horch and a male Horch wanted to mate, but since they were from the same gens, though not blood relatives, they couldn't. The various threads of the plot struck me as pretty universal; it was *Romeo and Juliet* combined with *Oedipus Rex* and a few snatches of Arthur Miller's *A View from the Bridge*. The male was a space pilot, the female some kind of a farmer. That didn't mean she dug seedlings into the mud with her toes. None of these Horch, however ancient in time, had to do much purely physical work. For that sort of thing they had machines. Those were pretty primitive compared to the latest Christmas-tree models, but they were good enough to free the Horch for more intellectual pursuits. Some of the characters in the play were artists, some philosophers, some teachers, some, as far as I could tell, engineers.

I can't say I followed every detail of the story. There were a lot of references that went right past me, but there are plenty of those in Shakespeare, too. The basic story was clear enough ... except that I kept thinking what a pity it was that I hadn't had this experience while I was in graduate school. What a hell of a doctoral dissertation I could have written—maybe even one that somebody might actually have wanted to read.

Pirraghiz had gone about her own business while I was watching the bowl. She timed her return perfectly, coming back in just as the story finished, and she wasn't alone. The male named Mrrranthoghrow was with her. After the two of them had greeted me, she looked at me apologetically. "Was any of that what you wanted to know?"

I came alive. "Not exactly. I was more interested in your field, technology, weapons, that sort of thing."

"Not weapons," he protested. "I have no experience with weapons. That is what the warriors and the Horch fighting machines are for."

"All right then." I pointed to the viewing bowl. "What makes that thing run?"

He scratched his beard. "Do you mean where the power

comes from? There is a small unit in the base which provides that. It is called a—" I heard the word he said, but it meant nothing to me.

"Something like a battery?" I guessed. I used the English word, because I didn't have one in Horch, but when I explained, "A device in which power from another source is stored, and released as needed," he shook his great head.

"I have never seen the *(incomprehensible)* charged up, Dannerman. I know nothing of such matters; I am a mechanic, trained in that alone. The power in each machine comes from—" he searched for a term I might understand, and came up with— "an accumulator, but what it accumulates, and what it accumulates it from, I do not know. Perhaps Djabeertapritch can tell you, if he wants to, but the Others had no reason to instruct me in such matters. When I disassembled and rebuilt the transit machine for the Horch, I knew what components needed to be connected in certain fashions, but I do not understand how it works."

Suddenly there was a rush of hot blood to my brain. I stared at him. "You worked on the transit machine?"

"With others, yes."

"And it is in working order?"

"Certainly. The cousin Horch use it all the time—for making copies, such as yourself, and also for tracing channels to other installations of the Others."

I swallowed, my throat tight. "Strictly as a theoretical question," I said—I didn't want to scare him off too soon—"would it be possible for me to use that machine to, say, transmit me back to my planet?"

He looked startled, and so did Pirraghiz. "Oh, Dannerman," she said sorrowfully, understanding at once what I was getting at.

So did Mrrranthoghrow. His voice was sympathetic as he said, "I am sorry, Dannerman. It is impossible."

I wasn't giving up, although my pulse was racing. "Why impossible? The Horch wouldn't have to know! You could just smuggle me in—"

He was shaking that great, moon-faced head. "I could not do that without their consent, Dannerman," he said gently. "But that is not the reason. It simply cannot be done. Nothing can be transmitted to any locus unless there is a receiver there, and the receiver in your Starlab has been destroyed."

PART FIVE

Marooned

There was another little period of time there that I'd just as soon forget. The next days passed, but they took a long time doing it. Pirraghiz clucked over me and tried to cheer me up. She proposed entertainments, promised that Beert would soon come back with good news, produced tasty new meals—she did everything she could to cheer me, but I didn't cheer. I was trying to adjust to the fact that I was marooned in this place for the rest of my life, while my world was going to hell . . . and there was nothing I could do about it.

I think I was a big frustration to Pirraghiz. She deserved better. She was my maid, valet, cook, washerwoman and all-day-long companion. Life with her around was like living in a five-star luxury hotel, with my personal Jeeves to care for all my needs. If she had a life of her own, she didn't let it interfere with her total attendance on me. She washed and mended my ragged clothes. She tended my chamber pot, whisking it away to be sterilized and cleaned before I had to use it again. She fed me about as well as I had ever been fed in my life—found new ways to improve the preserved swill from Starlab and added to it actual fresh vegetables, salads, soups, little cakes dripping with something like fruit-flavored honey. There was even milk. It didn't come from an actual cow, of course, because there weren't any of those within many light-years, but it was a sweetish, butterscotch-colored fluid that came, Pirraghiz said, from the females of one of the other captive species.

That startled me. "Don't they object when you take their milk away from them?"

She wagged her great head reprovingly. "Don't be foolish,

Dannerman. It is not 'taken.' It is bartered. They give us things we do not have, and we give them things of ours in return. These females are well repaid for what they have in plenty to spare."

I looked again at what was in my cup. But it still tasted good, and while I was checking it out Pirraghiz saw an opportunity. "I am glad that you are taking an interest in this, Dannerman. Would you like to know more about the other captive species?"

I considered that for a moment, then shrugged. "Why not?" I said, meaning, since I was going to be stuck here for the rest of my life, why not find out what that life was going to be like?

Pirraghiz beamed. "That is good, Dannerman. I thought you might feel so, and so I have prepared something for you. Wait one moment." She disappeared into her own room, and when she came back she was carrying the familiar helmet.

It wasn't what I had expected. I protested, "I've already seen all I need to see of what's happening back home."

"Oh, Dannerman," she sighed. "Do you think it was only your people who were bugged? That is not so. Sentient beings of many, many different species have worn the transmitters, species you have never seen, of kinds you cannot imagine, including some of those who shared captivity with you. I could not find all of those in the records," she said apologetically, "but I have selected a single individual from eight different species. Some of the species are here, some are not. Later on I can add others if you wish."

She waited for me to make up my mind. I hefted the helmet for a moment, indecisively. Curiosity won. Gingerly I put it on and pulled down the flaps. I heard Pirraghiz's voice giving last-minute instructions—"Simply say 'next' when you want to go to another subject, Dannerman, and I will make the change for you." And then the helmet took over.

▌was no longer myself. I wasn't in my chamber in the Horch nest.

I was surrounded by total blackness. There was nothing to be seen, smelled or felt, except that there before me, not two meters away, was an image of a creature that looked like a frog with the mouth of an alligator. Its skin was as fuzzy as a peach, and more or less the same color. On one bony arm it wore a thing like a wristwatch, but that was glowing with a pale blue light, and there were three golden bracelets on the other. It was dressed in tunic and leggings of a shimmery, silky material. It had four large ears on each side of its elongated head, and a cluster of bright pink feathers topping it off—probably a hat or a decoration, I thought, since the feathers didn't seem to be growing out of the creature's skull.

It wasn't moving at all. I figured that out easily enough; what I was looking at was just a picture, showing me what the first species Pirraghiz had selected for my viewing pleasure looked like; and in a moment the blackness winked away.

Now I wasn't looking at the creature anymore. Now I *was* that creature. What I was looking at—and smelling and hearing and feeling—was a warm, sunny seaside. Gentle ocean waves were breaking on a pebbly beach, where two or three ungainly-looking catamarans were drawn up. I was sitting—squatting, actually— on the side of another catamaran, eating something that crunched in my jaws and tasted richly of blood. I was not alone. There were two other alligator-frogs just below me on the beach, doing something or other with large nets—repairing them, I supposed. I was looking particularly at one of them, and it was giving me occasional sidelong glances in return. I was conscious of a kind of warm stirring that felt like sexual tension as I looked at—I guess, at her. Unless, of course, that one was male and the body I was inhabiting was female, but I could think of no good way of checking that.

People talk wistfully about wanting a change in their lives, generally meaning something like a better job, a new boyfriend, a week on some island resort—anything at all, as long as it is different. I know the sovereign recipe for that. Just slip one of the helmets on your head and tap into the mind of a truly alien being, and you'll never find anything more *different* as long as you live. It wasn't just the sights and smells that were different. My borrowed body interpreted them in ways that were completely foreign to me. There was a pervading stink of rotten fish in the air, powerful enough to make me hold my nose if I'd had one to hold. But I wasn't disliking it. It was actually making me hungry. My hearing was far better than ever before. Not only could I hear the distant sounds of insects and the lapping of the waves on the shore, I could hear precisely *where* they were; the frog's multiple ears were as directional as sonar. I could hear the other alligator-frogs calling to each other—deep baritone hissing, like a dragon's voice—but that was where the helmet's capacities ran out. I couldn't understand a word they said.

Then, *flick,* the scene changed. I was still in the creature's body, or in the body of one just like him, but I was in a series of different places, doing a variety of different things. Once my host was teamed with another frog, both of them wearing a kind of harness and pulling something that was heavy—but I couldn't see what it was—along a marshy dirt road between stands of head-high rushes. Once he and a couple of others were making a lot of noise—singing together or making threats, I couldn't tell which. Once he was asleep. None of it was very intelligible.

So I called, "Next!"

Frog gone away, blackness all around me. I was looking at another picture. This one was a fat, tentacle-nosed thing the general shape of a hippopotamus, and I knew what it was at once.

I was looking at a Wet One, one of the amphibians that had killed Patrice.

Perhaps, in the interests of scientific curiosity, I should have made the effort to understand what life was like for a Wet One. I didn't. I wasn't ready for going into that particular mind. As soon as I saw it I yelled, "Next!"

It took a moment for Pirraghiz to react—surprised, I guess,

that I wanted to cut that one so short. But then I felt the faint scrabbling of her talons as she poked at the controller on the side of the helmet, and I had a new bizarre creature to look at.

I kept going through the roster of diverse, but all nonhuman, beings that Pirraghiz had accessed for me. There was a Shelled Person, like the one I had seen in the compound. Very strange, that experience was, because the Shelled Person seemed to see other living things, like the Docs, as luminous, and it had two distinct ranges of odor-detecting senses, one for in the water and one for on land. I tried a thing that looked like a feathered gorilla, with batlike membranes that joined its arms to its body and let it leap and glide for short distances—on, I guess, a planet with a lesser gravity, because I did not think that would work on Earth. Number Five was a four-legged furry thing that made its home in a cave, with its mate and half a dozen young; why the Beloved Leaders had bothered to bug it, I didn't know, because it certainly didn't look very civilized to me. Number Six—

Number Six I knew very well.

Bewildered, I took the helmet off my head. It was unexpectedly dark in the room—evidently the sun had set while I was in the helmet—but I could see Pirraghiz. She wasn't hovering nearby, as I expected; she was over by the window, pulling the drapes back from the light-givers. She turned around questioningly. "I've just seen Dopey!" I told her. "The one who died."

She said comfortably, "Yes, of course. The talker. Did you simply see his image, Dannerman, or did you go on to experience him?"

"Seeing the image was plenty! He was just the way I saw him last, all tattered and beaten up, with that big turkey-gobbler thing of his drooping and all the colors gone. He's about to *die*, Pirraghiz, and I don't want to 'experience' any of that!"

"Dannerman, I would not ask you to. I chose that view of the talker on purpose so that it would be easy for you to recognize him. The tapes, however, are from other parts of his life."

I scowled at her. "What parts?"

"Oh, Dannerman. They are parts that I think will interest you. Why do you not put the helmet on and see?"

So there I was in Dopey's body. I knew it was so, because his head, the little cat head, was bent to look at the familiar, golden-mesh belly bag he wore. I could feel his little fingers, inside the muff, fiddling with what might have been a kind of keypad.

I wasn't comfortable in Dopey's body. His range of vision must have been different from mine, because the colors were odd. I felt odd, too. There was a sort of slow, rhythmic, muscle-flexing sensation at the base of my spine, but in my own body I don't have any muscles there. Perhaps it had something to do with that scaly peacock plume he carried, I thought, and then he looked up.

I caught my breath. What he was looking at was a screen, and on it were four or five figures—human figures—and the nearest of them was me.

It was something from my own life that I was seeing. There were the five of us—Pat and Rosaleen Artzybachova, Jimmy Lin, General Delasquez and myself, when we had first arrived in Starlab. We had come there—God, it seemed a century ago—in the hope of finding some kind of extraterrestrial technology that would make us rich, and what we were doing was squabbling over the division of the Beloved Leaders stuff we saw all around us. I remembered it well. I saw us yelling at each other, and I saw Jimmy Lin get hit on the head.

And then I felt Dopey's little hands scrabbling in his belly bag. There was a bluish flash on the screen. At once, all five of us stopped cold in the middle of the argument. We didn't fall down. We couldn't, being in Starlab's microgravity. But we went limp. We didn't speak anymore. We began to drift around the space in the orbiter.

Dopey had, somehow, put us all to sleep.

Then he got to work. He glanced back over his shoulder. For the first time I saw that there were two Docs standing immobile behind him, in a cramped little space I had never seen before. They began to move at once.

One of them pushed at a section of wall, which opened before him. The other picked Dopey up and carried him through that hidden door. Dopey's body felt pleased with itself; I could feel the warmth and sensual pleasure that emanated from the great peacock fan that my own body didn't have, but Dopey's did. As we glided down a passage, one mystery was solved. I caught a glimpse of the stenciled sign on the wall we had just come through. It was supposed to be a fuel tank. Dopey had emptied it out and made it into a hidey-hole so he could watch us without being seen.

I think I was in a kind of shock again. What happened next wasn't entirely comprehensible, but I couldn't stop watching. Dopey's Docs methodically lifted all five of us, one by one, and put us into the transit machine. Then, each time, without pause, they lifted us out again and went on to the next one. When we had all been transmitted—and copied!—they went to work on the next stage. One of the Docs held Rosaleen's unconscious form while the other opened a cupboard on the wall. He took out a coppery object the size and shape of an almond, while the first Doc, talons extended, slashed a little gash in the back of Rosaleen's neck.

I had never seen an implant put in before.

I saw it happen to Rosaleen. I saw it happen to Delasquez and Jimmy Lin, and I saw it happen to me.

And I saw it happen to Pat Adcock, the woman I loved. I could see her, unconscious and limp. I could almost touch her. I yearned for her. And when it was all over I took the helmet off my head and stared blindly at the room around me.

Pirraghiz said something to me, but I wasn't listening. I got up and walked over to the balcony door, slid it open and stepped outside.

It was full night now, and overhead was that spectacular, star-swarming sky. I wasn't looking at that, either. All I was seeing was Pat, once abandoned to Dopey and his Docs on the orbiter, now abandoned, with the rest of the human race, to whatever the Beloved Leaders chose to do with them.

I had never felt more helpless—and hopeless and useless—in my life.

A moment later I felt the wicker floor move in protest, and Pirraghiz stepped out beside me. I wondered for a moment if it would hold her great weight. Then I wondered whether that mattered at all. She said tentatively, "Dannerman? Was I wrong to show you what Dopey did to you on your Starlab?"

I thought that over for a moment, then I shook my head. "It isn't you who are wrong, Pirraghiz. What's wrong is that everything is going to hell and I can't do anything about it."

She said softly, "Yes. I know what you are going through."

That made me turn and stare at her. "Do you? Do you know what it feels like to see everyone I love about to be turned into robots, and to be able to do nothing about it?"

"Of course I do, Dannerman! I knew that for a very long time, for all the time I wore the Others' controller. I was even more helpless than you are now. I did their bidding! I had no hope at all—but then, you see, suddenly the Horch cousins came and I was free!"

"Oh? And do you think there's any chance that somebody will come charging along to help me?"

She looked at me for a long moment. I could see the struggle going on in her mind over what answer to give me.

Honesty won out over compassion. She said somberly, "No. In truth, Dannerman, I do not."

CHAPTER TWENTY-TWO

It wasn't easy for me to reconcile myself to spending the rest of my life—what might be a very long life—marooned with the Horch in this place. I tried to think of things I might usefully do. I couldn't think of any. Then I began to think of things that might make it more bearable for me. I'm not too proud of some of those, but—hell! For the first time in my life, I was *defeated*. I could see no way of helping anyone else, so my ideas began to get pretty selfish.

When Beert finally showed up, bubbling with good news, I made up my mind to try one of those selfish ideas out on him. All excitement, he told me the Greatmother would see me at last, and I put it to him. "That's great, Beert," I said, "but I've been thinking about something."

I don't know what Pirraghiz had told him about my state of funk. Everything, I guess, and he didn't seem patient with it. "About what?" he demanded.

"About a favor you could do me if you wanted to. If those other Horch let you have me as a, well, a pet . . . do you think they'd allow you to have another one?"

The snaky neck twisted around so that his eyes could peer into mine. I think I had hurt his feelings. "I do not like to ask my cousins to 'allow' me things, Dan. I do not understand what you mean."

"I mean Pat Adcock."

"Ah," he said. Well, it wasn't "ah," exactly, but it was the same sort of exhalation of breath, indicating that he comprehended. The breath was warm on my face. "You wish me to have a copy of your sexual partner made for you, is that it?"

His tone sounded disappointed in me. It made me defensive. "Is that too much to ask?"

He paused, the sinuous neck curling and straightening thoughtfully. "I don't know if it is too much. Tell me why you want this."

Now he was making me angry. "Why do you think? Because I'm frustrated and lonely and hopeless, that's why!"

"And you think it would make you happier to copy someone you care about, who then would herself become frustrated and lonely and hopeless?"

Well, it sounded all different when he put it like that, but he didn't give me a chance to try to defend myself. He took me firmly by the arm with one of those sinewy tentacles of his and said, "We will speak of this later, Dan, but now we must go. We must not keep the Greatmother waiting."

The Greatmother kept us waiting, though. We trudged to the topmost level of the nest, where a subadult Horch let us into a room, far larger than my own and with many more furnishings. There an ancient female Horch lay sprawled on an immense bed. She had an ungainly thing like a huge metallic corset wrapped around her midsection. It could not have been comfortable to sleep in, but she wasn't sleeping. Her long neck dangled limply off the side of the bed, her eyes half open but unseeing.

I whispered to Beert, "Is she all right?"

"Shh! Of course she is all right. She is simply accessing certain files. Her belly viewer is a thing like your helmet, do you understand?"

I did—after the moment it took me to figure out that the belly was where Horch kept their brains, since of course their heads were too small. I kept looking at Beert to see if he seemed to be getting receptive to my request, but his head was down low, staring at the floor. I couldn't tell what he was thinking; and just as I was making up my mind to ask him again, the Greatmother stirred. Her limbs straightened. Her head lifted to gaze at me, while her arms snaked down to the latches of her viewer.

That was the cue for Beert to spring forward to help her. When she had the thing unlatched he carefully stowed it away in its wicker container, turned his head toward me and said proudly, "The Greatmother will speak to you now."

The first thing she did was to direct Beert to lay out some food and drink for us. While I was munching on the only part that looked familiar she explained to me that she had been viewing some of the scenes of our life as captives of the others. It was all like a silent film for her, since she couldn't understand any of our talk, but Djabeertapritch had filled her in and she was full of questions. Did the Old Female Rosaleen Artzybachova possess among us the rightful dignity and authority that she herself had in her nest? Had I in fact bred with the young female Pat Adcock—that is, with one of the three young female Pat Adcocks—and if so, what had led me to choose that one over the identical other two? And if breeding was desirable, why had the Old Female not assigned a Pat to each of the other two males in our party so that all three might become pregnant?

When I told her there would be no young coming from our quick idyll, the idea of contraceptives startled her. "But why would this Pat not wish to gestate?" she asked incredulously.

I ran through all the reasons in my mind and settled on one that she might view sympathetically. "We did not wish to bear a child to suffer captivity in a place far from home," I said, and saw Beert's head swerve toward me thoughtfully.

She wriggled her neck at me in gentle reproof. "If our ancestors had thought that way when our planet was overrun, you and I would not be having this conversation. Life is worth saving, Dannerman. Offspring are worth having. Always." She flipped her neck in a complicated curve, and then asked politely, "Has

Djabeertapritch told you all you want to know about our nest?"

"Not everything," I said, and then I hesitated for a moment. Maybe I was a little annoyed with Beert for not promising to make me a Pat, but I didn't feel like being tactful. I said, right out, "I know this is a sensitive matter, but is it true that you don't get along with your cousins in the Beloved Leader base?"

Beert gave me a shocked, warning hiss, but the Greatmother answered at once. "We are all one folk, Dannerman. It is, however, true that some of the ways of our cousin Horch have changed greatly in the long, long time we have been separated from them, while this nest has kept to the old ways."

"The ways of your home planet?"

"Of our *particular* home planet, the Two Eights. There were many planets inhabited by our species when we were taken, Dannerman, and each had its own customs. Now there are even more. The Two Eights was one of the newest and smallest at the time, with only eight sixty-fours of sixty-fours of sixty-fours of sixty-fours of inhabitants." I calculated quickly: something less than 150 million. "Most of the other Horch planets were much larger. When the Others came—But perhaps Djabeertapritch has told you all this?"

"Not all, I think."

She gave Beert that quick, reproving neck-twist. He said hastily, "I have been busy with the cousins, Greatmother, as you know."

She patted his arm affectionately. "Of course. Well, you know, Dannerman, that all through our star-going history we Horch had met many strange species, a few of them nearly sentients. Those we always treated with kindness—as, you have seen, we in this nest have treated you yourself, Dannerman. When the Others' scoutship came to our world it was the first time another species had come through space to us. The ones who came to us were not the Others themselves. The Others were too frail to come to the surface of our planet, but they sent their subject species, and those were welcomed. All that they asked was given to them. They did tell us of the Eschaton; that was one gift of the Others. It was the only one."

She looked inquiringly at Beert, who was twitching restively. "They also gave us death," he growled.

She sighed. "Yes, that is so. It is what the Others often give, and they have many ways of giving it. They alter the reaction of a star, so that it goes nova, or change the orbit of a small planetoid so that it collides with the planet they would destroy. They can bring about an emission of poisonous gases from a planet's oceans if they choose. Or they can do what they did to our Two Eights. In their laboratories the Others developed a terrible new disease made out of the proteins of our own bodies, and they spread it secretly among us, and we began to die. Many, many of the people of our planet died. Nearly all. On the Two Eights fewer than sixty-four sixty-fours survived. Those were the ones who were brought here, and we are their descendants. Or," she corrected herself somberly, "the descendants of those who survived what happened here. The Others interrogated our first generations without mercy. Many of us died here as well, usually in great pain. Even when we no longer had any information to give, we were still valuable to the Others, because we were still genetically Horch. So from time to time they seized numbers of us and carried them away, to test new diseases and weapons on them; and that is what our lives were like, Dannerman, for eights of generations—until our cousins of the Eight Plus Three came and set us free."

Abruptly the Greatmother sat straighter on her bed. Her head sprang up to mine, until her pointy, hard-skinned nose was almost touching my own.

"Now I will give a more complete answer to your question, Dannerman. The Eight Plus Threes have treated us very well; they shared everything they have with us, and they offered to take anyone who wished to a Horch planet to live. Most of my nest did go, willingly. A few of us did not. Our cousins have had a long history of struggle and warfare, which we did not share. It has changed them, as our lifetimes of captivity have changed us. We in this nest wish to make a different life for ourselves, though we do not know how.

"But we intend to try.

"What you must remember is that we are all still Horch, Dannerman. We will never do anything to harm our cousins. Djabeertapritch understands this well. You must understand it, too."

CHAPTER TWENTY-THREE

When we left the Greatmother, Beert's bubbly mood was restored. "She likes you, Dan," he said on the way down the staircase, his neck dancing with pleasure. "Now we can act. Do you remember our earlier conversation?"

My heart leaped. "The one about Pat?"

"No, not the one about Pat," he said crossly. "We have had other conversations, have we not? I am speaking about the one in which I told you that you could help another person in a great matter."

As we walked out into the open air, I tried to remember. "Oh, that," I said, disappointed. "You mean the one where you didn't tell me what it was, or what I was supposed to do. How could I forget all that?"

Irony was wasted on him. "Yes, that conversation, exactly," he said abstractedly, glancing at that bent-tree sundial. He frowned. "The person who needs your help will be here shortly, but first we must go to my laboratory, if you don't mind."

I didn't mind. Didn't have much chance to object, either, because Beert was leading me rapidly toward his pink shed. I looked around apprehensively while he was opening the door, but the Christmas trees were absent. When he touched something just inside the doorway, bright lights sprang up, and he said with pride, "This is my personal workspace."

It was certainly something special. There weren't any luminous fungi here. The lights Beert had turned on came from the glowing walls themselves, with additional spotlights that were fixed on specific items, one a workbench, with several gadgets and tools on it, a couple of larger gadgets on the floor—and one other thing.

I swallowed. The other thing stood motionless against one wall, the light sparkling from its million little needles. It was a Christmas tree.

I must have made a sound, because Beert twisted his neck around from where he was taking objects out of a cabinet and tossing them into a basket. When he saw where I was looking, he reassured me. "I have told you that you need not fear the robots. This one in particular; I have taken it apart and rebuilt it, and now it does not even have a channel to the central controls."

"Um," I said, studying the thing. But it didn't move, so I decided to take him at his word. "Why do you bother?" I asked.

He seemed a little embarrassed, his face held low and not meeting my eyes. "I want to learn all that our cousin Horch know, Dan. It is the only way this nest can ever hope to stand on its own. And," he added, pride returning and his head lifting, "I have even been able to build some instruments for my own use. Like this."

He lifted one of the gadgets from the workbench and held it high. It was a sort of fish-shaped, flattened oval, looking rather like a metallically glittering flounder or sole. "It is a scrambler, Dan. It generates static which interferes with the communications channels of the Others. Instruments of this sort were very valuable to the cousins when they attacked this base."

I looked at it with more respect. "Valuable" was a conservative word for it; something like it would have come in very useful when we were captives. It wasn't the only thing around, either. Beert's lab was full of high-tech alien gadgets of all kind. It was exactly what I'd been looking for to take back to the Bureau's technicians, when I'd still had hope of that.

But I didn't have that hope anymore.

Beert was still talking. "This particular device is not exactly like theirs; I built it in a different shape, to serve the purposes it is planned for, and had to waterproof it to protect its power."

That reminded me. "And it's self-powered?"

He stared at me. "Of course. Why would it not be?"

"Well," I said, "I've been wondering about that. I've looked at some of your other gadgets, and I don't see any wires."

He made a hissing noise of exasperation. "There are no wires. Each device draws its energy from——"

That wasn't the end of his sentence, it was just the point at which it turned into gibberish and I couldn't understand it anymore. I asked, "What?"

"I said it draws its energy from the *garble* of the *garble garble* which is present in the *garblegarblegarble*."

That was no improvement. I shook my head apologetically. "I guess this translator thing doesn't work as well as I thought," I said, touching the thing behind my ear. "I didn't understand any of that."

He sighed, wriggling his neck regretfully. I said, "If you could just try to explain a little——"

"I did try," he said testily. "You simply do not have the background to understand the words, and I do not have time to teach you just now. The person I wish to help will be waiting for us." He put the scrambler in the basket with the other things and closed the lid, gesturing for us to leave the lab.

Outside, Beert slammed the door behind us and grabbed my arm. I let him lead me toward the stream that went through the grounds of the nest, and there, standing by one of those round little bridges, I saw the person Beert wanted me to help.

It was no friend of mine. The thing was a Wet One, one of the amphibians who had killed Patrice.

I didn't say anything to Beert. Well, maybe that's not true. I think I probably did say something like, "Screw this," under my breath, but I doubt that Beert heard me. I wrenched my arm free from his grip, turned around and walked away, not looking back . . . for no more than three or four meters.

Then I stopped.

Beert was a funny-looking little dinosaur, and his unpredictably fluctuating moods—his often *childish* moods—sometimes made that particular little dinosaur difficult to live with. But he had done his best to befriend me. Had, in fact, saved my life, just for starters. And if he was now asking me to help him, even to help him do something for a species I hated—didn't I owe him something?

"Oh, hell," I said, this time out loud, and turned around. Beert was peering after me.

I retraced my steps to the stream bank. "Exactly what is it that you want me to do?" I asked.

CHAPTER TWENTY-FOUR

I don't know if Beert had any idea of why I had walked away. He didn't comment. Maybe he figured it was just another bit of Earth-human queerness. He simply said, as though nothing had happened, "I will show you," and began pulling things out of his little basket and carefully setting them on the ground next to the Wet One.

Who was studying me intently with those bulging hippopotamus eyes that were set on the top of his head. I didn't speak. Neither did he. I did see that the tentacular electric organs that sprouted from his face were writhing restlessly. That didn't seem to be a friendly sign. It crossed my mind that Beert might have misjudged the situation, and I instinctively began looking around for something that might work as a weapon if the thing suddenly jumped me.

Beert's tap on my shoulder distracted me and I looked around. "Are you paying attention?" he asked crossly. "See, this is how the scrambler fits on the Wet One's body." He had it in his other hand, and began carefully to place it on the amphibian's gross belly, just behind its tiny mid-arms. I wondered what he was going to use for glue to make it stick to the Wet One's hide, but he didn't have to do that. He had something more effective than glue. A metal socket was actually embedded in the amphibian's flesh; the creature had evidently allowed someone to fasten the socket to his body surgically, right through the skin. There were two similar sockets flanking the one with the scrambler, and the next thing Beert did was to attach a couple of stout leather pouches to them.

Then he pulled the last of the basket's contents out.

It was a pair of handguns. *My* handguns. Two of the twenty-shot, Bureau-issued guns that had been my basic carry weapon ever since I became an agent.

I nearly lost it one more time, as the anger I had managed to push back out of sight boiled over again. If anybody was going to have my guns, it damn well ought to be me. I made a grab for them, snarling, "Hey! Those are *mine!*"

The amphibian slithered a half step away toward the stream, grunting a protest, but it didn't try to stop me. It didn't have to. Beert was fast as well as strong; he dropped the weapons, and his two rubbery arms clamped quick and hard around my wrists. He didn't raise his voice. "Actually," he said, "these two projectile weapons are for the Wet One. If you have a requirement for one, it can be copied for you, but I do not see any such necessity."

I wrenched free of his grip. He let me go, but his arms stayed near mine and his face danced before me. "They belong to me!" I complained. "That thing is a killer. How do I know he isn't going to shoot me with them?"

Beert said patiently, "He has no such intention."

That was when the amphibian spoke up, surprising me. He wasn't easy to understand. He spoke that same Horch language—naturally enough; I could see that he was wearing an implant of his own, tucked under his jaw. But he didn't have the same sort of vocal cords as I did, or even as the Horch did. The sounds he made were more like a hoarse, unpleasant kind of roaring than conversation, and I had to strain to make them out: "That is true. Shall I now speak of unfortunate past events?"

I guess the question was rhetorical, because the Wet One went right on talking. "The lethal pulsing of your female person should not have happened," he stated. "The sharp-object stabbing of our persons by yours should not have happened as well. The reason for these wrong happenings may be that my party was in Other Water, where we did not know its tastes. In Home Water," he explained, "where our females stay and the pups are reared, we know which tastes are persons and which are prey and which do not matter. In Other Water we may not know all the tastes. Yours were strange to us, and then your persons attacked us, so they were wrongly pulsed." He regarded me for a second with those knobbed eyes, then finished. "There is nothing else to speak on this matter."

I listened to his little speech impatiently, and turned to Beert. "What's he talking about?"

"He is telling you that the death of your friend was an accident," Beert said irritably. "As obviously it was. It is time you put this anger out of your mind."

I considered that for a moment, but damn him, Beert was right. I didn't much like being taught right from wrong by a snaky-headed monster from outer space, but I gave in. "But what the hell does he need my guns for?"

Beert gave me his approving neck-twist. "That is better, Dan. The reason to arm this person is that the Greatmothers have given permission to return him to his home planet, where he is going to resist the rule of the Others."

Resist the rule of the Others? That changed things.

It didn't necessarily make us friends. The first feeling that flooded my mind was simple, burning *envy*. This creature was going to go *home*, while I was stuck helplessly *here*. I was suddenly more jealous than I have ever felt in my life.

But the facts were plain. If I couldn't do anything to help my own human race, at least I might be able to do something to harm the damn Others. It was only revenge. But it was better than nothing.

Beert was picking one of the guns off the ground. He held it out to me gingerly. "It is for these that we need your help, Dan. The Wet One will be in grave danger when he arrives at his home planet. He needs a weapon. His ability to stun or kill other organisms with electrical shocks works only underwater and at close range. That is not good enough."

"Sure," I said, perplexed, "but why do you need one of my guns? Seems to me those Horch fighting machines had plenty of firepower."

Beert gave me that negative neck-wave. "He cannot use the energy weapons of our cousins. They would interfere with his electrical senses. These projectile things of yours might work, but we are not well sure of how to use them. Look, I have made these containers for them." He pulled one of those flexible sacks off its clamp, and I realized they were intended to be holsters for the guns. "Unfortunately," he said sadly, "the containers do not work well. Can you help?"

That put me right in familiar territory, so I grinned at him. "If there's one thing I'm good at," I said, "it's guns. Show me the problem."

He did. Actually, there wasn't a single problem, there were a lot of them. The first one was that Beert had put the holsters in on the wrong sides. I had heard that the flashier cowboy gunmen of the Old West—their TV versions, anyway—wore their guns like that, performing a lightning cross-draw when they had to kill some bad guy. That wouldn't work for the Wet One, because his anatomy wasn't up to the job. His short, skinny mid-arms were as conspicuously inadequate as the arms of a Tyrannosaur. They wouldn't stretch that far. When Beert reversed the holsters, we put the guns into them—after I made sure the safeties were well and truly on—and had the amphibian practice draws.

That was an improvement, but it suggested something else to me. "When he actually shoots a gun, he should fire with his arm straight out, otherwise he may get a broken bone. These twenty-shots don't have much recoil, but he doesn't have much arm." The Wet One, who was listening intently, immediately began trying that out. I sighed as I watched him. "Practice as much as you can before you go," I advised. "Another thing.

Where do you think you might be doing this shooting, in the water or out of it?"

Beert swirled his head at me in alarm. "Will immersion in water harm the weapon?"

"Oh, no, they're waterproof, all right. What about it?"

I was looking at the amphibian, who answered for himself. "In most cases, I think, in air."

"That's good. I'm worried about shooting the gun underwater. It's not made for that, and with the resistance of the water, it might blow up in your hand. Try not to do that. Now"—I crossed my fingers—"let's see how good a shot you are."

Unsurprisingly, he wasn't good at all.

The Horch had nothing like a firing range, but Beert produced a wad of some kind of packing material out of the basket; I wadded up some of it and tossed it in the stream for a target. When the amphibian reared up on his front flippers he had just enough clearance to draw the guns and fire them, his tentacles nervously elevated out of the line of fire.

Beert was taking notes, skipping nimbly out of the way when the amphibian's shots went wildest. Then, when the Wet One reached the point of being maybe able to hit the side of a barn if he were locked inside, I decided he was about as good as he was going to get. I told Beert, "The holster clasp is too tight; you'll have to ease it up a little. He'll need reloads, too. Have you got more ammunition?"

It took a moment to make Beert understand that the weapon did not produce its own endless supply of bullets, but then he gave me the head-twist. "We can copy as much as needed."

"Copy a lot; there isn't going to be a gun shop where he's going. And you'll have to make something for him to carry them in." I thought for a moment, then, with some reluctance, told the Wet One, "I think you'd better keep the safety off; you might have trouble handling it if you need to shoot in a hurry. Just don't touch that trigger until you want to fire. Now, let's see how good you are at reloading."

*   *   *

He wasn't good at that, either, but he eventually got the idea, after a fashion. That was as far as we got, because Beert was fidgeting. "I must go back to my laboratory to make these changes in the equipment," he told the Wet One. Who made no response, except to turn and head for the stream. Just as he was entering the water, he paused, turned ponderously around and spoke to me, in that horrible roaring voice:

"Your metal killing device may be valuable to me, also your instruction in its use. For this I owe you the debt of thanks. If I can repay it, I will."

Then he slipped into the stream and was gone. A couple of those electric-shock appendages appeared briefly above the water, fluttering in the air almost as though he were saying good-by. Then nothing showed but those two knobby eye sockets and a pair of V-shaped ripples in the water, leaving Beert and me looking after him.

Beert made that hissing sort of sigh. "He is a brave person," he informed me. I just nodded. I had formed that opinion of the Wet One myself—along with a fair amount of residual envy—and anyway, I had something else on my mind.

Beert wasn't giving me much chance to bring it up. "As soon as I am finished in the laboratory," he said happily, "I must go to my cousins to talk to the Greatmother of the Eight Plus Threes, so that we may schedule a time when Mrrranthoghrow may operate the transit machine for him. I will send Pirraghiz to you, Dan."

I swallowed and took the plunge. "There's one other thing," I said.

"Yes?"

"I've been thinking about what you said. You were right. So let's just forget about making that copy of Pat for me," I told him.

Horch can't smile, don't have the facial muscles for it, but I could have sworn he was looking at me in an affectionate way. "It is forgotten, Dan. I am glad." And he gave my arm a gentle pat before he turned and hurried away.

Listen, I'm only human. Get me depressed enough and you might see a person selfisher than you would have believed. But I didn't have to *stay* selfish all the time.

PART SIX

Fighting Back

There was another lesson that old drill instructor of mine had taught us, in between the pushups and the ten-kilometer runs. What she said was, "Listen, ass-holes. It's always better to do *something* than *nothing*, you hear me? If it don't do nothing else, it'll make you feel better."

She was right. It did. My situation hadn't improved a hair in any tangible way, but I felt different. I felt for the first time that I was playing some part, however insignificant, in an action that might cause the Beloved Leaders some aggravation, even if only a little. Morale-wise, that was a big plus. It almost made me feel as though this interminable lonely life that stretched ahead of me might be worth living after all.

So I decided to start looking for other ways to do the Others harm. I don't know exactly what I was thinking of. Maybe leading a charge of Horch fighting machines into some Beloved Leader stronghold, the way they had taken over the prison-planet base. But whatever I was going to do to the Others, the first step was to get to where the action was.

Beert was the logical person to talk to on that subject, but he wasn't available. When he wasn't over in the Horch base to negotiate with the cousins, he was locked up in his workshop, making the changes in the Wet One's armament. I decided to pester Pirraghiz about it. She was in her room, sterilizing my chamber pot for me, and Mrrranthoghrow was with her.

I hesitated in the doorway. Pirraghiz's room was no bigger than mine, but she had somehow found time to put in homey touches of her own: some of those tiny flowers in a planter, clothing neatly hung, her own much larger bed. She had turned the room into a very personal habitation and, belatedly, it crossed my mind that they might have preferred being alone in it.

Apparently not. As soon as Pirraghiz saw me she waved me in with a spare arm. "Are you hungry?" she asked at once, but I shook my head. I wasn't looking for food.

"I want to know about the Wet One," I said.

She looked surprised, but recited: "He is being sent back to his own planet, so that—"

"I know that. Tell me how he's getting there."

She looked at Mrrranthoghrow, who answered for her. "He will be transmitted on the captured transit machine of the Others, of course."

"And how does he know how to get there?"

"Ah," the Doc said, enlightened. "You want to know how the Wet One will find his way to his home. The Horch have been working on such problems ever since they occupied this base. Capturing a transit machine of the Others is very useful to them. Once we had it disassembled, the robots began tracing its channels."

"That is the one great advantage the Horch have over the Others," Pirraghiz added. "The Others are very strong, but the Horch have in some cases been able to enter the Others' channels, while the Others have never been able to enter theirs."

I mulled that over. I could see the strategic importance of that. "Does that mean there's a channel direct to the Wet One's planet?"

"Of course not, Dannerman," Mrrranthoghrow said. "Not from this outpost. But there are channels to a nexus, which has many channels. One will take the Wet One to his destination."

He was annoying me. "What is a 'nexus'?"

"It is a sort of center where many channels come together," he said patiently. "In this case it is a large installation which also was captured from the Others. Now it belongs to the Horch. There was great damage in the fighting, but much of its equipment is intact—just as is the case here."

"What kind of installation?"

He gave me one of those massive shrugs. "I had no reason to ask such a question, Dannerman. I only know that it is much larger than this installation here."

Pirraghiz had been silent, watching me, but then she spoke up. "Dannerman, I think you are jealous of the Wet One. Do you want to go with him?"

I started to shake my head, then decided to admit it. "I think I could help him fight against the Others. I'm a lot better with those guns than he is."

She made a clucking sound with those thin lips. "You would be discovered at once, Dannerman, and then you would die."

"It's my risk to take!"

"And his as well. His only hope is secrecy, Dannerman, and even so, he has very little chance to survive there. In company with someone as conspicuous as you, he would have no chance at all."

I said stubbornly, "I'm going to ask Beert if I can go along anyway. When will I see him?"

She waved that off impatiently. "Soon. This afternoon, I think, but what is the use of that? He will simply say no."

"And then I will ask him again, and keep on asking him, until he says yes. This is something I have to do. You don't understand what it's like not to be able to do anything for my friends."

She sighed. "Do I not? I am jealous of the Wet One, too."

I hadn't expected to hear that from her. "Because you'd like to try to rescue your own planet?" I guessed.

"Rescue it? But we have no planet anymore, Dannerman. It is long destroyed. Our people no longer exist except as slaves of the Others, countless numbers of them, all over the universe." She sighed. "No. I am jealous because he has a home to return to." She paused, fingering her little amulet, and then added somberly, "Even though it is certain that he will see it only long enough to die there."

*   *   *

didn't want to accept what Pir-
raghiz said, but I couldn't get rid of the sneaking suspicion that
she was right. Did it make any sense for me simply to get myself
killed on some planet not even my own? Would it even incon-
venience the Beloved Leaders at all?

Logically I had to agree that it would not. But did I have any
other way to strike a blow at them? I couldn't think of any.

I told Pirraghiz to call me when Beert was available and went
back to my room, and what I did there was to put on that helmet
again. Mrrranthoghrow had selected another set of taps on the
bugged people on Earth for me, and I wanted to see them. I think
maybe what I had in mind was to remind myself of what the
Beloved Leaders were doing to my own people.

It didn't work that way. The first person I saw was me, and
what I was doing was flying out of a transit machine. And when
the person whose eyes I was looking through turned, I saw Jimmy
Lin and Dopey and a pair of Docs, and Rosaleen Artzybachova
and Martin Delasquez and Pat. My Pat. Looking scared and worn
and generally shook up, but looking mostly very good indeed to
me.

It didn't take me long to figure out where I was. I was in
Starlab, and the bunch of us had just made our escape from the
prison planet. It was Patrice who I was eavesdropping on—had
to be, because she was the only one of us who was bugged at that
time. But it was Pat I wanted to see and touch, and be with.

I didn't switch to any other file. I stayed with that one. I
listened to us congratulating ourselves on having got away from
the damn Beloved Leaders, I watched myself destroy the transit
machine so we couldn't be followed, I listened as I—that other
I—called the Bureau on Starlab's ancient radio and painfully
worked out a way of communicating with them that the rest of
the world, and especially the Beloved Leaders, might not hear.
With all the rest of the gang I got into the rickety old crew-rescue

vehicle that had been berthed at Starlab since the last time any astronomer visited it. I stayed with them as its engines fired up and we started the long, bouncing, bucketing drop toward Earth, and I would have stayed a lot longer if I could, in spite of the fact that a suspicion was dawning in my mind.

What stopped me in the end wasn't that I got tired of seeing Pat, or that that new thought needed to be pursued. It was Pirraghiz. "Dannerman? I have brought you some food. And Beert is here now, if you want to see him."

I took the helmet off and blinked at her. She was taking little fruits and biscuits out of a coppery mesh bag and laying them before it. I ignored them. "Didn't you tell me that the transit machine on Starlab wasn't working anymore?"

She blinked back at me. "Why, yes, Dannerman. That is so."

"That's what I thought," I said—the other possibility having been that that other Dannerman hadn't done as thorough a job of destruction as he thought. "All right, let's go. I want to see Beert right away."

"To ask him if you can throw your life away with the Wet One? At least take the meal with you," she said, scooping it all back into the bag. As she handed it to me she said, "It is a foolish idea, and he will surely say no."

"You might be right," I agreed. "But maybe I have a better idea now."

CHAPTER TWENTY-SIX

When I knocked on the laboratory door Beert let me in at once. "Look here," he said, neck and arms awriggle. "I have taken your advice. Give me one of the ammunition carriers."

That last part was aimed at his Christmas tree, not me. The thing was hovering over a workbench, littered with the usual cryptic array of gadgets. The robot immediately picked one up and brought it over to hand to Beert. Who handed it happily to me. It was heavy. It was also streamlined and curved, like the other things Beert was attaching to the Wet One, and it had the same clamp arrangement to hold it in place. Which meant, I thought, that the Wet One would have had more sockets carved into his flesh. I admired his dedication. "See," Beert was saying proudly, reaching to touch the thing in my hand, "this release will fit the Wet One's digits. It is this button here; he needs only to touch it and it flies open." Beert did. It did, revealing half a dozen gleaming clips for the twenty-shot. "Also there are eight sixteens of additional clips and several others of the projectile weapons in those containers there—" gesturing at a pair of oblong boxes of that same rubbery material—"but those he will not be able to carry with him. Perhaps he can hide them somewhere, and come back to them when they are needed."

His little head was close to mine, the curly eyelashes fluttering excitedly. He was waiting for a compliment, I thought, so I obliged. "That's fine," I said, and glanced at the hovering robot. "Can you turn that thing off?" I asked.

Beert pulled his head away to regard me. "But I have told you, Dan, there is nothing to fear from this machine—"

I reached out and caught his neck, pulling his head toward me so that I could whisper. "I want to ask you about something I don't want the cousins to hear. I don't want that thing listening."

Beert went suddenly tense. He didn't pull away, as he easily could have, and I felt his warm breath on my face as he thought that over. "This robot does not interface with the others, as I have told you."

"Please, Beert."

He sighed. "Go into inactive mode," he ordered the Christmas tree. Then to me, warningly, "Dan, you recall what the Greatmother said to us. We do not agree with the cousins in all things, but they are still Horch."

"I don't want to harm the cousins. I just want a favor from you, and I think it is better if they don't know about it." I hesitated, looking at the Christmas tree, needles retracted, immobile— but could it still hear? I had to hope not. So I began. "Check me out on this, Beert. When the Wet One goes he won't be heading for his home planet; he'll be going to something they call a 'nexus,' where there are all sorts of channels that belong to the Others."

"Yes?"

"That's true, then? And another thing. When I was using the helmet I saw something funny," I went on. "I was in Patrice's mind, and we were in Starlab. I saw myself destroy the transit machine there. But I didn't lose contact even after it was destroyed. I think that means that there's another transit machine somewhere nearby that's still working—I don't know where. Maybe in the scout ship that found Earth in the first place? But still working, anyway, and somehow or other you're still tapping into that channel, I guess from this nexus."

"Yes, yes," Beert said testily. "I suppose all that is so, but I still do not know what favor you want of me."

And then he took a deep breath, because Beert was not a stupid being. By then he did know.

CHAPTER TWENTY-SEVEN

It took a lot of persuasion, and he fought me all the way. "Transmit you to this scout ship? But you do not know for sure even that it exists! The one that visited your planet's system may be long gone on some other errand."

"Or," I said doggedly, "it may not. At least there's some sort of contact, and what else could it be?"

"Oh, Dan," he said, sorrowful though sympathetic, "do you know what you ask? I do not believe the cousins would permit it."

"That's why I don't want them to know about it. But I give you my word, I mean no harm at all to the cousins."

"What about harm to yourself? A ship of the Others is not like your tiny Starlab orbiter. Such ships are quite large, and they are well guarded. There will be fighters of the Others standing by at the transit machine, watchful that they may be invaded by the cousins as this base was."

"I know. Pirraghiz told me all about the Others' ships."

"Then you also know that they will kill you as soon as you appear."

I shrugged. "Maybe I can kill them first."

"More likely you cannot, Dan," he scoffed. "You? Alone against well-armed fighters?"

"Oh," I said, "we Earth people have a pretty good combat record. Pirraghiz said so herself."

He waggled his neck at me reprovingly, then tried a different tack. "And even if they do not kill you, what can you accomplish? Do you think you can simply leap through space from the scout ship to your planet?"

"Whatever I can do, it will be more than I can do sitting here in your jail."

That silenced him for a moment. "I do not think of myself as your jailer, Dan," he said sorrowfully.

"Then set me free!"

He was silent again for quite a while, his head swerving indecisively about—darting toward the immobile robot as though about to start it up again, returning to search my face at close range.

While I—

I was estimating the distance to the nearest workbench.

I could see that there were all sorts of things there that I thought the Bureau's techs would have liked to play with. More immediately important, I saw a sort of chisel, a pink ceramic blade with a handle shaped for Beert's grip, not mine. But I thought I could hold it well enough in a pinch. What's more, I was pretty sure that the blade could cut right through that sinewy neck of his.

Well, let me make that clear. I certainly wasn't intending to kill Beert. I was merely hoping that he would believe I would, once I put the knife to his throat. The real question was whether threatening his life would force him to help me.

I wasn't proud of myself for thinking of taking a knife to a being who had befriended me. I wasn't even sure that I could bring myself to do it. But then I thought of what awaited my whole world—including Pat—and I inched a bit closer to the workbench.

Finally Beert gave one of his whispery sighs. "I do not see that this would directly threaten the interests of the cousins," he said reluctantly, "though perhaps it is better if they are not consulted. But even if I were willing to do what you wish, I do not know how to do it."

Well, I did. Or hoped I did, anyway. "When you transmit the Wet One to this nexus, transmit me too." I had been thinking it all out, as far as I could, and I laid it all out for Beert. The

Horch in this nexus probably could find a channel to the scout ship for me. If not, at least to whatever Beloved Leaders relay station was passing on the data from the bugged humans. If they could find the channel, presumably they could use it to send me there. And then I would take my chances.

Beert listened in brooding silence, then finally raised his serpentine arms to stop me. He said somberly, "Do you know, Dan, I was sure that, if I helped you at all, sooner or later you would ask me to do something that the cousins had not approved."

"Then why did you help me?"

Reflectively he rubbed his chin against the edge of the workbench. "I am not sure. Probably because I had seen so many of you die. Perhaps because you and I had both been captives of the Others. In any case, I thought it harmless to keep you alive, even to let you learn all you wished of our ways, since there was no possibility you could use that knowledge against us."

"I haven't really learned very much," I said, wheedling.

He lifted his head to gaze closely at me again. "You have learned enough to lie to me, haven't you? But very well. If I were you, I would fear the cousin Horch as much as I did the Others. Perhaps I do already. Let me find Mrrranthoghrow and tell him what he is to do."

PART SEVEN

The Nexus

The air-cushion van that took us to the old Beloved Leader base was big, but the eleven or twelve hundred kilograms of us, of one species or another, crowded it pretty tight. Beert's Christmas tree stood at the central control pedestal. Pirraghiz and Mrrranthoghrow sat one on each side of the vehicle, I guess for balance. The Wet One had the rear seat all to himself, while Beert and I were in front. Beert wasn't talking, his neck glumly waving from side to side, and I didn't press him. I took a piece of the stuff Pirraghiz had given me out of my pocket and began to eat it—it looked like a carrot, and crunched like one, but it had a sort of lemonade flavor.

Beert suddenly darted his head toward the copper-mesh bag between my feet and then up to confront me in my face. "What have you got there?" he asked suspiciously.

"Extra food," I said—untruthfully. I don't think I convinced him. To take his mind off it I jerked a thumb at the Christmas tree. "Do we have to have that thing with us?" I asked.

"It will carry the gear for the Wet One," he said grumpily, "and it will go with him to the nexus in case there are any problems." But he let it go at that, and then we were arriving.

We climbed a rise in that rust-red rock desert that seemed to be the prison planet's natural state, and the dilapidated buildings of the base were right in front of us. They looked naked. The Horch hadn't bothered to replace the silvery energy dome of the Beloved Leaders. The place looked like, and was, not much more than a junkyard of damaged Beloved Leaders machines.

As soon as we stopped, the Christmas tree silently gathered all the Wet One's possessions, guns and scrambler and ammunition boxes, and led the way outside. "Pick him up," Beert ordered, and Mrrranthoghrow obeyed. The Wet One was a lot of mass, and ungainly to handle, but the Doc lifted him and carried him out of the car, puffing slightly with the effort as Pirraghiz followed. Beert and I got out just behind them. Then, as the two Docs moved out of the way, I saw what was standing just inside the building line.

I froze. A silvery Horch fighting machine was poised there between a wrecked, man-high purple cylinder and a heap of coppery junk that might once have been anything at all. I knew all about those fighting machines. Two of them had done their best to kill me and all the others as we tried to escape the first time, and they had come pretty close. The good part was that they had turned out very vulnerable to a gunshot, having been designed to expect more sophisticated weapons, but that was not of immediate importance since I didn't have a gun. My adrenaline surged.

But the machine wasn't paying any attention to us. It stood like a statue on its spidery, wheeled legs, evidently abandoned there when the fighting was over. I breathed again, but I kept my eye on it as I sidled past, and that was what kept me from seeing the other Christmas tree, the one that was barring our path.

The first I knew of it was the sound of its little roller-skate wheels, but as I looked around it spoke. "Stop there," it ordered.

It didn't look hostile. Its needles were mostly retracted, but it didn't look as though it wanted to get out of our way, either. Beert shouldered his way past our own Christmas tree to confront it. "This Wet One is to be transmitted to his own world, for which the Greatmother of the Eight Plus Threes has given permission," he told it. "It cannot walk well on land, so these persons are here to carry it."

There was another noise of wheels coming from somewhere nearby, deeper and louder than a Christmas tree's skates, but the robot paid no attention. It extended a branch of needles toward me. "What is the reason for this other organism being here?" it asked.

If the question was meant for me, I didn't answer it. I was squinting down the passage, where a pair of those Horch three-wheeled velocipedes were rolling toward us. Each cart carried a single cousin Horch, their belly plates gleaming and their necks extended in curiosity toward us. I was wondering if my whole plan was going to collapse right there.

Beert answered for everyone. "This other organism is my project, for which the Greatmother has also given permission. I am investigating whether such a primitive person could learn to use advanced technology, or whether he is at too low a level to be a possible ally against the Others."

Whether the Christmas tree was buying that, I couldn't tell, but it didn't matter. One of the cousin Horch spoke up. "We have been called for nothing. It is only Djabeertapritch's puppy."

Well, he didn't say "puppy," exactly. What he said was more like "immature lower-form creature possessed for entertainment," and he sounded amused as he said it. But he went on to the Christmas tree: "He is harmless. Let them pass. Escort them to the transit machine in case they need help."

And the other cousin Horch said to Beert, equally amused, "You are still not used to the blessings of technology yourself, are you, Djabeertapritch? Imagine using organisms to carry another organism! You should have summoned a vehicle." And, with the Horch equivalent of chuckles, the two of them rolled away.

For the benefit of the glass robot, I did my best to look harmless, while, for Beert and the Docs, doing my best to prove the cousin Horch's estimate of me wrong. I hadn't cared for being called a puppy.

What I cared about was that the guard Christmas tree had been instructed to accompany us. It did. It rolled along in silence, apart from the occasional faint jingle of its needles. It paused when we paused, so that Mrrranthoghrow, panting, could turn the burden of the Wet One over to Pirraghiz for a while. It didn't seem to be paying any attention to us, other than that, though the sparkly ball at its top was flickering rapidly. It was just *there*, and it stayed there until we reached the space where the great green transit machine stood.

Two other Christmas trees stood there, apparently waiting for us. Worse still, one of the spider-legged fighting machines stood immobile against a wall. It seemed to be in standby mode, but I was pretty sure that it would come to life very quickly if needed. The only plus factor among those unwelcome negatives was that there were no living Horch cousins on the scene, but I wished their machines would go away. And they had no apparent intention of that.

When Pirraghiz had set the amphibian down, Beert looked around at the machines. "We have come to transmit this Wet One on his mission," he announced, in case they were interested. They didn't seem to be. I know of no way of telling what a Christmas tree is looking at—one configuration of needles is pretty much like another—but I didn't think they were even watching as Mrrranthoghrow opened a flap on the side of the transit machine and began rearranging its little rainbows of color. Beert's own Christmas tree was busy, too. It was expertly fitting all the Wet One's paraphernalia into its receptacles on the amphibian's body.

There was something I wanted there, so I walked over to where that was going on. The amphibian raised himself up, staring at me with those hippopotamus eyes. I patted his thick body encouragingly. "Good luck," I said, loudly enough so that everyone could hear, at the same time relieving him of one of his guns. That wasn't hard to do, since the holsters were made for quick release. I didn't think anyone had seen me.

Whether the amphibian had, I didn't know. Those electric Medusa snakes around his broad mouth were waving wildly, but not coming close to me. "I wish the same to you," he said thickly, and waddled over to the transit machine.

There was no ceremony. Mrrranthoghrow held the door

open. The amphibian climbed in. Beert's personal Christmas tree followed, lugging the ammunition cases. Mrrranthoghrow slammed the door shut and touched one of the colored lights.

And a moment later he opened the door again, and the chamber was empty. The Wet One was on his way.

That was when we came to the hard part.

I picked up my little copper-mesh bag of goodies and strolled to where Mrrranthoghrow was holding the door for me. "We will now transmit this other organism," Beert announced, and everything went bad at once.

All three of the robots spoke up. "No," said the violet one. "We have no instructions for more than one transmission."

"Why did this organism take the weapon from the Wet One?" the greenish one asked.

And the third one, the pale orange jobber that had stopped us in the first place, moved toward me. "What has the organism got in that bag? Has he been stealing from you, Djabeertapritch?"

The whole scheme was falling apart before my eyes. I could not let that happen, not when I was so close. "Wait!" Beert ordered, but the robots weren't waiting, and neither was I. I had the gun in my hand. I got the pale orange robot right in the globe at its top, first shot. I was drawing a bead on the second one when Pirraghiz grabbed me. She leaped into the machine, me and my bag in her arms, mewing at Mrrranthoghrow. Who put his hands on the controls. Beert bellowed in surprise and anger, but he was looking at the fighting machine, which had come to life and was advancing toward us.

I don't suppose Beert was thinking very clearly. What he did was jump into the transit machine with Pirraghiz and me, and the door closed.

I was on my way. To a place very far from Earth, as it happened. But on my way.

CHAPTER TWENTY-NINE

Travel in these alien go-machines was no trouble at all. You got in at one place, you came out at a different one. That was all there was to it.

This time the other place was really different. The first thing I noticed about it was that it was a microgravity environment, like Starlab's, where I weighed nothing at all.

No, that's wrong. The *first* thing I noticed about this "nexus" was that three ugly Horch fighting machines were standing there, looking ready to blow my head off. That's wrong, too, though, because they weren't standing. They were clinging to a network of cables that spanned the bare-metal-walled room we were in, and they hung there in three different orientations—heads up, tails up, every which way up—because the microgravity gave them no place to stand on. Beert, flailing around for something to grab on to, squawked, "Don't shoot!"

Mercifully, they didn't. I still had my twenty-shot in my hand, but I don't think I could have fired it to any effect if they had. Pirraghiz was holding me tight, but Pirraghiz was floating herself until she managed to catch on to a couple of the cables. Then things stopped whirling around for me; such were the advantages of a few extra arms.

By a doorway a couple of the glass robots were tugging the great bulk of the Wet One away. They stopped as we got there. One of them, an unfamiliar Prussian blue, shot out a crystalline tendril in our direction and spoke. "We were not informed of a second transmission. What is your purpose here?"

I didn't have a good answer for that, so I was glad that the

question seemed to be aimed at Beert. He didn't look as though
he had a good answer, either. He had caught one of the lines to
moor himself—upside down relative to me, as it happened—and
his neck was darting this way and that worriedly. That had me
worried, too. Could he forgive me for shooting up one of his
cousins' machines? And if he couldn't, what then?

The only thing I was sure of was that whatever might come
after that would not be good news for me.

As inconspicuously as possible, I jammed the gun in my
pocket to get it out of sight, but I kept that hand near it, just in
case. I was well aware that if Beert said the wrong word, one of
those fighting machines would start shooting, and that would be
the end of this particular Dan Dannerman. Of course, I would
certainly be shooting back. But it wouldn't do any good in the
long run, because I wasn't fool enough to think I could defeat
the whole Horch race single-handed.

Which would not have kept me from giving it a try.

The machine apologetically repeated its question, and Beert
finally bestirred himself. "I am Djabeertapritch of the Two
Eights," he said, sounding wretched but determined. "I was a
captive of the Others. My ancestors were caught there when the
Two Eights planet was invaded, and I am one of their descendants."

The Christmas tree silently processed that information for a
moment, then extended one branch toward Pirraghiz and me.
"And what are these organisms?"

"They are my servants. Since I am from a lost colony, we
have not had machine servers for many generations. I am used to
using living species to work for me. The larger of the two was
carrying the Wet One; the other is—a volunteer like the Wet
One," Beert said miserably, not looking at me. "He is to be
transmitted to his own planet to resist the Others."

The machine processed some more, and evidently did some
unheard communicating. After a bit it said, "You are welcome

here, Djabeertapritch of the Two Eights. The Greatmother of
this nest instructs me to provide you with quarters and whatever
else you need until she can come to welcome you in person."

Since Beert hadn't blown the whis-
tle on me, at least not yet, my chances of making it back to Earth
began to look a little better. That was when I remembered that
I didn't want to come back empty-handed. The little copper-
mesh bag of goodies I had swiped from Beert's lab was a good
start, but I wanted more.

There wasn't much more to be seen. The corridors we were
scudding through were starkly bare. I remembered being told that
this place, like the prison planet, had fairly recently been captured
from the Others; no doubt there had been a lot of wreckage, but
no doubt, too, that had been some time ago and the resident
Horch had had time to clean up. Nestled in one of Pirraghiz's
arms, I had every chance to look around, but there wasn't much
to look at.

We, on the other hand, must have been an interesting spec-
tacle for the locals. The two Christmas trees were making easy
work of tugging the Wet One along, though the amphibian himself was emitting snuffling noises of discomfort and complaint.
Pirraghiz had no trouble carrying me hand over hand along the
cables, even though behind us Beert had glumly wrapped both
his rubbery arms around one of her huge feet to be towed as well.
The corridors weren't entirely empty. Along the way we passed
half a dozen of the Christmas-tree robots, who simply got out of
the way but showed no sign of interest in us, and one or two
living Horch, who did. But, although the Horch goggled at us as
we passed, they didn't interfere.

There was a mix-up when we got to our destination. It was
in a better neighborhood—some of the rooms were occupied
here, and a couple of infant Horch stuck their heads out of the
doorways to see the sight—but the room the Christmas tree of-

fered Beert was small. Heaven knows what cattle pen the robot had had in mind for us lesser breeds, but Beert was having none of it. "They must all stay with me," he declared, in a tone that accepted no arguments. The robot didn't offer any, actually. It communed with itself for a moment or two—probably really was communicating with higher authority—and then led us to a larger suite.

It wasn't just large, it was handsomely furnished. It had a central reception area with those Horch bowl-shaped TVs and racks of the Horch glittery-tape books strapped in place so they wouldn't float away, and webbing to hold an occupant in place while he watched or read, and lighting that could be brightened or dimmed with switches that looked like mushroom caps. A couple of short passages led to other rooms, also nicely arranged. Evidently nothing was too good for a Horch who had suffered captivity under the Others.

Our robot guide indicated that the largest of the sleeping rooms was to be Beert's, so we underlings checked out the others. Each had sets of sleep-webbings attached to the walls, a good size for me but nowhere near adequate for Pirraghiz or the Wet One. Pirraghiz didn't complain. The amphibian did. "It is very dry here," it roared. "Is there no water anywhere? And why am I not already on my way to my home?"

I left Pirraghiz to try to placate him. I could hear Beert in his own room, talking to the robot, but I didn't want to see Beert just then, so I explored. What I was really looking for was some small additional bits of Horch technology to add to the store in my bag, but there wasn't much of that. I did find a nifty zero-G toilet—luckily, because the need was getting acute. Whether the technology was Horch or Beloved Leader, I couldn't tell, but it was kilometers better than anything on Starlab. I would have been glad to take that along if I could. Since I couldn't, I made do with another couple of the glitter-tape books.

When I got back to my room, Beert's Christmas tree was relieving the Wet One of his weapons and gadgets to stow away.

Then it came to me, a branch extended meaningfully. I hesitated, but Pirraghiz commanded, "Give the weapon to it," and I passed over my twenty-shot. When it had put the gun away I marked the place, but it was as well there as in my pocket, for the time being.

Then the Christmas tree ordered us into Beert's room. I found him nervously rubbing at a stain on his tunic, his long, supple neck dancing all around his body as he checked his outfit—like a debutante about to be presented to the queen, I thought, and found out how close I was. "It is the Greatmother of this nest," he told me. "She is actually coming here herself to see us! Be very respectful to her, Dan—and when she has gone, you and I have much to talk about."

CHAPTER THIRTY

The Greatmother did not travel alone. First came a couple of new Christmas trees, dexterously scrambling along the cables and bearing gifts. One had a variety of capsules and clumps of what appeared to be the food Beert had requested, the other a rubbery ovoid the size of a pig. That contained water, and when the Wet One found that out, he begged to have some of it sprayed on him. There wasn't time for that, for the next to enter was the Greatmother herself.

This one was even fatter than the Greatmother of Beert's nest, and a lot more fashionably dressed. She wore silvery body armor that covered not only her belly but nearly her whole torso. It struck me that that had to be uncomfortably heavy. Garments and all, the creature had to mass at least a quarter of a ton.

But not, of course, here. She came floating weightlessly into the reception chamber, towed by a pair of glass robots to save her the bother of swarming along the cables herself. Her long neck was covered with bangles like a Ubangi's, and it was dancing a hula of greeting. The Greatmother gave the most cursory of glances at the clutch of us lesser species, and addressed herself directly to Beert. "I welcome you, Djabeertapritch of the Two Eights," she declared, touching her nose almost to his. "We are glad to have you in our nest, but how does it happen that you come?"

It was clear that Beert was the one she was welcoming. I was sure that if Pirraghiz and I had turned up without a live Horch as company, our reception would have been a lot less hospitable. For Beert, she was different. The Greatmother was thrilled to meet a conspecific who had endured the vile captivity of the Others. She wasn't disposed to question Beert's stumbling explanation of his nest's history and the rapidly invented mix-up that had brought him here, either. Actually his rather creative description of the blunders that had made it happen amused her. She had a superior kind of tolerance of one planet in the Horch federation for another, reminding me of the way Canadians talked about New Zealanders in the British Commonwealth. "Well, what do you expect of a bunch of Eight Plus Threes?" she asked jovially. She cast a mildly disapproving eye at the amphibian and me. "It is odd, however," she added, "that Horch should concern themselves with the problems of lesser species."

"They are more worthy than they seem, Greatmother," Beert said humbly. "Permit me to introduce them——"

She shrugged that idea away impatiently, neck and arms all twisting at once. "My least of grandsons is interested in such other organisms. I am not. But tell me of your captivity, Djabeertapritch. You were allowed no machines at all? But how did you live?"

I am sure Beert had more urgent things to talk to her about than his nest's tribulations, but he was not capable of denying the request of a Greatmother. "We were Horch," he said simply. "We used what we had or could make. For building materials we took clay from the ground and long, thin shoots from the local vegetation——"

I didn't want to hear it all again, so I took a chance. "Excuse me," I said deferentially, addressing Beert. "The Wet One needs water, so if we may withdraw——?"

The Greatmother answered for him; it was the first time she had spoken to me directly. "Go, go," she said irritably. "But leave food for Djabeertapritch; the poor thing must be hungry."

We all crowded into one of the other rooms, or all but Beert and his personal robot, which remained behind to serve him his meal. I had two things on my mind. For one, I knew I was going to have that little talk with Beert before long, and I wasn't looking forward to it. I was definitely looking forward to the other, though. However much I tried to warn myself that there were many hurdles still to get across, I could almost taste the nearness of my escape to Earth. While Pirraghiz was taking charge of the food we had carried away with us, sniffing and tasting each item, I looked around the room for things that might be useful when I got back. By the time she had approved a few things for my meal, I decided there weren't any. But there might be information worth having.

Pirraghiz handed me a collection of fruits and spoke doubtfully to the amphibian. "I do not know if any of this is suitable for you, Wet One."

The Wet One waved a flipper at her. The robot with the sack of water was carefully spraying his rubbery skin, a squirt at a time, like Spanish peasants taking wine from a goatskin, while a second robot was busy mopping up the droplets that splashed away. The Wet One was wriggling with pleasure as his skin welcomed the damp, but it did not distract him from his purpose. "I do not need to eat now," he grumbled, in that thick, muddy voice. "I will eat well when I have been transmitted to my own planet. When will that happen?"

His bath boy-robot answered him. "The channels are being prepared. The Greatmother will give the order to transmit you when she wishes."

I thought that was a good opportunity to try to get some information, so I interrupted. "Can you tell us what kind of a place we're in?"

The spraying robot did not respond, but the one on mop-up detail stopped what it was doing and extruded a glittering branch of twiglets in my direction. "This is a nest of the Four and Ones, formerly occupied by the Others," it said.

That wasn't informative. I said, "I mean, what *is* it?" That was no better. The robot stood silent and impassive, only the glittering ball at its top flickering unhelpfully. Pirraghiz sighed, put down the loaf of something she was breaking into pieces for me and issued an order.

"Display the appearance of this artifact we are in," she commanded the Christmas tree.

It worked. The thing immediately went to the video bowl, fussed with the controls for a moment and did as commanded. An image sprang up in the bowl. It was obviously a space station of some kind, but what it looked like was a child's impromptu building-block construction, all jagged angles and bits and pieces tacked on. It gleamed of metal, though not very brightly. At first I thought it was a kind of engineering drawing, since it was displayed against a background of solid black, like the images I'd seen of other species in the helmet.

But then Pirraghiz said, "What are those things?" and I saw that the blackness was not quite complete. It was a sky, and not a kind of sky I had ever seen before. It was certainly nothing like the brilliant globular-cluster display of the prison planet. It wasn't even like a starry night on Earth. There were no stars at all. Instead there was a scattering of fuzzily glowing little scraps of light, hard to make out. Most were white, some bluish, one or two a ruddy orange in color. And apart from them there was nothing but blackness—total, unrelieved, unfriendly blackness.

I had not been in love with an astronomer for nothing. "My God," I said, "those are galaxies!"

Ever since the five of us found ourselves on the prison planet, I had been aware that we were far from home. Not *this* far, though. Not in intergalactic space! Even the globular cluster of stars that surrounded us could have been somewhere within that fuzzy whirlpool of stars that was our own galaxy, but now—

No. We weren't even that close anymore.

I know it's silly. If we had been close enough to see Earth as a star in the sky, say marooned on the surface of Mars, I still would have had no way of getting to it other than one of these alien transit machines. And with the machines, no distance was really far. Wherever I was, I was as close to home as a single step, no matter how many millions of light-years I had to cross to get there.

All the same, it *felt* different. It felt frightening.

It wasn't until Pirraghiz touched me on the shoulder that I realized I was still staring at that picture in the bowl. "Are you all right, Dannerman?" she asked anxiously. "You aren't eating."

I looked down at the crinkly pale fruit in my hand, then gave it back to her. "I'm not hungry," I said.

"You should eat," she said, "but if that is not what you want to do just now, perhaps you should go to Beert. Have you forgotten than he wanted to talk to you?"

Well, actually I had, at least for the moment. But it was something that needed to be done, so I headed for the reception room.

I was surprised to find that Beert was still talking; he had just got to the beginnings of the building of the nest and their invention of a kind of paper. And the Greatmother was absorbedly listening still, but when I came in she glanced at me, with the absent look a visitor might give the family cat as it slunk into a room, then shook herself. "I am being selfish, Djabeertapritch," she sighed. "All the nest will want to hear your story. We must have a banquet and sing so that you can teach them what Horch can do, however wretched their circumstances."

"I am honored by your visit, Greatmother," he said, lowering his head respectfully.

"Yes," she agreed. And as her personal Christmas tree began to bear her away she twisted her neck teasingly and added, "You will enjoy the banquet, Djabeertapritch. We will show you someone you have never seen before."

CHAPTER THIRTY-ONE

The talk with Beert didn't get off to a good start. What was on my mind was why we were so far from anything at all; what was on his was wonder about who this previously unknown "someone" might be. It turned out quickly that he couldn't answer my question, and naturally I hadn't a clue about his. So we got serious. I said, "I'm sorry if I got you in trouble, Beert."

He gave me one of those nose-to-nose looks for a moment, then pulled away. "You should not have destroyed one of the cousins' machines," he said, sorrowfully judicious. "The rest is my fault. Now show me what you have in that bag."

He caught me by surprise that time, but I sighed and retrieved the bag. There are times when you just have to throw in your hand and take what's coming to you.

When I loosened the drawstring and shook it gently, its contents spilled out: all the little odds and ends of Horchware that I had surreptitiously filled it with, tools stolen from Beert's laboratory, a batch of Pirraghiz's tapes and the ones I had taken from the room here. I had been careful when I opened it, but the things began to fly around the room. I caught as many as I could, and Beert reached out for others. He stared at the first one that came his way, a black oblong with rows of dimples along its side. "This is mine!" he said. I didn't answer, and he darted his head toward me. "You took it from my workshop!" I didn't say anything to that, either. I was busy cramming the loose items back in the bag. Beert didn't stop me. He even handed a couple of them back to me, but he wasn't meeting my eyes anymore. When I had everything stowed away again I cleared my throat.

"I didn't want to tell you about these things," I said.

"No, you would not," he agreed. "These are Horch technology! They came from the cousins. I did not think you would try to take such things with you. I do not think my Greatmother would approve."

I said miserably, "I didn't like doing it, Beert, but what choice did I have? Do you remember what you said? That in my place you would fear the cousin Horch as much as the Others? Well, I do!"

Beert gave me a look I couldn't read, then turned away. Well, "twisted away" is a better way to put it. He corkscrewed his neck around itself until it came to rest with his chin on his shoulder, or what would have been his shoulder if he'd had one, looking away from me. "I need to think," he said. "Leave me, Dan."

And I did.

Pirraghiz insisted that I eat, so I did. Then she urged me to sleep, because there was no knowing when I might get the chance again, so I tried to do that, too. Sleep didn't come quickly, though. What made it difficult was my conscience.

The difficulty was that although this Beert was a weird-looking creature with a snaky neck and the face of a rattlesnake—not to mention that he was also a member of that race who had just finished murdering a whole bunch of my fellow humans, one of whom (or several of whom) had been me—in spite of all that, he was something else. He was one of the only two friends I had left, anywhere in this part of the universe. And I had put him in the deep shit, and had every prospect of getting him in deeper still.

You might ask how I could do something like that to a friend.

I guess the only proper answer would be "practice," because actually I had had plenty of experience along those lines. Betraying friends was basically the job description of what I did for the National Bureau of Investigation. We called it "infiltration." In

order to get the goods on some gang of criminals or terrorists—
or whatever—my first step was to make some new friends, who
would remain my friends just as long as it took me to get the
evidence that would put them in prison for most of their adult
lives.

I had never had much of a problem with my conscience in
those days, because those "friends" weren't friends at all. They
were bad guys, and they needed to be put away. But Beert wasn't
a bad guy. Neither was my other new friend, Pirraghiz. And I
was definitely screwing up her life, too.

So I didn't get much sleep, hanging on to the webbing in my
alien room in this alien thing called a "nexus." Neither did anyone else, because it wasn't long until one of the Christmas trees
poked in on me and announced, "The channels for the Wet One
have been accessed. It may proceed now to its transmission."

CHAPTER THIRTY-TWO

I don't know if Beert had slept, either. When I got to where the Wet One was, Beert was there, too, painstakingly reattaching all the amphibian's gear to his body, but he didn't speak to me.

He didn't speak on the way back to the transit-machine chamber, either. The trip seemed shorter than it had coming the other way, maybe because my mind wasn't on what we were doing. What my mind was occupied with was wondering what Beert's mind was. I knew he was feeling guilty. I didn't know what he would do about it. If duty overcame friendship, he only had to speak a couple of words and my hopes of ever getting back to Earth would be right down the tube. Or if he dithered indecisively for very long, that would be nearly as bad. What I wanted was to be on my way before it occurred to anybody to put in a call to the Eight Plus Threes.

A couple of the Christmas trees were waiting for us at the transit machine. So was a living Horch—a very young Horch, I thought, because he was no more than half Beert's size, but handsomely decked out in a scaled-down version of his Greatmother's body armor. "I am Kofeeshtetch," he said—or something like that. He was talking to Beert, but his neck was swaying toward me and the Wet One. "I am the Greatmother's least grandson. Can these organisms talk?"

Kofeeshtetch turned out to be pretty nearly the best thing that had happened to me in a while. He was a pampered, and fairly well spoiled, youngster, and that was very good for us lower organisms. He wasn't just interested in us, he was *fascinated*. He was even more fascinated—no, the right word is "thrilled," thrilled enough to be peeing his pants if he'd had any—at what we two aborigines were planning to do. Invade strongholds of the Others! Do it single-handed! "When I myself am grown," he boasted breathlessly, "I too will command forces to capture stations and worlds from the Others, just as my parents did in this installation! But I will not, of course, be foolish enough to attempt it alone. Do you imagine that you have any hope of succeeding at all?"

I wasn't sure whether he was asking the Wet One or me, but I wanted to be the one who answered. "With the generous help of you Horch, yes!" I said.

Beert gave me a disapproving look, translated as *Shut up, you've made enough trouble*. "It is kind of you to take an interest, Kofeeshtetch," he said, doing his best to be polite to a grandson of a Greatmother, "but we have urgent business. This Wet One is most uncomfortable in this dry and weightless environment. He should begin his mission without delay."

The youth shrugged impatiently. "Of course, but first I wish to hear his plans in detail. Speak to me if you can, Wet One."

The amphibian's little electric whiskers were twisting about. For a moment I thought the Greatmother's least grandson was going to get a cattle-prod shock to hurry him along, but courtesy, and prudence, won out. The Wet One began telling his plans in his thick, slobbery voice.

Kofeeshtetch listened with a lot less courtesy, his neck drawn back from the Wet One in repugnance. "I can hardly understand this one," he remarked to Beert. "He speaks very poorly, as do you. I am disappointed." He turned to the nearest Christmas tree. "At least display for me what his planet looks like, also"—shooting one arm in my direction—"the planet of this one."

"We have not yet identified the other organism's home," the machine apologized.

"Do so! Meanwhile, the display!"

There was no doubt that Kofeeshtetch was used to having his

orders obeyed. They were. Another of the Christmas trees, the one hovering by the transit machine, quickly swung itself to a TV bowl in the wall and made adjustments.

As a picture sprang up in the bowl, the amphibian caught his breath in a sort of loud, abbreviated snore. To me, the picture was just a planet, and not a particularly interesting one. None of its few land masses looked anything like Earth, but it meant something to the amphibian. He croaked, "That is it! I believe that is my true Home Water!"

One of his shocking tendrils was resting on the image, touching a wide bay that looked like any other wide bay to me. It didn't seem to mean much to Kofeeshtetch, either. As he pulled himself closer, one of those mean-looking fighting machines got in his way, but he shoved it rudely aside. Then he made a sound of disgust. "This is a very tedious object, Wet One," he told the amphibian. "There is too much water. But if you wish to go there, then do so."

And he waved to the Christmas tree, who opened the door of the transit machine.

The amphibian crawled in, attachments and all, and the other robot tossed his ammunition boxes after him.

The door closed.

Kofeeshtetch made a gesture of dismissal. "I do not think that Wet One will survive for long," he remarked, and that was all there was to it.

After a moment Beert sighed. "I would have liked to wish him well on his venture," he said meditatively. "In any case, thank you for your help, Kofeeshtetch, but now I am quite tired. I think I will go to my chamber and rest before the banquet. Are you coming, Dan?"

I looked at the young Horch. He seemed poutily disappointed in the entertainment, but he hadn't left.

"You go ahead, Beert," I said. "I think Kofeeshtetch still has some questions for me, so I'll stay a bit."

* *· *

It took me about thirty seconds to get the kid juiced up again—he was, after all, a kid. All I had to do was to ask him if he would please grant me the favor of telling me how his ancestors had captured this installation. That did it. He was off, and then all I had to do was make the appropriate thrilled noises from time to time.

His story was full of Horch names that I didn't retain, and matters of who took precedence over whom that I didn't understand in the first place. Most of it, though, was blow-by-blow descriptions of how his parents' technicians had managed to insert their fighting forces into the Others' channel. And how the first wave of Horch fighting machines had been destroyed in a few moments. And how the Horch had sneaked a second wave in through a different transit machine while the defenders were distracted by what was happening at the first one. And—

And on and on. Kofeeshtetch loved the subject. He acted it out, with limbs and neck flying in all dirctions. It was interesting to me, too, as an insight into how the Horch did their fighting . . . but, at that moment, not very. I wanted to get on to my own problem, but I didn't want to interrupt.

When Kofeeshtetch got to the point where their Horch robots were mopping up the rags and tags of flesh that was all there was left of the Others' warriors, I began to hope for an ending. "The Greatmother has told me," he was saying proudly, "of how vile the stench of those decomposing corpses was, so that for a time it was difficult to breathe, even more difficult to eat without vomiting. To carry on the work of this installation was very hard."

Carry on? I did interrupt him then. "But this was an Others' installation. Why would you want to carry on their work?"

He gave me a scornful hiss, thrusting his head in my face. His breath was not nearly as inoffensive as Beert's. "Of course it had been operated by the Others. What of it? The Others are filthy vermin, but there are some few objectives we share in common. Do you want to hear the story of my parents or do you not?"

I wanted to hear what those common objectives were, but I wanted even more to get to my own desires. "Your parents were very, very brave," I said with admiration. "I only hope that I can be as brave, and as successful, when I too fight against the Others."

Kofeeshtetch swayed his neck indecisively back and forth for a moment. I could see that he was reluctant to give up his favorite subject, but he was torn.

I understood his dilemma. When my uncle Max Adcock, the not-very-successful buccaneer capitalist, told me about the next great stock raid or franchise operation that was going to make him rich at last, if only Uncle Cubby would help him out with a little seed capital, I always listened. To the ten-year-old I was at the time, it was exciting. I don't mean that I liked Uncle Max. Apart from the fact that he was my cousin Pat's father, I didn't have much use for the man. Kofeeshtetch didn't have a lot of use for lower organisms like me, either, but he had the same yearning to hear about exciting adventures. "Tell me your plan," he said sulkily.

Actually, the word "plan" was a lot more dignified than my hazy notions deserved, but I did my best. I said, "A scout ship of the Others is somewhere near my home planet. With your Greatmother's gracious permission, and assuming the proper channels can be accessed, I am going to invade it and kill everyone aboard."

"Hum," he said—actually, it was more like an approving growl. But he looked puzzled. "What do you mean by a 'scout ship'?"

It was my turn to be puzzled. Neither Beert nor Pirraghiz had had any difficulty knowing what I was talking about, so why did he? I floundered. "In order to discover civilizations like mine, the Others send out exploring vessels which travel slower than light speed. When they find one—"

"Yes, yes," he said, sounding impatient. "But such vessels come in many varieties, both for us Horch and the Others. Which kind do you mean?"

I winced. It had never occurred to me that there might be different kinds. But I said staunchly, "Whatever kind is there. It doesn't matter. I will slip aboard and start shooting. Only," I added, "there is a problem. I won't be able to do any of that unless I have weapons and a scrambler to disrupt their communications, like those the Wet One had. Now those are gone—"

Kofeeshtetch was waving his arms reprovingly. "You are so ignorant," he complained. "All such patterns are stored in the transit machine. It would be quite simple to make copies if there were any point to it, but is there? I am not satisfied that your plan is good."

He meditated for a moment, then gave a decisive neck-swirl. "I wish to see this scout ship for myself." He turned his head to the nearest Christmas tree and barked, "I am waiting! Haven't you found that planet for me yet?"

You wouldn't think a Christmas tree could look embarrassed, but this one's branches and twiglets hung low. "We have not yet made a positive identification."

That bugged me. "Of course you can do it! You've been relaying data from it for months!"

The robot didn't extend even one tiny spring in my direction. To Kofeeshtetch it said, "Relays occur automatically. We have traced all such, but there are two eights of planets transmitting this sort of data. Can this organism say whether his people use radio?"

I resisted an impulse to laugh. "Oh, yes. All the time," I said.

Still to the Horch: "That eliminates some. Then how many moons does this planet have?"

"One big one."

"Then, Kofeeshtetch," the robot said, shooting out a sprig of needles to touch the controls of the screen, "it is likely that this is the planet you seek."

And when the picture had formed in the bowl, it was.

I could see the dagger of India stabbing down into the Indian Ocean, with the little island of Sri Lanka dripping off its tip. As the planet slowly spun I could see Africa emerge, and the beginnings of Europe. There was something strange about the image, though. Tiny dots of reddish light that I had never seen before were sprinkled around the globe. But there was no doubt what I was looking at. I swallowed. "That's the Earth," I said, suddenly homesick.

Kofeeshtetch was not sentimental. "Not the planet!" he snapped at the robot. "Isn't there a survey vessel of the Others nearby?"

"We have identified one, yes. Here is a plot of its transit machines—"

Three or four of those reddish lights appeared, close together, against a background of stars. It was the stars, more than those little lights, that made me catch my breath. This was none of that awful intergalactic black, nor all those multicolored headlights of the globular cluster. These were my own stars, the very constellations you can see from Earth. I recognized at least one of them, the seven stars in a cup-and-handle pattern that every child knows as the Big Dipper.

Kofeeshtetch wasn't interested in stargazing. "So many transit machines," he muttered. "Can we see the ship itself?"

At once stars and ruddy lights vanished and we were looking at another set of children's Tinkertoys. "We have no view of the specific craft, but it is probable that it is this model," the robot said.

It looked to be smaller than the nexus itself, or at least a little less complicated, but it impressed Kofeeshtetch. "But this is no mere robot scout! It must be in fact a major vessel of the Others." He swung his head to face mine. "You could not possibly succeed in attacking it single-handed! It will be staffed with many, many warriors of the Others, all better armed than you. Such a venture would require a full-scale assault, almost as large as the one with which our nest stormed this place."

That was not at all what I wanted to hear. I think I'm more or less brave, but I'm not stupid. A one-man suicide venture against impossible odds didn't sound attractive—at least, unless there was nothing better on offer. I took a chance. "I don't suppose you could interest your Greatmother in, well, in launching such an attack?"

Kofeeshtetch laughed in my face, little raucous puffs of bad breath. He didn't say anything. He didn't have to. His laughter made it quite clear that the Horch were not going to launch a major battle to please a lower organism like me, especially over a pissant little planet like Earth.

What he did say was, "Your plan is not worth pursuing. Perhaps you should return to the Eight Plus Threes. I will leave you now to prepare for the feast the Greatmother is providing for Djabeertapritch."

He looked like he was getting ready to do it, too. I could feel my dreams collapsing around me, but one faint hope of an idea was percolating through my mind.

"Wait a minute," I begged. "Can I see the planet Earth again?"

I had nearly lost him. He was just a child, after all. If I wasn't about to pursue the feats of derring-do that fired up his kid imagination, he had no further use for me. He hung indecisively from his cable for a moment, then said petulantly, "Oh, very well, but do it quickly."

Quickly was how the robot did it. The planet had revolved a little more. Now we were looking at the Atlantic Ocean, South America bulging out into it and the East Coast of the United States just visible on the periphery. I peered at that unfamiliar scattering of red spots, clustered mostly along the shorelines. I pointed. "What are those?"

Kofeeshtetch gestured, and then the robot answered me. "We have no definite identification. They appear to be satellite installations, but we do not know their purpose."

"But they're smaller, and they're right on the surface of the Earth."

"That is not precisely accurate," the machine corrected me. "If you will observe, they are all in the water regions of the planet, close to the land masses but not on them."

"But still—" I began to argue.

I didn't finish. Kofeeshtetch waved me to silence. He was beginning to catch the spirit. "That might be a workable plan," he said thoughtfully. "A smaller installation. Only one transit machine each. Perhaps only operated by machines, certainly with a much smaller complement than the ship in space—yes! This may be worth considering. I will think on this, and perhaps seek advice from the Greatmother."

When I got back to my room, as jubilant as I dared be, Pirraghiz was waiting for me. She listened, but didn't comment, as I told her what had happened. "Where's Beert?" I asked. "I must tell him!"

"Djabeertapritch is sleeping, Dannerman. This has been exhausting for him."

She didn't sound excited at all, and she was bringing me down with her. "But he will want to hear all this!" I insisted.

She gave me one of those six-limbed shrugs. "You can speak to him when he wakes, Dannerman," she said firmly. "He has some important decisions to make, and he has ordered me to let him rest. It is better if you rest, also. Would you like to eat first?"

CHAPTER THIRTY-THREE

I didn't get a chance to talk to Beert after his sleep. I didn't get much sleep for myself, either, because Pirraghiz woke me up to tell me that the Greatmother's banquet was just about to happen and we'd better get a move on.

I could have wished for a little more warning. I really needed to talk to Beert, but when I tried to grab him he simply waggled his neck at me. "Later, Dan," he said, sounding distracted and not really all that interested. "We can't keep this Greatmother waiting." I was also conscious of really beginning to need a bath, and there wasn't anything of that sort in the chambers they'd given us. So, unwashed, I followed Beert and the Christmas tree along the roped passages, hoping that the Horch sense of smell was not acute. Because I was sure I was a lot less than fragrant just then.

I could hear the noise from the feast long before the banquet hall was in sight.

The hall was shaped like a pyramid—well, like a tetrahedron, with four triangular sides, none of which was either a floor or a ceiling—and it was big. It had to be. There were at least forty Horch present. They weren't sitting. They weren't even doing what Horch do instead of sitting down like a human being. They just hung there, clipped to one or another of the brightly glowing cords that were stretched across the volume of space, like strands of a 3-D spiderweb. And they were very loudly singing.

It is hard to say what a Horch group sing sounded like. It was a little like the howling of a pack of constipated wolves, a little like hogs grunting ferociously as they battled for tidbits in a pen. The big difference was that the Horch were doing all that in unison, and that there were lyrics to the tune they sang. They sang of the Greatest of Greatmothers, and of the undying delights—or of the later-on undying delights, that is, after they'd finished whatever other dying they had to get there—of living forever, cherished in the Greatest of Greatmother's love. Does that sound awful? Sure it does. It was.

They hadn't waited for us to arrive. They were eating as they sang. A squad of the glassy robots were busily slithering along the cords, hand over hand—well, branch over twig—to serve the diners with great gobs of something that looked like pink mashed potatoes, only gluey enough to hold together in a ball; clusters of figlike fruits that probably weren't fruits at all, because they were squirming; hinged food dishes containing stuff that I couldn't see, but could smell when the nearest Horch opened theirs; mesh bags of what might have been nuts or vegetables or—well, anything at all. All I could see through the mesh was varicolored lumps of God knew what. The other thing the Horch were doing was drinking, out of bagpipe-looking bladders with spouts on one end. The Horch took the spouts in their triangular little mouths when they wanted a drink, and then some of them pointed the spouts at friends nearby and squeezed. For fun, I guess. The thin streams of yellowish liquid, looking unpleasantly like urine, splashed when they hit another Horch and kept on going when they missed. It didn't matter which they did, though. The Christmas trees were diligently sucking the spilled liquid out of the air as they passed. These masters of the universe were having their fun at a kind of college fraternity brawl. I guess the overworked robots weren't enjoying it, but probably they weren't programmed to enjoy anything anyway.

Our personal robot first escorted Beert to the heart of the web. The Greatmother was there and eating industriously, pausing in her own consumption only, now and then, to stuff some particular delicacy into the mouth of her least grandson, Kofeeshtetch. Having their mouths full didn't keep them from singing along, welcomingly waving Beert to join in.

Pirraghiz and I weren't included in the invitation. We weren't given the good seats, either. A pair of serving robots dropped their waitering duties long enough to tug us to webs at one vertex of the tetrahedron. Then they scuttled away to fetch fresh delicacies for the Horch.

We weren't alone there. There were three or four Horch nearby, singing along lustily with the others though they couldn't have been very high ranking—our place was the exact equivalent of a table by the kitchen door in a human restaurant, even to the procession of serving robots that streamed back and forth past us. Our neighbors didn't stop singing. They darted their heads to glance at us as we arrived—not cordially. I could almost hear them asking each other what cretin had invited these nasty-looking lower orders to the feast. Especially ones who smelled as strange as Pirraghiz and, no doubt, me.

We weren't totally neglected. After a few moments the robots began dropping tidbits off for us, too. First there were a couple of net bags containing some of those things like green plums I remembered from my interrogation days, then a wine sack, then two lumps of that pink dough. They didn't hand them to us. They attached them, somehow, to the cables we were clinging to. I didn't see how, exactly, because I was trying to figure out what was going on up in the high-rent district.

The Greatmother's party wasn't singing anymore. The least grandson seemed to have left the group, but I could see Beert and the Greatmother talking to each other, necks intertwined in deep conversation. I was pretty sure what they were talking about. It was me. Every once in a while one or both of them would dart their heads in my direction, but what was being said, I couldn't guess. I could only hope that it had nothing to do with my destruction of valuable Horch machinery at the Eight Plus Threes.

Pirraghiz interrupted my fairly apprehensive thoughts about that by poking my shoulder. "Eat," she said.

That was easier said than done; I didn't see how I could hang on to the cable and eat at the same time. Pirraghiz solved the problem for me. She had linked herself to the cable with one of her lesser arms. Now she took a firm hold of my leg with another, thus safely mooring me, while she finished picking over the goodies the robots had left us with a couple more. Having six arms certainly had its points.

She drew me close enough to hear her over the noise of the singing, which was getting even more boisterous. "You can eat this," she said, offering me a lump of the pink dough. "Some of the fruits, too, after I pick the seeds out. Not the liquid. Not anything else."

The pink stuff was warm and soft and smelled a little like garlic. I nibbled at it to be polite. Although I was hungry, I still had the hope in my heart, now dwindlingly faint, that before long I would be where I could get a thick steak, with french fries and a few slices of red, ripe tomatoes, and maybe even a bottle of beer. . . .

"Look," Pirraghiz said, sounding surprised.

What she was pointing at was the least grandson, rapidly swinging himself in our direction, looking as though he had something to talk to us about.

He did. As soon as he was near he announced importantly, "I have solved the problem of the order of battle—theoretically, provided it is allowed to occur. Listen attentively."

He didn't have to say that. I was doing it already. He settled himself in, close to my head, and stared into my eyes.

"There are three eights and two of the vessels on your planet," he informed me. "One is considerably larger than the others, so we will not attack that one. To one of the smaller ones, first we will send in two waves of fighting machines, two at a time. I had thought," he said meditatively, "of perhaps using a pair of the warriors of the Others as a deception tactic for the first wave."

He surprised me. "You have some of their warriors?"

"Of course. Quite a few were still alive, though wounded, when this place was taken. Most did not survive, but some did, even after questioning. Later, when they had been removed from the control of the Others, the Greatmother gave them to me as pets. I possess a number of such creatures," he told me proudly. "I study them to learn what lesser organisms are like, so as to be prepared for dealing with them at the Eschaton. Perhaps sometime I will show some of them to you."

This particular lesser organism was getting impatient. I coughed to get him back on track. "That would be nice, but about your plan—?"

"Yes, the order of battle. I decided against using the organic warriors. Since they are no longer controlled, they have become quite cowardly and I do not trust their fighting skills. So we will use our machines in the first two waves. Then you and your— uh—associate"—he was looking at Pirraghiz—"will go in the third transmission, also armed with copies of your projectile weapons. By then the fighting machines should have neutralized whatever forces the Others have in place. Not many, I think. The Others will not expect us to bother them in a place like that. Then you will be free to act as you wish." I was rapturously hanging on every word. Then he brought me down. "Assuming, of course, that the Greatmother gives such orders. I believe she and Djabeertapritch of the Two Eights are discussing it now."

He twisted his neck to look in her direction. Then he said in sudden alarm, "I believe she is getting ready to speak! I must go! I will talk to you further later on. That is, I will if the project still seems feasible."

I could have wished for fewers ifs and maybes, but I could feel my heart speeding up. Pirraghiz was looking at me curiously. She had certainly heard every word, but if she wanted to say something about the exchange, she didn't have a chance, because just then the singing stopped at some signal I hadn't caught. Everyone was silent. Even the robots paused in their rounds for a moment, as the Greatmother began to speak.

"Nestmates and honored guest," she began—I noticed the "honored guest" was in the singular; Pirraghiz and I were not included. "We rejoice at this time at the reunion of a lost nest with the grand consortium of the Horch. We are greatly, and most pleasantly, surprised to have Djabeertapritch, descendant of our people of the Two Eights, with us. I have made him a promise, which I will keep at this celebration." She darted a coquettish look in Beert's direction. "What I have not decided," she went on, sounding like a teasing Santa Claus with a young child on his lap, "is whether it is better to prolong his suspense a bit longer or to reveal the surprise to him now." That brought on murmurs from the audience. I could hear that some of them were saying, "Now!" while others said, "No, make him wait," and a fair number were speaking what I took to be jocular obscenities. But they were all laughing about it, even the Greatmother. ("I believe they have had a great deal of the intoxicating liquid," Pirraghiz whispered in my ear.)

The Greatmother bent her neck to her least grandson, who was tugging at her arm. I noticed that Kofeeshtetch was hanging upside down relative to her, but she didn't seem to care—well, that didn't matter as much for the Horch as it would for us, since their heads could go every which way.

Then she lifted her head, giggling. "My least grandson asks to have the surprise now," she announced. "Djabeertapritch? Do you agree?"

Beert wasn't doing any of the laughing, seemed to have something serious on his mind, but he rose to the occasion. "I will be pleased with whatever pleases the Greatmother," he said diplomatically.

"Yes, of course. Very well. This surprise is a very great fool, Djabeertapritch. She was unwise enough to come to this place after the fighting had begun, and we did not allow her to leave." The Greatmother paused for dramatic effect, then issued an order to the robots. "Bring the prisoner in!"

CHAPTER THIRTY-FOUR

Every Horch head in the banquet hall turned toward one of the vertices of the tetrahedron, where the diners were scrambling to get out of the way. They needed to, for what entered was a procession.

First came a fighting machine in full combat alert, backing into the room with its weapons trained on what followed. That was a couple: a Christmas tree chained to a creature with spindly legs and arms and a head like a jack-o'-lantern. Another fighting machine brought up the rear, also with dead aim on the captive.

I knew what she was at once.

I was in the presence of one of the Others. One of Dopey's Beloved Leaders. A member of the species that, at this very moment, was casually deciding whether it would be more advantageous to annihilate everyone I knew and loved, or turn them into abject slaves.

When Pirrzghiz put one worried arm on me I realized I was shaking. I gave her a nod to reassure her, but I couldn't stop.

I wasn't the only one affected. For most of the Horch this poor captive was old news, but not for Beert. His neck and both arms were stretched out toward her, frozen motionless, and his little snake mouth was open in shock.

The Greatmother made that choking, staccato sound that was a Horch laugh. "Well, Djabeertapritch," she said, delighted with her effect. "How do you like your surprise? Would you like to speak to her? Ask her some questions about how it feels to be a captive, as you were to her people?"

He managed to make a slow, negative shake of his head, but

that was it. The female Beloved Leader was not so reluctant. She turned that great, round, scarecrow head toward Beert and spoke through her huge teeth. "I excrete into the mouth of your Greatmother," she said in a shrill, piping, venomous voice. "I will do the same to all of you when the Eschaton comes and you organisms are all shrieking in pain as we trample you under our feet."

She was speaking perfect Horch, far better than Beert's farmboy drawl. I saw the reason: one of those ribbed, golden scabs tucked under the swell of the pumpkin where it joined the skinny neck. When she leaned forward to hiss at Beert, I saw, too, that the last link of the chain that held her to the Christmas tree had actually been grafted into her flesh. They were taking no chances with this representative of the ultimate enemy.

The Greatmother was switching her head about ominously. I thought for a moment there was going to be a major hissing match between the two of them, if not something more physical. Beert prevented it. He spoke up.

"Prisoner," he said, "the Greatmother called you a fool, but you are an even bigger fool than you know. You will not win. We Horch are stronger and braver and wiser than you, and even the lower species are going to rise against you." He turned to the Greatmother. "Have I permission to speak now?"

She graciously waved her neck in assent, and he began to talk. I hung there in suspense, almost dreading to hear what he was going to say.

He began, "I speak to you from the belly, revered Greatmother, and to all you Horch of the Four and Ones. I am Djabeertapritch of the Two Eights, which is no more."

That was a letdown for me, right there. Beert wasn't delivering any casual talk, it was an oration! I was willing to bet that the son of a bitch had been rehearsing it to himself all along. Discouraged, I slumped back, waiting for him to get to a point, but I was the only one in the room who felt that way. Every one of the Horch had stopped their foolery and were listening with their little mouths wide-open.

Beert seemed to intend to give the whole history of his nest: "When the Horch came to the Two Eights they slew us by the sixteens of sixteens of sixteens, most cruelly and treacherously. . . ." Well, I had heard all of that. And about how the survivors had been taken to the prison planet, and what happened to them there. However, the Four and Ones were eating it up. They hissed and moaned when he spoke of how people from their nest had been studied and used for experimental purposes, and when he came to their rescue by the Eight Plus Threes there were scattered cheers.

I might have cheered myself, because that was when he got to what I wanted to hear. "Then our little nest was free at last. As were the members of those other species whom the Others had imprisoned there. And it is of those other species that I would speak, revered Greatmother."

Now he had my full attention, all right. "Some of you have seen the Wet One, whom we have helped return to his own planet to do battle with the Others who have enslaved it. His species was fortunate—a little fortunate—because their planet still exists. Not all were that lucky.

"You all know the species of the large one with many limbs"—his neck was outthrust toward Pirraghiz—"because some of them were here when you bravely captured this place. Their fate may be the worst of all. Not only were they compelled for a long, long time to be the servants of the Others, but their planet is long lost.

"The planet of the four-limbed one, whose name is Dan, is yet free, but perhaps not for long. The Others have already begun to infiltrate it. Dan wishes to be returned there so that he can help fight them off."

He hesitated, eyeing me with a look I couldn't interpret. Then he said, "Dan's are a simple people, Greatmother. Their machines are crude. They have little wisdom. And they are not a peaceful race. I say only of·them that their people are divided among themselves, with many 'nations' which make their own customs and laws, and sometimes actually go to war with each other." Shocked stir among the Horch; Beert went bravely on, overriding the mutterings. "Nevertheless, they do not deserve to be made slaves of the Others. It is not their fault that their limbs are stiff and their brains are imprisoned in a box of bone on their necks. They are not animals. Their brains are in some ways almost the equal of our own. So I ask you to help him in this cause, revered Greatmother, and"—he hesitated, then got it out—"I ask you for more than that. I wish to go with him myself, to do what I can to prevent what happened to my planet from happening to his. Greatmother, will you grant me this wish?"

When Beert finished speaking there was a stir among the assembled Horch. Our nearest neighbors craned their necks to study Pirraghiz and me curiously, silently at first. Then not so silent. One of them abruptly clapped his hinged feeding dish against his belly armor. Then another did. Then they were all doing it, rhythmically, like the kind of we-want-a-touchdown thing that people do at football games. And then they began to sing again, first one or two, then the whole damn collection of them at once.

I don't think it was the same song I had heard before, but I wasn't paying attention to the words. I was staring at Beert.

The guy had taken me by surprise. Not only had he chosen not to denounce me as a capricious destroyer of Horch machines, but what was this about coming to Earth with us? That had never been part of the plan.

I realized Pirraghiz was shaking my leg. I blinked at her. "The Greatmother is beckoning us," she whispered. "I think she wants us to come to her."

*   *   *

They were all looking at us, as a matter of fact, even the Greatmother. As soon as I was close she darted her head at mine, inspecting me at close range far more thoroughly than before. But I was looking at the female Other. At close range I could see that the creature had not had an easy life lately. Her clothing was smudged and torn, and there were recent scars on the bulbous pumpkin face. As Pirraghiz set me down, not two meters away, the Other rattled her chains and hissed venomously at me. The Greatmother didn't even look at her. "I tire of this filth's presence," she said to the air. "Remove her!"

As the crystal robots were dragging the Other away, the Greatmother twisted her neck to look at Beert. "You are determined to do this?" she asked. "To risk your life for the sake of some lower organisms?"

He didn't look at me. "I am determined," he said.

Then she sighed. "It will be done. My least grandson has prepared a plan which we will follow." And added, "You are very brave, Djabeertapritch."

And so he was, in more ways than the Greatmother knew.

PART EIGHT

Going Home

When the Greatmother said "Do it" she didn't mean do it on Tuesday. She didn't even mean do it when the feast was over. Kofeeshtetch disappeared at once, promising to meet us at the transit machine, and then it was maybe five minutes before a pair of Christmas trees came charging along the cords to drag me and Beert away, Pirraghiz following. Cheers broke out as we left, and then another burst of raucous song. I was glad enough not to have to stay for that.

We stopped by the rooms to collect Beert's personal glass robot. That was useful, since it gave me a chance to pick up my little mesh bag of Horch goodies. Beert gave me a dark look but didn't say anything, and we were at the transit machine long before Kofeeshtetch and the troops.

Our Christmas trees deserted us then to fiddle with the machine, and I finally got the chance to ask Beert the question on my mind. "Why, Beert? Why are you coming with us?"

He swung his face partly toward mine, then away. To the air he said, "I want to be able to go back to my own nest."

That didn't make sense. "Why not just jump in that thing and go home?"

This time he did look at me. "And if I did that, what would I tell my Greatmother? That I turned loose somebody who had destroyed a Horch machine, with a bag of Horch material, and no way to know what you do with it? No, Dan. I can't go home yet, though I wish with all my belly I could."

"But—" I began, trying to be reasonable, but then I ran out of time for being reasonable as Kofeeshtetch made his entrance.

The kid had an entourage with him, not only the four deadly

Horch fighting machines but a large, ugly alien which had four or five tiny, different aliens clinging to his fur. I had seen them in pictures before, but never alive: the Bashfuls and the Happies, as the comics had named them on Earth.

"I promised to show you my other species," Kofeeshtetch said proudly. "This large being is a warrior of the Others; the little ones are used for delicate work by them. Do not fear the warrior," he added kindly. "He has been freed of his bondage and will do you no harm." Kofeeshtetch allowed us a moment to admire his menagerie, then waved them off and gave one of the robots his orders.

Then he turned to us and got down to business. He extended one arm toward the TV, which the robot had made to display the globe of Earth again, and said: "Of the three eights and two vessels of the Others which are on your planet, I have chosen this one for your mission."

I looked where he was pointing. The thing was down in the Gulf of 'Aqaba, of all places. I demanded, "Why?"

He looked almost embarrassed. "It is not near any of the others. Also I liked the look of that funny-looking land mass."

"No," I said strongly, and then remembered to add, "Please. Do you remember what Djabeertapritch said about our many independent countries? Well, that one's in the wrong country." I stabbed at the map, in the vague direction of the East Coast of the United States. "Over here would be better. Can you enlarge this part of the globe?"

The Christmas tree did, and I saw the Eastern Seaboard swell up before me. There were four or five of those ruddy dots between Florida and Newfoundland. The best-looking one was not far from the alligator shape of Long Island, as close to the Bureau headquarters in Virginia as I could get. I pointed at it. "That one . . . please."

"Oh, very well," Kofeeshtetch said sulkily, and gave an order to the Christmas tree by the machine, which began to fiddle with the controls. "Anyway," he said, brightening, "now it is time!

Remember the order of battle! These two fighters first; they have their orders. Then two more to mop up. Then you, Djabeertapritch, with—ah—the 'Dan.' I wish you all good luck."

Pirraghiz stirred. "Wait a minute," she said. "I'm going too. Also Djabeertapritch will want his own personal robot with him."

Kofeeshtetch gave her an angry look. "It is very foolish to make trivial changes in a battle plan just before the engagement," he complained.

"But it would be better that way," Beert said, his tone placating. "Perhaps my robot could go with the second wave of fighting machines, then us, then—"

"No, Djabeertapritch," Pirraghiz said firmly. "I will go before you. We do not know what the conditions will be when we arrive."

Kofeeshtetch looked at Beert, who nodded agreement then gave up. "All right," he said. "Now, if you're ready? First wave! Go!"

It was the quietest beginning of a battle I can imagine. The first two fighters entered the machine, the door closed; it opened again; the second wave entered with Beert's Christmas tree. It closed.

As Pirraghiz was going into the machine I checked my twenty-shots, one in each hand. Then I remembered something. "Oh, Kofeeshtetch! You were going to tell me what this installation was for."

He blinked his little snake eyes at me, his mind clearly changing gears. He threw a look at the transit machine, already yawning open for Beert and me. "You are upsetting the timetable," he said pettishly. "Why, the installation is for the Eschaton, of course. Now go!"

CHAPTER THIRTY-SIX

It was peaceful when we got into the transit machine. It wasn't when we got out. Whatever we had arrived in—a chamber the size of an eighteen-wheeler truck, metal walls filled with displays and gadgets—it stank. Partly it smelled of scorched protein, like an ancient fish-and-chips store after a long, busy winter night, when nobody had cared to open a window. Partly it smelled of seared metal and destruction. It looked that way, too. The fighting seemed to be over, though most of our first-wave fighting machines had already become sizzling junk. In the first quick glance I saw an unfamiliar Doc, with a copper blanket over his head—I recognized my goodies bag—a distraught Dopey perched at one end of the chamber and a couple of dead Beloved Leader warrior-Bashfuls. The place was suffocatingly hot. And it was noisier than I would have believed.

Most of the noise didn't come from the crackling metal or the whimpering Dopey perched at one end of the compartment as he gazed with horror at the Horch, Beert. The deafening part came from my friend Pirraghiz. Bafflingly, she was shrieking at the top of her lungs, a long, meowing garble in her own impenetrable language. She sounded either terrified or in pain. I swore to myself in alarm and staggered toward her in the sudden Earth gravity, looking for the wound that was causing her such agony. There didn't seem to be any. Still screaming, she shook me off, at the same time gesturing to the strange Doc with the copper blanket over his head. I had no idea what she wanted from him, but after a moment he did. Wounded as he was—one of his lesser arms was terribly burned—he limped over to the control boards and quickly played his clawed hands over the colored dots.

When the Doc said something to Pirraghiz she stopped screaming at once and gave him a quick hug of greeting. Then she bent to examine his burned arm and tsk-tsked over it—in her case it was actually a sort of *bup-bup* sound—before she turned to me. "Wrahrrgherfoozh"—I think that's what she said the Doc's name was—"needs attention! I fear he may lose that arm! I must try to help him!"

"Well, sure," I said, "but what was all the screaming about?"

Pirraghiz was already delicately probing the skin around the Doc's—well, shoulder; at least, around the little bony bump where his burned lesser arm joined his torso. Her full attention was on his injuries, and she didn't look up. "I didn't want the Others to know what was happening," she said, still gently working away on him. "So as soon as the machines and I got him neutralized with the mesh, I turned off the scrambler and began to scream—yelling that there were explosions, water was coming in, all that sort of thing. My intention was to make the Others believe we had some kind of a terrible accident," she explained. "Then, as you saw, we turned off the communicator and the transit machine. Is that all right?"

It was a hell of a lot better than all right. I wished I had thought of it myself. What I said was an inadequate, "Thank you."

She spared me a quick glance. "Yes. But, Dannerman, what do we do now?"

That was what I needed to figure out. It was great to be back on Earth again, but I was still a long way from Arlington.

I took a moment to get a better idea of what I had to work with. The Horch fighting machines had been surgically efficient in their assault. As far as I could tell, none of the fittings of the sub had been damaged, but I didn't see much that was helpful. There had been two Beloved Leader warriors on the sub, both now dead. There had been four Horch fighting machines, three of which were now scrap; the Bashfuls had put up a pretty good fight before they died. Beert's personal robot seemed unharmed. So did the Dopey, who had stopped his terrified whining and was staring from one to the other of us as Pirraghiz and I talked.

There was something I needed to know about that Dopey. So, watching him, what I said to Pirraghiz was, "The first thing we do is kill the Dopey, so he can't make any trouble."

Pirraghiz stiffened in surprise. The Dopey didn't. He just kept looking back and forth at the two of us, with an occasional frightened glance at Beert. Even his tail plume didn't change color. So either he was a wonderful actor, or he didn't understand the Horch language we were speaking.

As Pirraghiz began to object I said, "Cancel that." I pointed to the wounded Doc. "Can he drive this thing?"

She gave me a strange look, but then she mewed at the Doc and he mewed back. "Yes, he can. Wrahrrgherfoozh is engineer for this vessel. He can operate any part of it, but he wants to know where to drive to."

Another good question. If I can see some kind of a map, I'll tell him.

More mewing. Then, "The locators are turned off, Dannerman," she reported. "They are part of the communication system." While I was absorbing the notion that we were somewhere in the Atlantic Ocean, and blind, she added, "However, Wrahrrgherfoozh says it is possible for him to alter the system to receive only and not to transmit. But that will take some time."

That lifted a huge weight from my soul. "Tell him to do it, then!"

"He is badly hurt, Dannerman. I do not think we can save that arm."

That was when Beert spoke up. He had been quietly talking to his Christmas tree, and he said, "Dan. I have used my machine to work on many devices of the Others. Perhaps it can help."

I looked at Pirraghiz. "Can it?" And when she nodded, "Then tell them to get on with it! I mean, please."

The Christmas tree scuttled over to the board, Pirraghiz explained to the Doc what was going on, and I had my first chance to say anything to Beert. He was standing silent, his head darting this way and that, his arms slumped by his side. He looked dejected.

I said, "Beert? Listen, I'm sorry that I got you into this."

He turned the head toward me, but all he said was, "Yes."

There was nothing to be done for the dead warriors. The one surviving fighting machine was poking at the ruins of the other three, but it didn't look like they were going to be repairable for a good long time. If ever.

By then the Dopey had managed to collect himself. He fixed his little kitten eyes on me and spoke up. *"Sprechen-sie Deutsch?"* he asked. He was looking at me. *"Panamayoo Paruski? Parlez-vous—"*

I cut him off, "Try English."

He switched at once, gazing at me intently. "I must ask, why are you here? Do you have any understanding of what fate awaits you for daring to bring a filthy Horch into a vessel of the Beloved Leaders?"

"They have to catch us first," I said. It was oddly pleasing to be speaking my own language again, even with this creature.

"But they surely will," he said reasonably. "Then it will be terrible for you. You have only one chance to avoid the worst of the punishment, and that is to destroy the Horch and his machine with that projectile weapon of yours. At once. And then—"

"Forget it," I said.

"But—"

I put it more strongly. "What I mean is, shut up. I'll talk to you later, but if you don't keep quiet now, I will turn you over to the filthy Horch."

That didn't stop him, either. I turned my back on his arguments and spoke in his own language to Beert: "Do you think you could get your fighter to scare him? Not kill him. Just make him be quiet."

Beert's head lifted to gaze at me. "Then you don't really want him killed?"

"Of course I don't, Beert. What use is he dead? I want him alive to be interrogated. Do you think I would actually murder an unarmed person?"

He gazed at me in silence for a moment. Then he said, "I was not sure."

CHAPTER THIRTY-SEVEN

It didn't take the Doc and the Christmas tree as long as I feared to get some of the systems running, and then the wall over the controls blossomed into a display. A golden dot marked our position. There weren't any other dots nearby, which I thought was good, and at the top of the picture was an irregular mass which I took to be the coast.

I grunted at him as I tried to figure out what to do. Back in those New Jersey summers with Uncle Cubby, my parents had sometimes taken me out for a fishing trip in Uncle Cubby's seldom-used cabin cruiser. I wished I had paid more attention to the charts. What I saw looked nothing like any coastline I remembered.

Then I saw one of the problems. I was accustomed to maps in which up was always north. Evidently the Beloved Leaders had no such prejudice. I guessed the land had to be east, and—once I craned my neck to peer at it sidewise and got the Doc to widen the view—it made sense. Island that forked at one end, like an alligator's opened jaws, narrow body of water behind it and then the mainland—"Long Island," I announced. "Great! That water over on the left has to be New York Bay. That's where we want to go! Tell the Doc, Pirraghiz!"

She didn't move right away. She was looking at me puzzledly again. So was Beert, and I realized I had used the English names for what I saw, since the Horch language didn't have any. When I explained to them that "New York Bay" was one of the busiest harbors on Earth, and we would have no trouble making contact there, Beert swung his neck around closer to me. "First answer a question for me, Dan. What will you do when you get there?"

"Call the Bureau," I said promptly. "See if they can get this sub under wraps before the Others can see what we're doing—"

I stopped there; what I had just said didn't sound right to me. Before I could figure out what it was, Beert went on. "And then?"

To tell the truth, I hadn't thought much about that "then." Especially about what *then* would mean for him and Pirraghiz. "Why," I said, "I guess we'll let the Bureau figure out what to do next."

"What you mean," he said meditatively, "is that you will turn this vehicle, and us, over to your human spy organization. Who will question us, and no doubt do their best to copy its technology, both Others and Horch."

"I guess that's about the size of it," I admitted.

He sighed—that shrill Horch whistle of released breath that meant resignation. He didn't say anything. He just nodded to Pirraghiz, who spoke to Wrahrrgherfoozh.

The Doc touched only a few dots on the board, but I felt the results at once. The submarine was turning and beginning to accelerate. The picture on the wall whirled to a new orientation, and we were beginning to go home.

That felt good. It felt like things were going to work out after all. It even felt as though I were going to get that steak before long, and sleep that night in a real bed . . . and maybe even see Pat . . .

But we weren't there yet.

The air fresheners had removed a certain amount of the stench from the sub, and things were quieting down. Cowed by the Horch fighting machine looming over him, the Dopey was still muttering—but softly, and to himself. Pirraghiz and the other Doc were in close conversation with each other. It looked as though they had left the navigation to Beert's Christmas tree. Beert himself was standing by the control board, gazing at the changing display that showed where we were moving. I didn't think he was seeing it, though. His neck was waving a slow sine, as though he were deep in thought.

When he saw me looking at him he turned his head toward me. "I have reasoned out," he announced, "that your order to kill the little one was a ruse of some kind, not an actual intention."

"That's right, Beert. It was a trick," I admitted. "We Bureau agents are full of tricks, but listen, Beert, I don't mean to trick you. When we get to the Bureau they will know how much we all owe to you and Pirraghiz, because I'll damn sure make sure they understand."

"I will be grateful for that," he said sadly.

And made me feel like a rat. Or, more accurately, made me feel that he was feeling the way I had when the Horch machines were working me over. Alone. Depressed. Pretty near hopeless. And all of it my fault.

There wasn't anything I could do about it, though. I tried to take his mind off it by changing the subject. "Listen, Beert, I've been meaning to ask you. What did Kofeeshtetch mean about the nexus thing helping the Eschaton?"

It didn't cheer him up. He gave me a three-snake shrug. "Perhaps it is something to be used when the Eschaton comes."

"Yeah, but," I said, "nothing physical is going to survive to the Eschaton, is it? Isn't everything supposed to go back into a kind of a point at the Big Crunch? So how would they get it there without its turning into a mess of quarks or something?"

He shrugged again. "I do not know. The cousins have not yet shared that kind of knowledge with me."

Pirraghiz didn't know, either. Neither did the wounded Doc. If the Dopey knew, he wasn't telling. I added that to the lengthening list of questions I was not likely to get answers to any time soon.

Anyway, other things were beginning to jostle for attention in my mind.

Like Pat. Very much like Pat. I was deeply, excitingly aware that every minute that passed was getting me closer and closer to the minute when I could actually see and touch her again.

And although that was fine, it wasn't all fine. Another itchy little needle of reality was beginning to force itself upon me.

Pat already had a Dan Dannerman. What was she going to do with me?

As we approached New York's Lower Bay I got one more of those nasty little stabs of reality.

Pirraghiz assured me that the other Doc had assured her that, yes, it would be possible to bring the sub close enough to the surface to be awash, and yes, there was a hatch that I could use to get out of, and then—

Well, then what should I do? Wave to a passing Staten Island ferry and hitch a ride to shore? Use a flashlight—if I could find anything like a flashlight—to send a message in Morse code—if I could remember the Morse code—to—

Well, to whom?

And what about security?

The sub's display was really great stuff. I could see the wide-open mouth of the bay, Coney Island on one side, Sandy Hook on the other; I could see little splotches that had to be Ellis Island and Liberty Island; I could even see the long old piers that stuck out into the Hudson from every side. And I could also see objects moving around that I supposed were tankers and cruise liners and excursion boats, and what was I going to be doing about them? Not to mention any U.S. Coast Guard stuff that might be patrolling against just such a Horch sub as ourselves; no doubt the human race had figured out that the Beloved Leaders had sneaked in underwater vessels that had given them the opportunity to kidnap and bug a lot of mariners.

According to Wrahrrgherfoozh, the Horch stealth capabilities were a lot more effective than any primitive human sonars. But

I didn't want to take the chance of being depth-bombed by some jumpy lieutenant in a Coast Guard corvette.

I studied the display. "Change of plan," I said.

Both Beert and Pirraghiz turned to me, Pirraghiz's expression wondering, Beert's merely resigned.

"I don't think we'd better get into all that traffic," I told them. "Better if we can find some quiet bay somewhere along the shore. Show me what's down—here."·

I put my finger on the barrier island that began around the Highlands and went south. Why did I pick there? I don't know. Maybe I thought we might just pull in at Uncle Cubby's old boat dock and knock on his door.

I didn't think it long. Uncle Cubby was long dead. I had no idea who owned his house, and didn't want to investigate. "There's a bay," I said, pointing between the Sea Bright barrier island and the shore. "Let's take a look."

CHAPTER THIRTY-EIGHT

It wasn't a bay. It was the mouth of a river that I had forgotten about, but that was just as good.

Slowly and carefully the Christmas tree piloted us upstream on this nice, wide river with no boats visible anywhere on its surface. I never took my eyes off the display. Not far ahead I saw something that stretched clear across the river, which worried me for a moment. A dam? So we'd have to go back and try again?

But it was a bridge. And off to one side of it was a system of docks with small objects moored to them: a boat basin.

"That'll do," I said, hoping I was right.

In fact, it did very well. The Christmas tree brought us to the surface, the robot opened the hatch and I climbed out into a cold, wet—but Earthly!—drizzle.

I saw lights up on the road. I found a little driveway that led up to them, and when I was at street level, there, right across the road, was a large and lighted seafood restaurant.

When I was inside the cashier gave me a thoroughly funny look—reasonably enough; I was tattered, unwashed and long unshaven—but she pointed me to a telephone anyway. There was a scattering of diners in the place; curiously, most of them in uniform. They were staring at me, too. I turned my back on them.

Naturally I had no encryption facilities. I didn't even have a payment card, and the restaurant's smells of good, hot human food were driving me crazy. But I managed to get a collect call through to the Bureau in Arlington.

The duty officer must have thought I was crazy, too, but she listened as I talked: "This is Senior Agent James Daniel Dannerman calling. I'm the one that—ah"—I tried to figure out how to put it—"the one you haven't seen for quite a while because I've been away. A long way away. Relay this information immediately to Colonel Hilda Morrisey or Deputy Director Marcus Pell. I require immediate pickup and a full squad to take charge of important assets."

There was a moment's silence while she thought that over. "I thought Brigadier Morrisey was dead," she said doubtfully.

I don't know which shook me up more, Hilda dead or Hilda a brigadier. But I didn't have time to think about it. "Tell *somebody* in authority at once," I ordered, and got the restaurant cashier to tell me where I was so I could pass it along. "And most of all," I finished, "tell them *no shooting*."

I guess she did pass the word along, because in about twenty minutes half the helicopters in the world seemed to be jockeying to land in the restaurant parking lot, and I could hear sirens coming toward us from the highway.

It's amazing what the Bureau can do when it puts its mind to it. Although the gaggle of Bureau people who popped out of the first two choppers claimed to be from the New York office, I didn't know a soul among them. But they knew me. "Jesus, Dannerman, how the hell many of you guys are there, anyway?" one of them asked wonderingly, and didn't wait for an answer. "Never mind. Let's get some damage control going here."

They did. Faster than I would have believed possible, the next few choppers of federal police and the co-opted local cops had the place sealed off. They blocked the bridge at both ends, with roadblocks on our side to keep anybody from getting near the boat basin. A couple of uniformed noncoms were going from table to table in the restaurant to tell the late diners that everything was all right, they just couldn't leave just yet because (showing a lot of imagination) there was a boat down there with a leaky fuel tank and they didn't want anybody hurt in a possible explosion. They were erecting screens around the sub itself, and a Bureau colonel named Makalanos, this one by then already up from Arlington, was on the phone to arrange for a Navy submarine to tow the Horch ship to a secure place, underwater.

It was this Colonel Makalanos who got back into the sub with me.

I don't know what he had expected to find, but his eyes popped when he saw the Dopey, the Docs, the Horch machines . . . and Beert. "Mother of God," he whispered, and then pulled himself together. "Tell the Meows and those other things what's going on, Dannerman," he ordered. "They'll all go with the sub, and I'll put a couple of guards on board, too. You? No, not you, Dannerman. I'm taking you straight to Arlington so you can explain all this to the deputy director."

I don't know what Beert had expected, either. He didn't say. He just listened while I told him what the colonel wanted, his neck down around his midsection, his head tipped upward to regard me sorrowfully. "I'll come back to you as soon as I can," I promised. "Just don't let the machines do anything, all right?"

He didn't answer that. He had stopped looking at me and was staring at the four husky Bureau people who were climbing in, their weapons at the ready.

"Ah, Beert," I said. "Listen, everybody's going to be really grateful to you for your help against the Others. It'll be all right."

He twisted his neck to look at me again. "I hope that is so," he said.

PART NINE

Home at Last

CHAPTER THIRTY-NINE

Twenty-four hours later I wasn't so enthusiastic about the Bureau's efficiency, because they had spent those hours very efficiently questioning me. They did it in relays, three or four of them at a time, and they questioned me *hard*. They didn't give up a thing in return, either, no matter how much I begged to be told what was happening here on Earth. Or what they were doing with Beert and Pirraghiz or the sub. Or anything.

It took me right back to those good old days with the Christmas trees and the helmet. This time my interrogators weren't causing me any actual physical pain, true. But, you know, interrogation is interrogation whoever does it. If the interrogators are really serious about it, it's no fun at all for the party being interrogated.

The place I was in was what we called "the Pit of Pain," one of the Bureau's interrogation chambers. They had me and the interrogators down in the bare little working space where the action took place: a table and a few straight-backed chairs and nothing else. I knew there were people observing us in the gallery seats that surrounded the pit, but I couldn't see them. They were hidden behind the one-way mirror walls.

The first question the Bureau's goons asked me was, "What's that thing on your neck?" They didn't like the look of it, and they didn't like my answer, either. When I said it was just so I could understand Horch, not a bit like those Beloved Leader spy bugs, they weren't believing a word of it. They suspended questioning for a moment, just left me with the interrogators glowering at me in silence until someone came back with a couple of strips of coppery mesh which they wound around my head and neck. Then they wanted to know everything, and I mean *every-thing*, starting with when the Dopey and I popped out of the transit machine.

The questioning was pretty much nonstop. They did let me pee a couple of times—not giving me any decent privacy while I did it, of course; a Bureau goon stood alertly behind me every minute, in case I had some kind of evil trick to play with the urinal. They even let me eat once or twice, dry ham sandwiches that looked as though they'd been salvaged from somebody's lunch meeting and black coffee out of the same urn the interrogators used. It was not the homecoming meal I had been dreaming about. What they wouldn't let me do at all was sleep. When I began getting woozy they handed me a glass of tepid water and a couple of those Bureau-issue wake-up pills. The things woke me right up, but I would rather have got horizontal. Even the Christmas trees had been kinder than that.

I thought I'd seen the woman who handed me the wake-up pills around the headquarters before. I pressed my luck. While I was still swallowing, I asked her, "What about my friends in the sub, are they all right?"

She might have answered. She opened her mouth as though she intended to, but one of the other interrogators shouldered her aside. He took the glass from my hand and said, "Don't worry about your buddies, we're taking care of them. Now, tell us about these Horch that you say are good guys." So I told them about the Two Eights and their nest, and why they were different from the cousin Horch.

It kept going until, along about the third or fourth wake-up pill, there was a change. My interrogators all stopped talking at once, turning toward the mirror wall. I knew why: they'd all heard something on their little earphones. At once a little door in the wall opened. Someone I knew walked in, looking both irritated and grim. It was the way Deputy Director Marcus Pell usually looked.

I stood up and offered him a hand to shake. "I'm Agent Dannerman," I told him.

The deputy director didn't answer at first. He ignored the hand and took one of the straight-backed chairs—its previous occupant getting up and out of the way fast—and regarded me for a moment. "That remains to be seen," he said. "How do we know you're who you say you are?"

I guessed, "Fingerprints? Retinal scan?" I think I was getting a little light-headed by then, regardless of the pills.

"Not good enough," he said judiciously. "I understand the Scarecrows can make an exact copy of anybody or anything they like. You could be a Scarecrow brain wearing a human body, for all I know."

"I'm not," I said wearily, and couldn't help adding, "For that matter, so could you."

He didn't take offense. He just nodded and said, "I think we need confirmation of your identity. Brigadier Morrisey! Come in, please."

The door that opened this time wasn't to the auditorium seats; it was the one that allowed suspects and interrogators to get in and out from the corridors outside. In a moment a clumsy-looking thing like a white-enameled kitchen refrigerator on wheels rolled in. I frowned at it, puzzled about what the deputy director was bringing this big metal thing in for, annoyed because it was blocking my view; I couldn't see my old boss, Hilda Morrisey, at all. Even when the thing rolled up close to me and I could see the door behind it closing again, there was no sign of Hilda.

Then a voice that I knew came out of the box. "Tell me, Danno, what was the name of the Kraut broad from the Mad King Ludwigs you were shacking up with?"

"Oh, my God," I said. "Hilda! They told me you were dead! What the hell are you doing in that thing?"

It—she—came to a full stop right across the table from me. There was nothing that looked human about the box. It had no face, only a rectangle of mirror glass at head height; I could not see what was behind it. But the voice was Hilda's, all right—a little fainter than I was used to, a little breathier, but definitely Hilda. "I'm not quite dead, Danno. I got shot up a little, is all, and the reason I'm still alive is that I've got this box to keep me going. Answer the question."

Evidently we wouldn't be catching up on each other's news for a while. "You mean Ilse?" I asked.

"Last name too," she ordered.

I cudgeled my memory. "Keinwasser? Something like that. I never heard her real name until somebody, I think it was you, told me about it after she was arrested, and I wasn't paying a lot of attention. If you remember, I was in Intensive Care at the time."

She didn't comment, just rapped out: "The name of my sergeant when you were working on the dope ring in New York."

"Uh. McEvoy? He was a master sergeant, but I don't know his first name."

"Your mother's birthday?" And when I told her that, she wanted the names of all my fellow lodgers in Rita Gummidge's rooming house, and the date of my promotion to senior agent, and the address of the little theater in Coney Island where my then girlfriend, Anita Berman, worked as ticket clerk when she didn't have a part in whatever play they were doing at the time. Hilda was thorough—maybe a little more thorough than the deputy director enjoyed, because he was drumming his fingers on the table before she was through.

Then she turned the big box to face him. "Looks all right as far as I can tell, Marcus," she said cautiously. "We'll get a better fix when the other witness gets here. I suggest we let him get some sleep."

She caught the deputy director in the middle of a yawn of his own. He suppressed it and said, "Very well. Put him in a cell."

That didn't sound good to me. Or to Hilda. "We can do better than that, Marcus," she said. "If he's him, he's entitled to a little something. I've reserved one of the VIP suites downstairs for him."

I think because he was too sleepy to object, Pell only shrugged. "Put a double guard on it. Now take him away."

The VIP suites were what they sounded like, plush little accommodations for high-ranking or otherwise important visitors who might need to be put up temporarily by the Bureau. They had comfortable beds and private baths and all the fixings. I didn't pay much attention to the niceties, though. I fell into the sack and, wake-up pills or none, in two minutes I was gone.

When I woke up there was an orderly standing by my bed, a coffee tray in his hand. "They want you to be ready to leave for another destination shortly, Agent Dannerman. There are clean clothes hanging behind the bathroom door."

Of course I asked him what this other destination I was supposed to be leaving for was, but the door was already closing behind him by the time I got the question out. I swallowed one whole cup of the coffee, scalding as it was, and headed for the shower. While I was dressing I got my first good look at myself in a human mirror. I looked skinny, and the beard I'd grown in captivity needed either trimming or shaving off entirely, I wasn't sure which. I was a good many months behind a haircut, too. I came out of the bathroom, wondering absently if the Bureau was going to have a barber wherever I was going. . . .

A woman was standing by my unmade bed. Not just any woman; this one had the face and form of the one I had been dreaming about. I gaped at her unbelievingly. "Pat?" I croaked.

That seemed to annoy her. "Actually I'm Patrice," she said. "The Pat you're talking about is over at Camp Smolley, and by the way, you might be interested to know that she's married now. Married to you, as a matter of fact." She didn't give me time to absorb that, but went right on. "Listen, I'm starved. Put your babushka back on and let's get some breakfast while we talk."

CHAPTER FORTY

I hadn't had anywhere near enough sleep, and the question of what the Bureau was doing with Beert and Pirraghiz and the sub hung heavy in my mind. But right then, not *very* heavy, because I had more personal things to distract me. Partly it was the presence of Patrice Adcock. She was a lot cleaner and better-dressed than the last time I'd seen her, with her more or less reddish hair curled around her pretty face and looking so *exactly* like Pat that I had to remind myself that she wasn't *really* Pat. That was confusing, and I had too many other things on my mind to want to be confused about the woman I loved.

The other part of it was food. I didn't hear any order given, but almost immediately two Bureau noncoms appeared at the door, rolling in breakfast tables that were covered with hot plates and cold. I think the meal must have been prepared in the deputy director's private kitchen, because it was *fine*. There were eggs, four of them, lightly fried with their perfect golden yolks staring up at me. Hash browns, crisp and oniony. A liter or so of orange juice that had obviously been squeezed within the hour. Crisp bacon. Crackly-crusted sausages. Pancakes with melted butter and hot syrup dribbling down their sides. More coffee—more of everything, in fact.

It was the precise kind of meal I had been dreaming about for a long time.

The metal-mesh babushka kept getting in the way of my mouth, but I didn't let that slow me down. I managed to get down a good share of everything in sight as we talked, while Patrice contented herself with picking at some toast and half a papaya. "The reason I'm here," she told me, "is they wanted somebody who knew you to check you out, and who better than me? So let's get down to it. What was the name of Uncle Cubby's cat?"

That made me grin, with my mouth full of sausage. "Starting right out with trick questions, are we, Patrice? Uncle Cubby didn't have a cat. Grandma Dannerman was allergic to them. The cook had a little yellow dog, but it wasn't ever allowed out of the servants' quarters. I think its name was Molly."

She made a face at me. "Was it? I don't remember. So tell me how old you were when we first met, and what rooms we had in Uncle Cubby's house."

So I told her that and, when she went on to ask, told her what it was like to swim in the muddy-bottomed river below the house, and the names of Uncle Cubby's servants, or as many of them as either of us could remember, and what games we used to play. Except that when I started to mention the games she and I had played under Uncle Cubby's big front porch she cleared her throat and changed the subject. Well, I knew why that was. I had no doubt that every word we spoke and every expression on our faces was monitored so that the Bureau's gumshoes watching us wouldn't miss a thing, and there were things Patrice didn't choose to discuss in front of strangers.

By the time I had reached the point where I couldn't eat any more, she had run out of questions. "All right," she said, and looked away. She spoke to the air. "Hilda? If he's a fake, he's a damn good one. Come on in."

The door opened at once, and Hilda's mobile life support rolled in. The big white box stopped right in front of me, so she could take another good look at my face, but when she spoke it was to Patrice. "You're sure about him?"

Patrice shrugged. "As sure as I can be in twenty minutes. I think it's him, all right."

Hilda meditated for a moment, then sighed. "All right, Patrice, but you'd better come along with us to double-check. The chopper's waiting."

Patrice frowned as if she might be about to object to the idea. I didn't give her a chance. All this talk about good times in the old days had put more urgent matters out of my mind, but they came flooding back. "Hold it," I said. "What's happening with my friends and the sub? And where are we going?"

"We're going to Camp Smolley," Hilda informed me. "Ever been there? The old biowar research plant? That's where the action is on trying to reverse-engineer Scarecrow artifacts these days."

"My friends—"

Her voice got harsh. "I said the chopper's waiting, Danno. We'll see your pals when we get there. The Navy towed the sub to Hampton Roads for security reasons, and now they're flying it to Smolley."

I stared at her. That huge thing? Flying it? But when I tried to ask her about it she wasn't patient anymore. "You'll see when we get there. Now get your ass in gear."

CHAPTER FORTY-ONE

Outside it was still dark and there were a few stars in the sky—unusually, for foggy, cloudy northern Virginia. I didn't think it was going to stay dark for long. I didn't have any good idea of the time, but a full moon was down near the western horizon and daybreak couldn't be far away.

Getting into the helicopter took a little longer than I would have guessed. The problem was Hilda's life-support system; we had to wait while they brought up the kind of lift they use to bring meals into passenger jets. She rolled her white box onto the lift, it elevated her, she rolled onto the chopper, two attendants guiding her. Then Patrice and I were allowed to board. The rotors began to turn before they'd finished strapping Hilda down, and we were airborne.

I had about a million more serious questions—*really* serious ones—on my mind, but I couldn't help it. First I had to clear up what she had said. "Patrice? You said Pat was married?"

As she was buckling herself in she paused to give me what struck me as an unsympathetic look, I could not guess why. "Pat One, you're talking about. Yes, she's definitely married. To Dan M.—M for mustache, see? That's what we call that particular Dan because he's got a mustache. He's the one who was with us on the prison planet. And Dan S.—the clean-shaved one, the one that never got there—he's married, too, to that little girl you were romancing from the theater. I guess all your other Dans have been taking all your old girlfriends out of circulation while you were away." She gave me a considering look. I wasn't sure what was in her mind, but what she said was, "Maybe you should tidy up that beard a little and keep it for a while, Dan. So we can tell you apart. We could call you Dan B., for beard."

She went on to explain some of the other problems of nomenclature for all us identical copies. She was still Patrice, just as Rosaleen had named her back on the prison planet. The Pat I had been thinking of as my own particular Pat was now called Pat One. The one who had been pregnant was still Pat Five (and no, she wasn't pregnant anymore; she had given birth to triplets, three little girls). And the Pat who had been returned to Earth with a bug in her head and never got to the prison planet with the rest of us had flatly refused to be given any number, so she was called P. J.

While she was telling me how to tell the Pats apart by sight— it had to do with the colors they wore—I remembered the important stuff. I broke in on her explanations with, "What about the Beloved Leaders?"

She looked startled, then relaxed. "I haven't heard them called that for a while. The Scarecrows, we call them now. What about them?"

"Jesus, Patrice! Nobody's said a word about them, but you must know they're planning to kill off a lot of people. Whatever you call them, why aren't you worried?"

She considered that for a moment. "Well, I do worry, a little bit, sometimes," she admitted, "but not much. The situation is under control, Dan. Honest. The Scarecrows call in every once in a while—lots of bluster, warnings, demands we let them come down to talk to us—but it's just talk. They sneaked in those damn submarines that caught a lot of people and bugged them a while ago—the same way I was, remember? So they could use the people as spies? But we've located most of those people and debugged them. The Scarecrows haven't done anything aggressive since then, not even their submarines."

I frowned. "How did you know they had subs on Earth?"

"Figured it out, Dan. All the bugged people turned out to

have been at sea. The only Scarecrow object from the scout ship landed in the sea. Had to be. Only," she said without pleasure, "the damn things aren't easy to find. Every navy in the world's been looking. No luck. There was this one Turkish destroyer that thought it had one and depth-bombed it, only it turned out to be an Italian submarine. But nobody ever actually saw one—well, until you brought us yours, I mean. We don't even know how many of the things there are—probably at least a dozen—"

"Twenty-six," I said. "Twenty-five besides the one I brought in."

"Oh," she said, dampened. "Well, if you've got some way of locating them, probably they could be depth-bombed for real."

I stared at her. "Are you crazy? The subs aren't the problem. The Belov—The *Scarecrow* are the problem! They can wipe us out any time they like!"

She gave me a strangely indulgent look. "Not really, Dan. We know what they're capable of. Dopey told us. What he said," she went on, sounding a lot like a mother telling her two-year-old that there aren't really any monsters under the bed, "was that the Scarecrows could tweak a big near-Earth-passing asteroid out of its orbit and dump it on the Earth and kill us all that way. You know. Like the old KT event that killed the dinosaurs. Well, that's what Threat Watch is all about, Dan. You don't know what Threat Watch is, though, do you? It's what's been keeping us busy at the Observatory; I was working there, keeping track of all the findings, when they called me about you. Every decent telescope in the world is searching for objects with orbits that can come anywhere near us. We've mapped just about everything bigger than a panel truck for ten or twelve AU in every direction, whether they're asteroids or comets or can't-tell-which. I promise there's absolutely nothing big that's in an orbit that can come anywhere near hitting us for a minimum of two years. And there isn't any tweaking going on, either. Threat Watch hasn't found a single object that shows any signs of interference with its ballistic orbit."

I wasn't willing to be convinced. "All right, but that isn't the only weapon they've got, Patrice. They've turned some suns into novas—"

She was smiling tolerantly at me. "*Our* sun, Dan? You're not much of an astrophysicist, are you? Can't happen. Our sun isn't that kind of star."

She seemed so confident. I stared at her. "You're sure?"

"As sure as I can be. No, the asteroid impact is the only scenario that makes sense, and trust me, we've definitely got at least two years grace on that one, Dan. Every observatory's computer models agree on that."

Two years. I thought about two years for a bit. It was a lot better than no margin at all, but I couldn't help asking, "And then?"

She gave my hand a reassuring pat. "Ah, by then we'll be ready for them, Dan. There are big new spaceships building all over the world. Fighters. High-mass ships with plenty of delta-V. And weapons!"

I frowned. "So if the Scarecrows nudge an asteroid, we'll nudge it back?"

"Better than that, Dan. We're going to go after the poppa. I said 'fighters'; we've located the Scarecrows' scout ship, and when we're ready we'll go out and blow the damn thing up. *Then* we'll nudge any asteroid that looks like trouble out of the way." She gave my arm a friendly squeeze. "It's okay, Dan. Honest. We haven't just been sitting still and waiting for the bomb to hit. We'll be ready when the time comes."

So that was good news, right? If Patrice was correct, and she sounded really sure of herself, the human race wasn't just going to let itself be taken over or wiped out without a fight—exactly as I had boasted to Pirraghiz and Beert.

But the funny thing was that it didn't feel as good as it ought to. I mean, to me personally. What it felt like was that I'd been

filling myself full of magnolious notions of coming back a hero
to save the world, and it wasn't looking that way at all. The damn
situation seemed to be saving itself just fine without me.

While all that was soaking in I felt the chopper change course.
A minute later the pilot got on the horn. "Folks," he said, his
voice sounding peculiarly amused, "we're only a couple of
minutes from the Camp Smolley landing pad, but they've told
us we have to orbit for a while. There seems to be some tricky
traffic ahead of us. Matter of fact, if you look out of your left-
hand windows, you can probably see it as we turn."

We did look, and boy, we saw it, all right. I'd never seen
anything like it in my life. It was a giant blimp-copter, shaped
like an immense fat sausage, its red and green lights blinking, and
it was settling down toward the earth.

I don't mean I'd never seen blimp-copters before. Actually
I'd even been in one, years earlier, when we were retrieving some
wreckage for evidence from a bombed-out survivalist compound.
This one was a whole lot bigger. In the early dawn light it looked
like an airborne ocean liner, and the funniest part was that slung
under it was some other large thing that was shrouded in tarpau-
lins. It took me a moment to figure it out, but then I sucked in
my breath. "My God," I whispered. "That's my submarine!"

Up ahead Hilda was complaining furiously to the pilot because the way her life-support box was strapped down, she
couldn't turn and look out. I didn't blame her. It was something
to see.

The blimp-copter pilot seemed to be pretty good at his job.
Slowly his whirly blades pulled the big bag down, jockeying this
way and that, a meter or two at a time, until his load was resting
on a wheeled metal cradle between two low buildings. Then the
aircraft sat there without moving for two or three minutes. Nothing seemed to be happening, except that the envelope of the big
sausage wrinkled and shrank a little, almost invisibly.

If I hadn't seen a blimp-copter in action before, I wouldn't
have known what was going on, but I was able to explain it to

Patrice, who had loosened her seat belt and leaned over me to get a better look. "He's pumping some of the helium back into the high-pressure tanks to cut the lift," I said into her ear. "Otherwise he wouldn't have neutral buoyancy when he lets go of the load, and the rotors couldn't handle it."

"Wow," she said, craning her neck. She was practically in my lap. It had been a long time since I had had so much woman so close, so warm and smelling so good. I put my hand on her shoulder—to steady her—and she turned her head to look quizzically up at me.

I thought—no, I still think—that what had crossed her mind just then was something about kissing. It certainly crossed mine. Kissing Pat Adcock had been a dream, yearned for most thoroughly for a long time, and now our lips were not much more than twenty centimeters apart.

They didn't get any closer. She didn't move any nearer and neither did I. She was Pat Adcock, all right, but she was a different Pat Adcock, and I couldn't sort that out.

Then the moment passed. The pilot was already on the horn again. "Okay, people, they say we can come in to land now. Make sure your seat belts are fastened, will you?" And Patrice straightened up and did as ordered. So did I, and that particular conundrum had to be set aside again.

The blimp-copter pilot had eased his big ship down another meter or two, until the cables that held his load went slack. Workmen on the ground had quickly released them, and the blimp-copter lifted and went sailing away into the sunrise. I lost sight of it as our own pilot was setting us down on the pad a few dozen meters away.

While we were waiting for somebody to bring up a forklift to get Hilda's box to the ground, I could see that the handlers had already hooked a little tractor to the cradle the sub was on. They weren't wasting any time. The machine was pulling the whole thing, sub and all, into a cavernous loading dock the size of a hotel ballroom.

As soon as we were off the chopper a couple of Bureau guards were waving us inside. Next to me Patrice stumbled and frowned; she was looking curiously toward the perimeter of Camp Smolley. Some sort of argument was going on there, Bureau guards and a couple of soldiers in unfamiliar blue berets yelling at each other. But what the squabble was about, I could not see.

The Bureau people weren't just beckoning us inside, they were *rushing* us inside. As soon as the sub and we were in the loading dock, its big steel door folded itself down to shut us off from the outside world, and the workmen began pulling the tarps off the submarine.

CHAPTER FORTY-TWO

Even in that moment I noticed something funny. The workmen weren't the usual uniformed grunts the Bureau used for heavy lifting. They were high-ranking officers. I recognized some of them as upper brass from the Arlington headquarters, and they didn't seem to like being used as manual labor.

I didn't spend much time thinking about that; there was something more important. It was the first time I'd seen the whole Scarecrow submarine exposed. It didn't look a bit like any vessel I'd seen before.

When the tarps came off at one end of the sub they revealed a squared-off stern with three great openings, making a triangle, looking like exhaust nozzles on a huge rocket. There was neither propeller nor rudder. At the bow end was a group of tightly nested jointed rods, for what purpose, I could not say. A whitely gleaming squarish thing was between them; it looked vaguely familiar, but I couldn't quite place it. The rest of the hull was featureless, metal, marked only by the hatch on the upper deck.

I heard my name called and turned around. It was Deputy Director Marcus Pell, looking recently slept and freshly bathed. From behind me Hilda's voice said, "He wants you at the sub. Go!"

I went. The brigadiers and department subheads were rolling a wheeled ladder up to the sub's side and Pell was standing impatiently beside it. "Up you go, Dannerman," he snapped. "See if you can keep those freaks of yours from making any more trouble."

I did as ordered, somewhat confused because I had no idea what kind of trouble Pell was talking about. Then the people on the desk opened the hatch and it got a lot more confusing than that.

The first thing that came out of the sub was the stink, worse than ever and with some unpleasant new ingredients added. The second thing was a uniformed police lieutenant, looking as if he'd had a hard ride. He glowered at me. "Who the hell are you?" he demanded, and didn't wait for an answer. He turned to the deputy director, who had followed me up. "Is there somebody who can talk to those freaks? They wouldn't let us touch the machinery at all. Then kept getting in Dr. Evergood's way when she was trying to take care of the Doc with the burned arm and . . . and Sergeant Coughlan was airsick all the way here," he finished bitterly.

That explained the new aroma. It didn't explain the fact that the second person out of the sub was a portly black woman in a stained white smock, whom I'd never seen before. The deputy director didn't give me a chance to ask questions. "You heard what the lieutenant said, Dannerman," he snapped. "Get in there and straighten the freaks out!"

As soon as I lowered myself inside, Beert and Pirraghiz came clamoring around me for news and explanations. "Give me a minute," I begged—in Horch, of course—while I looked around. Part of the stink came from three Bureau-issue body bags stacked one on top of the other—four body bags, actually; two bags had been put together to hold a larger carcass. That would be the dead Doc; the other bags would be holding the bodies of the two dead Scarecrow warriors. Another component of the stench was a couple of drying puddles of vomit on the floor, just under the perch where the ship's Dopey was fastidiously shielding his face with his fan and squawking his own raucous complaints at me—in English, this time. The sergeant who had been airsick gave me an aggrieved look and said faintly, "He's been going on like that the whole time. They all have."

They all still were. The surviving Doc was holding up his ruined arm, now neatly bandaged and a lot shorter than it had been, and mewing earnestly to Pirraghiz. The only things capable of speech or action that weren't demanding attention at once were the two machines, Beert's Christmas tree and the surviving robot fighter. They stood totally silent and unmoving in a corner of the sub's cabin. I appreciated that.

I raised a hand and said loudly, in English: "Shut up." Then in Horch, "I'm sorry if you had a rough trip, but it's over now. Pirraghiz? What happened to your friend?"

She was standing next to him, with one big hand on his shoulder for comforting. "At the other nest—the first place they took us to, I don't know where it was—the human female amputated most of his stump," she told me. "She did an excellent job, I think."

I blinked at that. "You let her operate on him?"

"I had no choice, Dannerman. It was clear that she knew what she was doing, and the medical attention was urgently needed. Then she came with us to care for him on the trip."

"But I thought you were the medical one—"

"Only for dealing with your species, Dannerman. I have been given no skills for my own."

Beert had been standing behind me, listening. Now his neck snaked over my shoulder and his little head twisted to peer sidewise into mine. "May I speak now, Dan?" he asked, sounding sorrowful but resigned. "I do not complain, but can you tell me what place we have arrived at? And for what purpose?"

It was a tall order, but I did my best to pass on to him—adding apologies every few sentences—what Hilda and Patrice had explained to me: We were at a research facility devoted to analyzing the technology of the Others, where he and the Docs would be—I took a moment over the choice of words—would be cared for, I said. I didn't want to say "imprisoned."

The hard part of answering his question was when it came to purpose. I didn't know what the Bureau had in mind for him, and didn't much like my suspicions. While I was stumbling over that, the deputy director stuck his nose down the hatch. "What's going on?" he demanded suspiciously. "Come on out of there! Bring those—things—out with you."

That sounded like a good idea. The stink was getting to me. Beert and the Docs followed me up the ladder agilely enough and in a moment we were all standing uneasily on the slippery, rounded deck of the sub, which had not been intended for anybody to stand on. I could see Patrice standing down below, a few feet from the big wheeled dolly the sub was resting on. The plump black woman was beside her, and Patrice's mouth was open in wonder as she saw Beert. Pell nudged me, pointing to the exterior ladder. "Get them down there!" he ordered. And when I added a few sentences to the Horch translation of his order, trying to reassure them, Pell demanded, even more suspiciously than before: "What are you saying to them?"

"I'm telling them what you said," I informed him.

"All right," he grumbled, "but I want you to translate every damn word both ways, do you hear me? Now move it, all of you."

When we were all on the ground he hadn't finished giving orders. "You!" he barked at me. "Go see the doctor."

He was pointing to the black woman standing with Patrice. Pell did not choose to mention what I was supposed to see her about. Before I could ask, he was already stalking away, barking orders at everyone in sight. When I got there, Beert and the Docs trailing after, Patrice's eyes were all on Beert, but she hadn't forgotten her manners. "This is Colonel Marsha Evergood, Dan. She's a neurosurgeon."

I shook her hand. "I hear you have a side specialty in amputating Doc limbs," I said.

She acknowledged the remark with a grin. "It happens I'm

the world's greatest expert on Doc anatomy, Agent Dannerman. I didn't plan it that way, but I've debugged one and autopsied another. Now will you hold still for a minute?"

She didn't wait for an answer. She reached under my babushka to run her fingers over the thing behind my right ear. Marcus Pell came up behind me as she felt and peered and poked. "Well?" he demanded testily.

The doctor withdrew her hand and gave me a friendly pat on the shoulder. She pursed her lips, considering. "I can't say for sure without X rays and an ultrasound and maybe a little exploratory surgery, but I'd say it's architecturally similar to the Scarecrow bugs. If so, it has probably invaded a lot of tissue. I doubt I could remove it without risking serious brain damage."

"Hey," I squawked, pulling away. Pell didn't even look at me.

"So you think he's transmitting everything he sees?" he asked.

Marsha Evergood shrugged, so I answered for her. "No! I'm not transmitting anything! It's nothing like that. It isn't a spy bug! It's made by the Horch, not the, uh, Scarecrows, and all it does is give me their language."

He gave me a glance that time, but didn't respond. The doctor patted my hand reassuringly. I thought what she was trying to tell me was that she wasn't going to turn me into a slobbering idiot with her scalpels, no matter what Marcus Pell wanted. At least I hoped so.

Anyway, whatever decision he might have wanted to make got deferred by another call on his attention. The duty crew had been carrying bits and pieces of loose equipment—including my sack of Horch goodies—out of the sub. They were stacking it all on the floor next to a Bureau van, but they came to a stop. The officer in charge hurried over, looking worried. "Deputy Director? I don't think we can lift the big cadaver without more men, and we'd better get it into refrigeration pretty fast."

For a moment it occurred to me to volunteer the Docs for the job, which they could have handled easily, but Pell was already gone to sort this new problem out. Anyway, I wasn't in a mood to do him any favors, and I had something else I wanted to do. I beckoned Pirraghiz and Beert to come forward. "Patrice," I said, "I'd like you to meet my two best friends."

She stumbled over their names, but gamely stuck her hand out. Being a considerate person, Pirraghiz barely touched Patrice's hand with her enormous, taloned fist, but Beert wrapped one snaky arm around it. He kept his eyes on her but slid his head up close to mine, whispering. When I answered Patrice spoke up. "What were you saying?" she demanded.

"Oh, well," I said, trying to think of a lie, deciding to tell her the truth, "he, uh, wanted to know if you were the human female I was talking about back in his nest."

"And you said?"

I shrugged and stuck with the truth. "I said, more or less."

"Ah," she said, nodding. "More or less." Then she added, in a tone of friendly curiosity, "Tell me something, Dan. Why do you wriggle your arms and neck that way when you talk to your friends?"

She caught me by surprise. "Do I? I never noticed it. Maybe I'm just sort of copying the way Beert talks."

"You ought to try to stop it. It looks pretty dumb." And the look she was giving me that time had no suggestion of kissing in it.

By then the cleanup crew had loaded the casualties onto a couple of waiting gurneys—and a hand truck for the dead Doc—and Marcus Pell was peremptorily calling my name again. "Those robot machine things in the sub," he said, sounding harried. "The crew's afraid to touch them. Can you make them come out?"

I shook my head. "No, but Beert can. Give me a minute."

Beert and I climbed back onto the deck, and he called his orders down through the hatch. Both the robots immediately came to life. I wasn't sure how the Christmas tree was going to manage the two ladders, up and down, but it simply extruded four or five more branches and whisked itself along, the fighter robot following briskly.

"Tell them to get in the van," Pell ordered when they were down. I opened my mouth to ask why, but he didn't give me a chance. "Do it!" he barked. And while they were doing it, impassive as ever, he climbed onto a crate. "Listen up, all of you!" he called. Those high-ranking workmen stopped what they were doing and turned toward him. "You will not, repeat not, ever under any circumstances mention to anyone at all the fact that you have seen any of this Horch technology. The Scarecrow stuff is different; that's covered by the treaty, and in a minute we'll let the UN people and everybody else in this project in to see it. Nothing about the Horch! Understand me? This is a national security matter, and violation carries a death penalty. Plus," he added savagely, "I will make you pray for the firing squad long before the sentence is carried out." He met the eyes of everybody in the loading area, then jumped down and turned to me. "Tell your Horch friend to get in the van, too," he ordered.

That was pushing it a step too far. I didn't know what Pell was up to, but I didn't feel like going along with it. I said, "No."

Pell looked as astonished as though a waiter had turned down his request for a clean spoon. "What the hell do you mean, no? That's an order!"

"No," I said again. "Beert stays with me. I promised him."

The deputy director's expression changed. He didn't look angrier; he looked as though he had suddenly turned to ice. "I don't give a shit what you promised that thing, Dannerman! I want him out of here before anybody else sees him. Do you want me to put you under arrest right now?"

Out of the corner of my eye I saw Hilda's life-support box

rolling toward me dangerously, but I ignored her. I said, "Well, Deputy Director, if that's what you want to do, I guess I can't stop you. I ought to remind you, though, that I'm the only one who can speak to these people. I don't see how I could do that for you if you put me in a detention cell." He stood silent for a moment, swallowing what I had said to him. It looked as though it might choke him. I went on, "Anyway, what's the point? Why do you want this stuff taken away?"

He glanced at Hilda, standing silently by, but didn't say anything until he had finished processing the situation in his head. When he had made up his mind all he said was, "The Horch can stay. Just keep your mouth shut about the equipment."

I could feel Hilda's warning eyes on me in spite of her one-way glass. I persisted anyway, "Yes, but why?"

"Security," he snapped.

That puzzled me. "I don't see the problem. Isn't this place secure from the Scarecrows?"

Pell had regained his composure. When he answered it was as though our little head-to-head had never happened. "It's secure from the Scarecrows, sure—I hope. That's not the problem. Camp Smolley is full of UN personnel and I don't want them nosing around the Horch matériel. It's bad enough we have to share the Scarecrow technology with them."

That was even more of a puzzle. "Why are you worrying about the UN? I thought the Scarecrows were the enemy."

Pell gave me the kind of look a kindergarten teacher might give to a child who hadn't covered his coughs and sneezes. "They're the *present* enemy, Dannerman. Who knows who our friends are going to be when this is over? Remember what country pays your salary, and keep your priorities straight!"

That was the end of the discussion. Pell turned away and gestured to the van driver, who started up and drove away through a smaller door to the outside.

Then, paying no further attention to me, Pell called to the guard at the inside door: "Open up! Let's let the rest of the team come in and see what we've got!"

CHAPTER FORTY-THREE

I don't know how many people had been waiting impatiently on the other side of those doors, maybe a hundred or more. They came pouring in, full of indignation at being kept outside, even more full of astonishment when they saw what was waiting for them. The ones in front stopped short, goggling, until the ones behind pushed them forward. There was a curious sort of collective sigh. Then some rushed toward the sub and a dozen or so zeroed in on Marcus Pell, full of complaints and accusations. A tall woman in a sari got to him first. "I must protest this unnecessary delay, Deputy Director Pell!" she snapped sternly. "Under the terms of the UN covenant we are entitled to immediate access to every item of Scarecrow technology, without delay!" And a man, in the uniform of some army I didn't recognize but wearing a blue United Nations beret, backed her up: "I have already filed a protest because your people did not allow UN observers to be present when this submarine was landed!"

Pell wasn't fazed. He'd had plenty of practice in dealing with indignant foreigners who were pissed off at something the Bureau had done. He spread his hands benignly. "I understand your concerns, Major Korman, Doctor Tal, but these are exceptional circumstances. The Scarecrows don't know we have captured this sub, and they mustn't find out. So we have had to take unusual security precautions—"

He didn't stop there, but I stopped listening. I had a nearer problem. Several dozen of the new people had circled my little group, staring in fascination at their first sight of a real, live Horch. A couple of them were cameramen, shooting from every angle, and when Beert saw the lenses pointing at him he couldn't help flinching away. Pirraghiz and the wounded Doc, Wrahrrgh-erfoozh, saw what was happening and moved to surround Beert protectively, but the audience was all raucously shouting questions: Did they speak English? What happened to the big one's arm? How come the other Doc was wearing *clothes*? Were they dangerous?

I tried to reassure Beert and Pirraghiz and at the same time keep the more adventurous of the spectators from reaching out to touch Beert, but it was Hilda, the expert in crowd control, who rescued us. She produced four Bureau police to surround us and then—she must have turned up the gain on her internal microphone—she thundered at the people:

"Don't come too close! There's a risk of communicable diseases." With the help of the police, that made them fall back a little. She added, more civilly, "When they've been examined you will have your proper access to them, and before that we'll arrange for Agent Dannerman to meet with you in the auditorium to tell his story."

She didn't give me a chance to react to that. While the police were moving the spectators away she came up close to me and said softly, "I'd go easy on telling Marcus to go screw himself if I were you, Danno. You're not making any friends for yourself that way."

She was telling me what I knew already. I shrugged. "I already have all the friends I need."

She was silent for a moment. Then she said, "Maybe you do. It's a good thing for you that I'm one of them." And then, with a change of tone, "Anyway, here comes our transportation."

The transportation was one of those electric-motored people carriers you see in airports. It was big enough to hold all of us—including the Docs, though just barely. With a couple of Bureau uniformed police ahead of us to clear the way we moved pretty fast out of the loading area, through the halls of Camp Smolley. Hilda wasn't on the vehicle and didn't need to be; her box's wheels kept up easily as she rolled along behind us. Behind her still half a dozen more guards were following, half-trotting to keep up; most of them wore the blue UN berets. All the way the two Docs were mewing to each other, taking a lively interest in the rooms they passed, the fire extinguishers on the walls, the water fountains, the ceiling-mounted TV screens at every intersection that were all displaying the scene in the loading dock, though no human beings were present in the halls to watch them because everybody who could get there was there already. Beert was darting his head in every direction, too, and full of questions. I couldn't tell him much. I'd never been in Camp Smolley before either.

I knew right away when we got to the rooms they had reserved for my friends, though, because two people were standing in front of one of the doors. One was a blue-beret guard, looking uneasy, and the huge figure next to him was unmistakably a Doc. I was astonished to see him there, but Pirraghiz saw him at the same moment I did and her reaction was a lot more violent. She screamed something and leaped off the carrier—I thought she was going to overturn the thing—and flung herself into the other one's arms, the two of them mewing at high volume at each other. I got off, too, turning to Hilda. "Oh, right," I said, memory returning at last. "There were a couple of Docs with the bunch that escaped from the prison planet, the escape party, weren't there?"

"Two of them. The other one's dead," she said shortly. "This one we call Meow; he's been helping out figuring how the Scarecrow stuff works—can't talk so anybody can understand him, but he's good at drawing pictures. Tell your Horch friend this is where he's going to live for a while."

For a while. When I looked inside I hoped that "for a while" would be really brief, because the room they wanted him in was

not attractive. It was a damn jail cell, is what it was. It had bars
on its one window, and a lidless open toilet, and a washstand,
and a narrow cot. That was all.

Hilda was watching my face. "Tell him it's only temporary,"
she suggested.

I looked at her. "Yeah, sure," I said. I did tell Beert that.
What I didn't tell him was how long "only temporary" was likely
to be in government practice. I glossed it over as fast as I could,
and tried to explain to him how the toilet worked, and offered
to get more blankets for his cot if he wanted them, and promised
I would see him as often as I could—I didn't then realize how
intensive the questioning was that lay ahead of us, and therefore
how often that would be.

Beert listened in silence, head hung low, ropy arms wrapped
around his belly for protection. All he said, his voice low-pitched
and somber, was, "What about food, Dan?"

That took me aback. "Oh, hell," I said. "Right. Food." I
hadn't given that little problem any thought at all.

So I asked Hilda for help. She wasn't, much. "There's plenty
for the Docs and the Dopeys," she told me. "The Scarecrows sent
some food down for them—that's how they sneaked their subs
along. I don't know about the Horch. What does he eat?"

I turned to Pirraghiz for help. That took a little doing, because all three of the Docs were still excitedly mewing to each
other. Wrahrrgherfoozh and the one they called Meow were hugging each other at that moment—by no means with the same
passion as Pirraghiz had shown, but you can do a lot of hugging
with six arms apiece, even if one of them is only a stump. When
I got Pirraghiz's attention and explained the problem, she looked
remorseful. "I did not think, Dannerman," she said sadly. "Let
me ask the others." They chattered back and forth for a moment,
then she shook her massive head at me. "I am not sure," she said.
"Perhaps I can do for Djabeertapritch what I did for you in the
nest of the Two Eights—get samples of all the foods your species

eats, and see what among them resembles the foods of the Horch."

"I understand Meow has food of his own," I said, pointing at the other Doc. "Maybe some of that can be used, or the food for the Dopeys."

She looked puzzled. "Perhaps," she said, "but why do you call him that? It is Mrrranthoghrow."

I stared at her, slack-jawed. "Mrrranthoghrow?"

"Exactly he," she said happily. You would not think that a six-armed creature with a face like a bearded full moon could look coquettish, but she managed it. "He is a copy of the one we knew in the Two Eights, of course, but it is Mrrranthoghrow whom the Others copied for this mission and he remembers me well from earlier times. But you surprise me, Dannerman. Did you think I would be so affectionate with a total stranger?"

Next stop for me was my press conference—well, there was certainly no press there, but that was what it felt like to the person in the hot seat. I climbed up onto the platform, before the hundreds of staring eyes, and gave them a sketchy outline of my adventures with the Horch. Then I opened the floor for questions. That was a mistake. There were about a million of them, and all the time I was searching the hundred or more faces in the room for Patrice.

When I found her, squeezed into almost the last row, I managed an inconspicuous wave. She waved back, all right, but there was something about her that seemed wrong.

I took me a moment to figure that out. It was the clothes and the hairdo. Patrice had been wearing a pretty pants suit; this one was in Bureau coveralls. All right, she could have changed her clothes—not very likely, but possible—but she hadn't had time to let her hair grow into a long ponytail.

There was only one possible explanation. The woman I was

looking at wasn't Patrice. She had to be Pat! The *real* Pat. And
sitting beside her was a man who looked a lot like me, except that
he wore a mustache, and I realized I was looking at the other me,
Danny M., the man who was married to Pat.

That did not help my concentration.

When the deputy director, sitting behind me on the platform,
saw that I was stumbling through the next couple of questions,
he took pity on me—or, more likely, was afraid that I was getting
tired enough to say something he didn't want said. He got up
and preempted the mike. "No more questions, please," he said.
"Agent Dannerman has had a very exhausting time. We must see
that he is fed, and allowed to rest. As he is debriefed over the
next few days the records and transcripts will be made available
to all of you, under the terms of the UN agreement. Please leave
now."

There was a rumble of discontent from the audience at that,
but they left—or I guess they did; Pell had me by the arm and
escorted me backstage before I could see. Hilda was waiting there
amid the tangle of ropes and discarded pieces of sets. "Nice job,
Danno," she informed me. "The way you duck the questions you
don't want to answer, you'll make a good administrator someday."

The deputy director gave her an opaque look, but all he said
was, "Have you got a schedule for Dannerman yet?"

"Working on it, Marcus. He's got to eat first, though."

He looked surprised, as though that sort of pampering had
never crossed his mind. Then he looked resigned. "Take care of
it," he ordered, and left without another word—to catch up on
his harassing of somebody else, no doubt.

I looked at Hilda. I hadn't realized I was hungry until she
put it in my mind, but I was. "You mentioned food?"

"Right next door," she said, rolling away. I followed her down
a steep ramp, through a doorway, and came out in a little room—
I suppose a dressing room at one time, now set up with a table
and four chairs. Three of the chairs were occupied already: the

Pat in the Bureau coveralls, that other Dannerman and old Rosaleen Artzybachova. "I thought you'd like company while you
ate," Hilda said indulgently. Then, less indulgent: "You've got
forty-five minutes."

As she left us I fixed my gaze on the Pat. "Patrice?" I guessed,
very unsure of myself in more ways than one. She shook her head.

"No, Patrice went back to the Observatory to work on the
Threat Watch," she said. "I'm Pat—Pat One—but won't I do
for now?"

The food was typical Bureau on-duty
fare: platters of sandwich materials, a big bowl of salad, coffee,
fruit for dessert. I was hungry again and I ate, but I wasn't paying
much attention to it. I had never had the experience of sitting
down at a table with myself before.

They began at once to tell me all the news that I hadn't heard
from Patrice, what a commotion they'd made when they got back,
how this Dan and this Pat had been put in charge of their Dopey
and Meow—"His name is actually Mrrranthoghrow," I told
them, and they practiced that for a while without a lot of
success—and thus assigned to Camp Smolley. And all the while
I kept looking at the two of them, and trying to figure out just
what I was feeling.

Odd. That was how I was feeling. Not uncomfortable, exactly. Just odd. I guess it showed, because the other Dan grinned
at me, then looked serious and said, "Weird, right? But you'll get
used to it."

And Pat said sympathetically. "We all did."

"Except in my case," Rosaleen put in, "because I didn't have
anything of that sort to get used to. When I returned I learned
that the other of me had died while we were away. That was more
than simply a bizarre feeling, Dan. It was quite distressing. But
as Dan says—as Dan M. says—one gets used to it."

Then Pat—Pat One—began to show me pictures of Pat

Five's triplets; they looked like rather ordinary little girls to me, somewhat Asian-looking. As was to be expected, considering that what got Pat Five pregnant was some of the Beloved Leaders' experimentation with sperm from their copy of Jimmy Lin. Who had managed to secure visitation rights, after a lot of high-level and acrimonious diplomatic discussion between the United States and the People's Republic, and was surprisingly turning out to be a fondly besotted new father. And Pat Five was doing fine, too, except that the drugs she was taking to enhance her milk flow—three babies sucking away six times a day each!—had made her breasts so sensitive that she complained of being horny all the time. And how busy Patrice and P. J. were at the Observatory, with the Threat Watch using up so much of their resources, and the Observatory's scientific staff constantly pissing and moaning because they weren't getting enough observing time to do any real science since the world's telescopes were kept busy hunting comets that might be a threat.

All the time, out of the corner of my eye, I was watching Pat, my true love whom I had been missing so urgently, for so long. And what I was thinking was how much she looked like Patrice, with all of Patrice's mannerisms and every bit of Patrice's looks. I cleared my throat. "Will she be coming back soon, do you think?"

That made them all look at each other. "I don't know," Dan M. said at last.

And Pat bit her lip, and then leaned toward me confidentially. "I guess you know," she said, "back in the prison planet Patrice, well, had a kind of crush on you—that is, *you*, I mean"—pointing a forefinger at each of us Dan Dannermans.

I blinked at that. "She did?"

Rosaleen was laughing, a dry old chuckle. "Of course she did, Dan, as did we all," she said kindly. "Do not let it make you conceited. You were simply the only worthwhile man for many light-years in any direction. What did you expect?" She gave me

a demure look. "Perhaps I should confess that I even had some
sorts of foolish old-woman thoughts about you myself."

"You did?" That was astonishing, too, but in a different way.

"Patrice didn't exactly get over it, either," Pat went on. "So
when she heard you were here—well, look, I'm telling tales out
of school, but we're all kind of family here, aren't we? And now
you've just kind of hurt her feelings, you know."

That baffled me. "What did I do?"

"Something you said, I'm not sure what. Did you say she was
just a copy of me? Because we're all a little bit sensitive about
that."

Well, I hadn't done that. Not ex-
actly, anyway. What I had done was to admit to her that I'd told
Pirraghiz she was "more or less" the woman in my dreams, but
what was so bad about that? It was true, wasn't it?

They all kept talking, mostly Dan M. telling me about the
religious nut who had wormed her way into Hilda's confidence
and repaid it by shooting her and three or four other people. I
listened and responded. But I was still mulling over the Patrice
problem when Hilda herself rolled in.

"Finished, Danno?" she asked. "You better be. Wipe the
crumbs off your face, because family time is over and the debriefers are waiting to get at you."

PART TEN

The Most Important Man in the World

CHAPTER FORTY-FOUR

There were half a dozen people impatiently waiting for me in the debriefing room, some male, some female, some wearing the blue UN beret and some in Bureau tans. They didn't waste time. They started in right away—"Describe in more detail the robots you called 'Christmas trees,' " one of them commanded, and we were off.

It didn't stop, either. It didn't even slow down. After I told them how the robots had acted I had to tell them what their needles felt like when I touched them, and what they had done to me with their damned helmet, and what they had been doing to the Dopey. The questioning didn't even pause for breath— my breath, I mean; the debriefers had plenty of breathing space because they took turns with the questions—until Hilda's great white refrigerator box rolled back into the room. "Time's up for this segment," she said. "You go to the sub now, Danno."

"Slow down a little, Hilda," I begged. "I have to go to the bathroom."

"Sure you do, Danno. I've got you down for a pee break right after the next session. You can hold it until then, can't you?"

And rolled away, leaving me to follow her, without waiting to hear whether I could or couldn't.

There were more questions at the submarine, but this time they weren't for me. They were for the two Docs who waited there, Pirraghiz and the recent amputee, Wrahrrgherfoozh, and all I had to do was translate. The head debriefer seemed to be a middle-aged, red-haired woman I sort of knew—Daisy Fennell, her name was, one of the Bureau higher-ups. She started with the questions before I was all the way inside.

They'd had the sense to leave the hatch open, and so the sub smelled a little better. Someone had also cleaned up the airsick guard's puke, but outside of that nothing much had been touched. There was one woman in there as we climbed down, operating three or four cameras that were methodically scanning around. "Watch where she's shooting," Fennel ordered. "We want to know the function of every piece of equipment in this vehicle, also as much as these, ah, persons can tell us about how it works. Understand? Start with this one."

She was pointing where one of the cameras was pointing, to a sort of Chinese lantern, twelve or fifteen centimeters high, that was fixed to one wall. It glowed with a pale green light and was softly humming to itself. I passed the question on to Pirraghiz, who mewed to Wrahrrgherfoozh, who spoke at some length. When Pirraghiz translated for me, it came out as, "Wrahrrgher-foozh says it monitors the lighting system. I don't know why that's necessary, do you?" And while I was putting that into English for the debriefers, she kept on going. "He also told me what systems are inside it, but I did not understand the terms he used."

"One moment, please," one of the debriefers said, while I was adding that. He looked unhappy. "Will you please make sure you give us exact wording in every case? Also ask Pir—Pirr—the one with the purry name to do the same when she translates for you."

I opened my mouth to ask why, but Daisy Fennell was already talking. "Do as she says, Dannerman," she commanded. "Dr. Hausman and Dr. Tiempe are linguists; the deputy director has given them permission to record your translations so they can work on learning these languages."

"Like a sort of Rosetta stone; do you know what that is?" Dr. Hausman said eagerly. "That's why verbatim translations are so important. Once we can match up individual words, we can build a vocabulary, and then we can start trying to identify a grammar.

We've been trying to do that with Meow, but it's been very slow."

Fennel flagged her down. "Another time, Dr. Hausman. We've got business here. Dannerman! I thought there was supposed to be some kind of chart here that showed where all the other subs were, but I don't see it."

I looked around and spotted the place where it had been, but now it was only a sort of glassy oval that displayed nothing at all. "There. I guess it's turned off for some reason."

"*Why* is it turned off?"

I put the question to Pirraghiz and got the answer from Wrahrrgherfoozh. "He says it's because the way the systems are hooked up—"

"Please!" the linguist begged. "Exact words! Also the Doc's when he speaks to Pirraghiz, if you don't mind."

I didn't, particularly. Pirraghiz was less obliging when I told her about it. "It is very tedious this way," she sniffed. "If these other persons wish to speak the Horch language, why do you not implant them with language modules of their own?"

When I translated that, there was an amused titter all around, though she hadn't sounded to me as though she were joking. But Fennell wasn't amused. "Get the hell on with it, Dannerman," she ordered. "Cut the comedy!"

So I did, as best I could. Trying to translate word for word made the job about twice as tedious, and it was tedious enough already. Still, we finally got that message cleared up. Wrahrrgherfoozh had cut the sub's communications out completely when we took over. That was good, since the Scarecrows stopped receiving data from us, and thus wouldn't know what had happened, but it was also bad because we stopped receiving anything from them at the same time. Nothing was incoming. No talk on the circuits between subs, no data to locate the other subs on the screen. No nothing at all.

But when I asked, Pirraghiz conferred with Wrahrrgherfoozh and reported that, yes, he'd never done it before but he thought he could maybe rejigger the sub's communications systems so that we could receive without transmitting. It wasn't an easy job, but if he could get Mrrranthoghrow to help him, maybe, in a day or two.

Fennell didn't enjoy that news. "Meow's needed elsewhere," she said.

I shrugged. "If you think so. If you want my opinion, I'd say he's needed here. We don't know what the Scarecrows are doing, do we? If Pirraghiz could listen in, we might be able to find out whether they've really bought the idea of an accident, and the sooner the better."

I guess my tone wasn't very deferential, because she gave me a hard look. "I'll take it up with the deputy director," she said. "Get back to work."

So I did, and we had named and more or less described about half the visible gadgets on the sub when Hilda called in to say that it was time for me to go to my next appointment. As I came down the ladder, Pirraghiz and the linguistics team following, Hilda studied me for a minute. "Are you deliberately trying to piss Daisy Fennell off?" she demanded.

I shrugged. "Not deliberately."

"Well, you're doing a good job of it," she said, and then she made a little sound that must have been a chuckle. "On the other hand, I guess it doesn't matter much, since she can't get along without you. Hey, I guess none of us can really, can we, Danno? How does it feel to be the most important man in the world?"

The most important man in the world. It had a nice sound. I pondered over it between pauses for translations at the next stop, which was in a kind of laboratory.

I'd seen the Bureau's forensic lab at the headquarters in Arlington. The one at Camp Smolley was a lot bigger. It was a twenty-four-hour operation, and it was bustling with all kinds of activity. In one room technicians were doing mass spectroscopy, its door closed but the nasty, dentist's-drill sound leaking through as they sputtered ions off samples of Scarecrow metals. In another the chemists had other samples bubbling and fizzing under glass hoods. The place Hilda took us to was a larger room, filled with rows of workbenches. Each of them held its own piece of Scarecrow gimmickry being investigated, with a handful of techs poking and prodding at its innards.

We stopped where Mrrranthoghrow was waiting with two or three techs, one of them wearing the UN blue beret. While Pirraghiz was hugging her long-lost friend in greeting, I got a look at what was on the bench. It was a huge thing, the size of Hilda's mobile box, but it wasn't on wheels, and instead of being refrigerator white, it was iridescently greenish. When Mrranthoghrow finished hugging Pirraghiz he picked up a sheaf of carefully executed drawings and thrust them at me, mewing earnestly.

"This is a part of a transit machine of the Others," Pirraghiz translated. "It comes from the human astronomical orbiter called Starlab and Mrrranthoghrow has made these sketches of its parts, which these people wish to discuss when one more person arrives."

By the time I had translated that, the one more person was arriving, speeding along in her wheelchair with an apologetic expression on her face. It was Rosaleen Artzybachova. "Sorry if I've kept you waiting," she said. "I didn't expect you to be on time, I'm afraid. Hello, Meow."

She was speaking to Mrrranthoghrow, and the surprising part was that he replied with "Hello, Rosaleen" in English. Well, almost in English. It came out, "Uh-woh, Wozzaweeeen," but close enough.

Hilda, of course, was having none of that. "We are seven minutes behind schedule, Dr. Artzybachova," she said crisply. "Please do not delay us any more."

"Of course," Rosaleen said. "Here, Dan." She plucked a couple of the carefully executed drawings out of my hand and pointed to the sketch of a round object with a partly serrated edge. "Ask him if this thing is meant to fit in with this other one—" pointing to another sheet with a detail of something that looked like a clamshell.

And on and on. Well, there's no sense describing every last thing I did around then, because there were many too many things to be done.

See, I was the only one who could talk to Beert or Pirraghiz, and through her to the other Docs. There was a lot of talking to be done, and every bit of it required my participation.

It wasn't much of a stretch for Hilda to call me the most important man in the world. The busiest, anyway. So it isn't really surprising that some really important matters just sort of slipped my mind.

CHAPTER FORTY-FIVE

I don't know if you've ever found yourself in a situation like mine. By that I mean finding yourself back on your home planet when you'd pretty much given up hope of ever seeing it again. And meeting once more the girl of your dreams . . . more or less. And worrying about what your human associates were going to do to your best friend, who happened to be a Horch. And trying to catch up on food, sleep and news, the accumulated news of a world I hadn't seen for many months. And all day long answering questions and asking them—of Pirraghiz and Beert—and always, every minute, hustled from one interrogation place to another with little time to eat and barely enough for sleeping.

The worst part was the constant interruptions. We would go from trying to figure out whether Mrrranthoghrow was talking about magnetism or electricity or something entirely different to an emergency trip to the sub, where Daisy Fennell was having hysterics because the Doc had begun ripping one whole panel out of the sub's wall. By the time we finished convincing her that he was just doing what he was told to do up the chain of communication (Wrahrrgherfoozh, Pirraghiz, me, Fennell) and she finished demanding that he let Bureau mechanics observe and record every move (back down the same chain—four or five times each way), Hilda was already getting calls from the reverse-engineering people to complain that their allotted time was being frittered away. And when we got back to the hunk of Scarecrow transit machine, Mrrranthoghrow was in the middle of trying to explain the way the thing's laserlike weaponry was generated and Rosaleen Artzybachova was begging to be told where the power came from. And while we were trying to deal with that, the head of the UN detachment showed up to protest that some of the semiorganic Scarecrow matériel was making fizzing noises and seemed to be rotting away, and why were we wasting time with hardware when valuable stuff was being lost because they didn't know how to preserve it?

It was pretty hectic. Trust me on that. The only ones who were enjoying it all were the linguists, and they were in heaven. After months of effort, they'd picked up only a few words of Doc; now they had their Rosetta stone, me, and a completely different new language, Horch. Two new languages! Not just "new" in the sense that some newly discovered African hill tribe's language was "new" to, at least, Western linguists, but wholly new in provenance, languages that had developed with no ancestors in common with any language any human being had ever heard before, all the way back to the earliest presentient screeches and grunts. I could almost smell their ecstatic daydreaming about the papers they would someday contribute to the linguistics journals.

I was glad they were having fun. Nobody else was. Definitely I was not, and least happy of all was my friend, Beert. When they brought me in to question him he was belly-down on his army cot, head held dejectedly low.

The way I looked at it, he had a lot to be dejected about. The room he was in was Spartan and not at all private; two wall-mounted cameras followed him wherever he went. Which was never very far, since the cell was only about two meters by three altogether. When we all piled in, there was hardly room to move at all.

"They want me to ask you some questions, Beert," I told him.

His neck had swerved to the two armed guards in UN blue helmets. "Yes, I supposed that they would," he said absently, and then asked, "Those persons with the blue metal on their heads, are they your cousins?"

"Something like that," I said, but that was all the chitchat we were allowed. And before we could get down to business the translators were on my case again for verbatim translations of everything we had said.

When the debriefers' questions began he stayed dejected, but answered civilly enough. It wasn't a very useful interview, though. The first things the debriefers wanted to know about were weaponry, and Beert complained that he had had no experience in that area. "My robot may have more of that data," he said, "but I think not much." And then when I translated that, Hilda cleared her throat.

"Since we don't have one of his robots to ask," she said warningly, "let's go on to some other subject."

I took the hint. When, disappointed, the interrogators switched to questions about other kinds of Horch technology, Beert complained several times that his robot was the one to be asked of such matters, but I simply didn't translate. Technology wasn't a productive area anyway; even when Beert had answers, the terms he used meant nothing to me. Or to the debriefers.

That didn't stop them from asking, though. They were entitled to a full hour, they said. They claimed every minute of it, although the need for sleep was catching up with me and I was yawning long before Hilda announced time was up and hustled me out of the room.

For once the linguists didn't follow. That puzzled me, but when I asked Hilda she said, "You don't need to take them to bed with you, do you?"

"Bed?" I had almost given up on the hope of being allowed to go to bed.

"Bed, Danno," she confirmed. "You'll need your rest. You've got a long day ahead of you tomorrow." Then she added approvingly, "You did good in there, Danno. Just remember: Scarecrow stuff, tell them everything. What you saw and did, tell them everything. The Horch stuff at Arlington, you don't tell them anything about it at all."

"Um," I said, meaning, you've told me all this before and I'm too tired to hear it again. Then I said, "Can't you do better for Beert than that dump? Remember, we owe him—"

"I do remember," she said crossly. "We'll do the best we can. Give it a rest."

I stopped, turned and peered into her one-way glass, which made her recoil a little. "What the hell are you up to now, Danno?" she demanded.

"I'm trying to see if you still have a heart."

"As much as I ever did," she snapped. "Back off, Danno. You have to get over this nasty little curiosity about what I look like inside this box. I can see out, but you can't see in, and that's the way I want it. Now go to bed. You're going to have a full day tomorrow."

When the door closed behind me, I looked around. My room wasn't much better than Beert's, except that it did have a TV set and washstand, and there was a lid on the toilet. I thought about turning on the TV to catch a little news before I went to sleep, but I lay down to think about it, and then I didn't want to get up again. I wondered what Pat was doing just then. Then I wondered what Patrice was doing. Then I wondered what it was that was niggling for attention at the edges of my mind. Then I fell asleep, and when I woke up I had forgotten that there was anything like that at all.

CHAPTER FORTY-SIX

I knew my new life with the Bureau was not going to be any bed of roses. I found out just how tough it was going to be as soon as I was awake. I was eating the breakfast an orderly had delivered—a lot less pleasing than the last human breakfast I had had, with its room-temperature eggs and not-quite-crisp bacon—when my TV screen beeped at me and displayed my schedule for the day:

0700	Reveille
0800–0915	Debriefing, solo
0915–1000	Break and medical
1000–1130	Debriefing with Horch
1130–1430	Lunch
1430–1500	Debriefing, submarine, with Docs
1500–1715	Translation, technical, with Docs
1715–1730	Break and medical
1730–1930	Debriefing, solo
1930–2100	Dinner
2100–2200	Debriefing, submarine, with Docs
2200–2230	Administrative conference
2230	Medical, and retire for night

It looked pretty formidable, apart from that one surprising exception. When Hilda came to hustle me over to *Debriefing, solo* I said gratefully, "I guess you do have a heart, Hilda. Thanks for that long lunch hour."

"Oh, that," she said, turning slightly to see if we were alone. We weren't. She was silent for a moment, then said in a lowered tone, "Yes. Well, I'll explain about that part when we come to it."

That was the Hilda I knew. There was going to be a catch to her generosity. And, of course, there was.

We got through *Debriefing, solo,* with its million questions about Beert's lab and Horch technology in general, and *Break and Medical*—five minutes for me to go to the bathroom, ten more for a couple of medics to peer down my throat and squirt something nasty-tasting into it so I wouldn't lose my voice—and *Debriefing with Horch,* where they asked the same sort of questions of Beert, with me translating. And, of course, wherever we went, our entourage trailed along.

The linguists did their best to stay out of the way, but we now had an additional group keeping us company, mostly United Nations MPs. They didn't wear blue berets like the technicians, they wore blue helmets, and they were everywhere, watching everything, muttering reports into their pocket screens, acting suspicious of everything that was done with the Scarecrow stuff. (Suspicious of the Bureau! How very strange. I couldn't think why.)

But they didn't stay with us when the questioning of Beert was over. Hilda shooed them off. "Agent Dannerman must have his time for relaxation," she said firmly, and they went. As soon as they were out of sight she turned to me. "We're going," she said briefly. "Bring your Horch friend along."

"What—" I started to ask, but didn't bother finishing. Hilda wasn't answering questions just then. I sighed and told Beert to come along, and when he asked what I would have asked, I just shook my head. A couple of Bureau cops were waiting for us, and they led the way to an outside door. A van was waiting for us there; and when it had taken us to the chopper pad, a helicopter was waiting for the van.

Then I guessed.

"We're going to Arlington, aren't we?" I asked Hilda.

And all she said was, "Where else?"

*   *   *

Well, we did get lunch there, such as it was. It amounted to no more than the trademark Bureau sandwiches and coffee for me, and a few scraps of what looked like stewed rhubarb for Beert, all that Pirraghiz had been able to sort out in the time available. We weren't given much time to enjoy it, either.

The Bureau's forensic laboratory was built to do whatever might be needed in any Bureau operation—everything from dissecting a spray bomb full of radionuclides in its containment ovens to analyzing the toxins in an assassin's needle-tipped umbrella or picking apart the linings in a smuggler's suitcase. The place they gave us to eat in smelled of ancient ashes and acids, but nothing was going on there at the moment but our lunch. Nor was much happening in most of the lab chambers we passed on the way in, but when Hilda informed us lunchtime was over and escorted us to a locked wing of the lab, there was plenty. At three or four work stations technicians—all Bureau people, not a single blue UN beret in sight—were delicately prizing apart pieces of the wrecked Scarecrow fighters. At a couple of other benches the objects being examined were the bits and pieces I had stolen from Beert and Pirraghiz—her books, his instruments. Beert snorted sadly as he saw them, but Hilda didn't let us linger. "Keep moving," she ordered. "We're going to see the live ones."

The Bureau wasn't taking any chances with the live ones. The room the fighting machine and the Christmas tree were in was steel-walled. A couple of senior Bureau technicians were waiting for us, gathered around a monitor screen that let them see inside. There a pair of Bureau sharpshooters were covering the machines from separate angles in case either of them made some sudden hostile move. They weren't making any, apart from an occasional twitch.

That made Hilda ask why they were doing that, and when I asked Beert he said somberly, "They are simply running routine systems checks, to be sure everything is functioning in case of need. There is nothing to fear."

She mulled that over for a moment, then sighed. All she said was, "Let's get on with it."

When we were inside the chamber the sharpshooters came to attention. "You have to stay out of our line of fire, Brigadier," one of them warned.

"Yes, yes," she said testily, but she obediently rolled to one corner of the room and let the technicians take over.

They knew what they wanted. Evidently they had studied everything I had said in debriefing about what the Christmas trees were capable of, and one by one they asked to have the machine put through its paces: extend branches down to the tiniest twiglets, display its recording lenses, speak. One of the techs was recording every move while the other gave me orders. Which I passed on to Beert to repeat, until he got tired of that and sulkily told the Christmas tree, "Do as Dan orders." Then it went a little faster . . . but still interminable.

When they had seen everything the Christmas tree could do—at least twice—they turned to the fighting machine. That made the sharpshooters more nervous, but the machine obediently turned, moved and displayed its weaponry for a good twenty minutes. Then the technicians paused, looking at each other. "We'd like to see it fire its weapons," one of them said. "Do you think we could take it out to the range?"

"You damn well could *not*," Hilda barked from her corner. "Neither of these things is leaving this room."

The tech sighed. "All right, but we need to know its effective killing distance, firing rate, all that sort of thing."

But when I asked Beert those questions all I got from him was some violent neck-twisting. "Do not forget, Dan," he said obstinately, "I came late to this world of high technology. I know nothing of weapons."

I wasn't sure I believed him. I didn't want to call my old friend a liar, though, so I simply translated his words with a straight face. The way I looked at it, Beert was entitled to an occasional lie when his conscience didn't want him to tell the truth. After all, he had given me pretty much the same kind of slack when I was in his nest.

When it was time to leave I was surprised to see that we'd had an audience. Marcus Pell was standing outside the cell, watching the machines on the monitor. He gave me a quick look. "I remind you, Agent Dannerman, that none of this is to be spoken of to anyone, especially those UN people. This is a Bureau matter. The only person outside the Bureau who knows anything about it is the President of the United States."

"Yes, sir," I said, a little surprised that he had bothered to take the President into his confidence.

Inside the cell the machines were twitching slightly again, and he jerked a thumb at them. "Do they have to be doing that?"

"Beert says it's just systems checks," I told him, though I knew he had been told that before.

"Well, I don't like it," the deputy director said. "Can't he turn them off?"

When I put the question to Beert it seemed to bother him. He studied my face at close range for a moment before he said glumly, "Yes, Dan, I could do that. Why should I?"

"Because they scare the hell out of some of the people here."

"I do not mind that that is so, Dan. Do you remember that I am alone on this planet? These machines are the only security I have."

"It isn't much, Beert," I told him. "First suspicious move either of them makes, the guards will destroy it."

"Even so," he said flatly, closing the discussion. So I told the deputy director:

"He can't do it."

He didn't believe me. "So what was all that palaver about?" he demanded.

"He was telling me all the reasons he couldn't do it. I didn't understand most of it."

He gave me one of those deputy director looks. "Do you know what I think, Dannerman?" he asked. "I think your pal isn't being entirely frank with us. Maybe he needs a little encouragement."

I didn't like the way his mind was going. "If you're talking about beating the piss out of him, that's against Bureau policy, isn't it?"

"Only against human beings, Dannerman. Nobody ever said anything about space freaks."

It was impossible for me to tell how serious he was. So I reminded him that not only was Beert a good friend to whom we owed a debt, but we knew so little of his anatomy that torture might kill him. He sniffed, meaning I did not know what. "Time's up," he said. "You're needed back at Camp Smolley." And that was all he said.

On the way back we had to wait for the dolly to lift Hilda into the chopper. I took advantage of the moment of privacy to try to get back on the sort of fellowship I owed Beert. I tried to tell him I knew how he must be feeling, but he didn't let me get very far.

"Do you indeed, Dan?" he asked angrily, but then collected himself. "I suppose you do. Do not concern yourself about it. This is my personal worry, not yours."

"What worry do you mean?"

He waved both arms and neck unhappily. "It is simply that I feel I may have made a mistake. I think I will never see my Greatmother again . . . and that may be as well, for I think she would not approve."

CHAPTER FORTY-SEVEN

Between the 1730–1930 *Debriefing, solo* and the 2100–2200 *Debriefing, submarine, with Docs* there was an hour and a half marked for dinner. This time it was real. Hilda not only gave me all that time for a leisurely meal, she let me have it in the little apartment belonging to Pat and Dan M., and she left us alone for it.

It wasn't exactly a home-cooked meal. It seemed they didn't do much cooking, because both of them worked for a living. Dan—*that* Dan—was in charge of Camp Smolley's resident aliens, their Dopey and Mrrranthoghrow; he told me that right now the job mostly amounted to monitoring all the Dopey's contacts to keep him from learning anything about the captured sub and Beert. It wasn't a demanding job. The Dopey's contacts were few; he had been well and truly interrogated long since, and there weren't many questions left to ask him.

Dan M. was waiting for me when I got to the apartment. He offered me a drink, and I took it gladly—it was the first I'd been allowed since I got back. "Pat'll be along in a minute," he told me, as he poured the Canadian and ginger ale—naturally he didn't have to ask what I preferred. As I was holding the copper-mesh babushka out of the way with one hand in order to lift the glass to my lips, he gave me a disapproving look. "Why don't you take that thing off?" he asked. "We aren't going to be talking any military secrets here, are we?"

"Well, Hilda said—" I began, and then reconsidered. Hilda, after all, wasn't there, and the thing certainly was a damned nuisance. I slipped it off and set it down on the floor next to my chair.

"Better?" he asked. "Fine. Now you can look over the menu

and see what you like." He scrolled the screen for me, offering comments. The gazpacho was more or less all right, but they made it with canned tomatoes; the soup of the day, though generally canned, was better. He didn't recommend any of the fish, but the steaks were pretty good. So I studied the menu with care, not so much because I was having trouble making up my mind as because I was feeling a little uneasy. It was the first time the other Dan and I had been alone together.

It didn't seem to be bothering him much—well, he'd had the practice. He freshened my drink without being asked, and politely offered to show me around the apartment. I said no. I could see the workroom and bathroom from where I sat; the kitchen was only a little appendage off the main room, and I had no interest in visiting the bedroom he and Pat shared. I don't mean that I was consumed with jealousy, exactly. I just didn't choose to look at their bed.

While he was placing our orders with the kitchen Pat came in, looking exactly as I expected her to look. "Sorry," she said. "Pell is such a pain in the ass sometimes." She took a quick look at the screen, made her choices and then sat down next to me, explaining what Marcus Pell had done to make her late. It was her job to take the Threat Watch synoptics as they came in from the Observatory and dumb them down enough for Marcus Pell to understand. That was a tricky tightrope for her to walk. If she didn't make them simple enough for him to grasp at the first hearing, he complained she was wasting his time. If she simplified them too much—as tonight—he got suspicious and demanded to know what she was leaving out.

I listened to her story, but not attentively. What was mostly on my mind was less what she was saying than the mere presence of Pat herself beside me. This was the precise Pat I loved, the Pat I had made love to back on the prison planet; this was the exact, specific, identical physical body that I had undressed and explored, and had yearned to do the same to again for all that long time I spent with the Horch.

Of course, so had this other Dan Dannerman with the mustache.

I wondered if he felt any jealousy, with me sitting right there in the room with them. For that matter, I wondered if I did. I definitely felt *something*. When Pat passed me the salt and our fingers touched, I was aware that that was the hand that had caressed me. . . .

And, of course, the same hand that had caressed him as well.

That was a jolting thought. On the other hand, Dan M. was definitely me, wasn't he? And was it possible for me to be jealous of myself?

I didn't know the answer. This whole question of living in a world that contained more than one of me took a lot of getting used to, and I was nowhere near that point.

I don't know what Dan M. made of my absentmindedness, but he surely noticed it. What he said after a moment, kindly, was, "I guess you'd like Patrice to come back, wouldn't you?"

I thought for a moment, then came to a conclusion. I did want her to come back, if only to sort out what, if anything, I felt for the carbon copy of the woman I loved. I said, "Yes."

"She didn't really want to leave, Dan," Pat said reassuringly. "She didn't have any choice about getting back to the Observatory. We're all working for the Bureau now, Patrice, too; she has to keep me posted on Threat Watch so I can pass the data along."

I mulled that over. "Aren't there a couple of you Pats there already?"

She gave me a forgiving smile. "Pat Five has her hands pretty full with the triplets, and it needs both Patrice and P. J. to handle the job at the Observatory, Dan. They work in shifts. There's all the administrative work to do, the stuff I used to hate—signing payroll checks, travel vouchers have to be approved, somebody has to keep the interns in line—especially keep them from flirting with the Bureau spooks these days. And then there's the regular staff, Kip Papathanassiou and Pete Schneyman and all. Some ways, they're the hardest part of the job. Patrice says they keep barging in on her at all hours, all of them, because they're not getting the observing time to keep up with their Cepheid counts or gravitational-lensing studies or whatever. Observing time! They know perfectly well that every big telescope is fully committed on Threat Watch. . . . And then there's Threat Watch itself. Patrice and P. J. have the synoptics to prepare every six hours and send me so I can tell the deputy director what's going on. Now and then, when there's something special, I even get to brief the President." She nodded her head approvingly. "That's the good part of the job. The President isn't a bad guy, for a politician. And he always treats me as though I were a human being— not like Marcus Pell."

I chewed away on my steak, listening. Something had crossed my mind about this Threat Watch thing, but there was something else on my mind that drove it out. "About Patrice," I said when Pat paused for a moment, getting the subject back to what interested me. "You said I hurt her feelings."

"Well, you did. You shouldn't have said she was 'more or less' me, Dan," Pat informed me. "Patrice isn't more or less anybody. She's herself. And also me, of course, but none of us like to be told we're part of a matched set. Even if we are. It's better if we just think of ourselves as family, isn't it? Saves a lot of confusion."

But it didn't. Not for me, anyway. Thinking of us as family didn't make it easier to handle for me, because I had had no experience in that area. I had never had a family to get used to. No siblings, parents long dead, no one to call a relative but Cousin Pat . . . and that was in the days when there was only one Cousin Pat.

The fact was that I didn't have much time to be part of a

family, anyway. I didn't have much time for anything at all. Hilda made sure of that. She came to collect me right on the dot, hurrying me to my last session of the day, this one at the submarine.

I guess the talk had made me a little absentminded. We got through the session at the sub without my noticing anything was wrong—work coming along well, Wrahrrgherfoozh promising the sub's incoming comm systems would be back on line in a day or so—and it wasn't until we were in the final talk session between Hilda and me that I put up my hand to scratch my head and said, "Oh, shit."

Hilda interrupted herself in the middle of telling me that I really had to press Beert and the Docs harder for information to ask, "Now what, Danno?" Then she saw for herself. "Oh, Christ! Where's your damn Faraday shawl?"

I said apologetically, "I guess I forgot to put it back on when I was having dinner. I'm sorry."

"Sorry!"

"Well, hell, Hilda, I didn't do it on purpose. But look, if I really was transmitting data to somebody, I've done it, haven't I? So why don't we just forget about the damn babushka?"

And after a certain amount of chewing me out, she sighed and said, "Oh, what the hell. Maybe we could."

CHAPTER FORTY-EIGHT

Naturally, the deputy director blew a fuse. But in the long run he had to admit that if there was any damage to be done by letting me off wearing the babushka, it was done already. And that was the way my life went. Debriefing, translation, more debriefing, more translation . . . and bed. Apart from the fact that my head was babushkaless now—and that Hilda squeezed twenty minutes in the next day for me to get a haircut and a beard trim—every day the same.

It wasn't all that unlike the days when the Christmas trees were pumping me for everything I knew about the human race.

I did now have better food and a more comfortable bed, and even a little entertainment. There wasn't much variety to the entertainment, though. Every morning I turned on the news channels, and every morning the news was the same. There were stories about plane crashes and stock-market gyrations; there were senators denouncing the opposition party for not responding to the Scarecrow threat vigorously enough, and opposition leaders denouncing those senators for recklessly damaging national unity in this time of crisis. There were sports scores and weather forecasts and about a million other kinds of news items that the media thought worth passing on, but there was not ever a single word of any kind about the captured submarine, the Horch or the unexpected arrival of another Dan Dannerman.

So security was holding. Whatever the faults of the National Bureau of Investigation, it was still outstanding at keeping its secrets buried.

There was something else that wasn't there, and when I had a free moment with Hilda I asked her about it. "Don't they have traffic advisories anymore? I didn't see anything at all about terrorists on the news."

"Oh," she said offhandedly, "those are last year's worries. The nuts've all calmed down, now that they've got something else to worry about. We haven't had a terrorist scare in weeks. Now get a move on, they want us at the submarine."

That stopped me in midthought. "The schedule says we're supposed to be doing solo debriefing," I protested, not liking the sound of a break in the routine.

Hilda wasn't patient. "Let me worry about scheduling, will you, Danno? It's the submarine now. They've got the stuff working."

When we got there Hilda waited outside as I climbed up to the sub's hatch, the linguists trailing as always. As always, the congestion inside the vessel was acute: all three Docs, the linguists, the technicians and me.

But it was worth the crowding. Wrahrrgherfoozh and Mrrranthoghrow had finally finished the job of rebuilding the sub's communications for receiving only—would have had it done a lot faster, Mrrranthoghrow said, sounding aggrieved, if all those Bureau and UN techs hadn't kept getting in the way. Well, I couldn't blame the techs for that. It was their best chance ever to watch people who knew what they were doing in the actual process of repairing a piece of Scarecrow machinery.

The two Docs had done a good job. The display screen was alight again, with all its red dots showing the location of every Scarecrow sub. The pattern wasn't the same as before, as far as I could remember—I hadn't had time for careful scrutiny in the excitement of invading the sub—and Wrahrrgherfoozh confirmed that some of them had changed stations, for what reason he could not say. More important, the two of them had restored the message circuits, so that now we could listen in on communications between the ships. There weren't many of those, though; Wrahrrgherfoozh informed us that crews were discouraged from talking to each other except in emergencies. What did come in were occasional bursts of gibberish which, Wrahrrgherfoozh said, were instrumentation reports that were in a machine code unreadable for any of us, even himself.

"I think they are sensor readings," he said, and explained. "Now and then we would get orders from the scout ship to go to a certain point on the sea bottom, always near a land mass and at shallow depth, and deploy sensors through the forward hatch. Then the sensor readings are automatically transmitted to the scout ship. What do the sensors sense? I do not know that, Dannerman. We simply did as ordered."

That stirred the technicians right up. They demanded to be shown how these "sensors" were extended and controlled, and when Wrahrrgherfoozh had done that they demanded that he extend them. "But not right away," they ordered. "Wait till we get a camera outside so we can see what's happening."

So the techs split up. A couple of them went out for a camera while others handed a portable screen down through the hatch, and all the time they were giving me orders to pass on to Wrahrrgherfoozh about what they wanted him to do, and he was telling them why he couldn't do some of it, and they kept me busy translating back and forth. Then, when camera and screen were in place, it got even worse. The part they most wanted to see was the sensor, but in order to reveal that, Wrahrrgherfoozh had to deploy four or five of the nested handling rods to get them out of the way.

I'd seen it before, but I couldn't help sneaking looks at the screen as the rods moved. They looked a lot like the tentacles of a squid. I wondered what they were intended for—"to handle objects," Wrahrrgherfoozh had said, but what objects were to be handled, he didn't know; that hadn't come up yet in his orders from the scout ship. That didn't stop the techs from asking him all over again—about the handling tentacles, about the sensor that looked a little like Beert's snaky head and mouth—about everything; and trying to keep up with questions and answers and explanations.

Halfway through, Pirraghiz looked at me curiously. "Tell me something, Dannerman. This is very difficult for you. Why do you not do as I have suggested and implant a translation module in some of these others?"

I glanced at the linguists to see if they were about to become annoyed at a little untranslated chatter. It didn't look that way; they were murmuring to each other and letting the recorders handle our talk. I said cautiously, "I've been thinking about that, but the trouble is that I don't have one to implant. Will you ask Wrahrrgherfoozh something for me? Ask him if it would be possible to build one out of whatever materials are available here."

She looked surprised but obediently mewed at Wrahrrgherfoozh. The conversation between the two of them went on for some time before she reported, "He says, yes, he thinks it may be possible, but quite difficult. Certain metals and other substances may not exist at all here, so they would have to be synthesized, or perhaps cannibalized from other pieces of equipment."

Actually, that wasn't any worse than I had expected. "How long does he think it would take?"

"Oh, very long, Dannerman. Some sixteens of days at least. But why do you wish to make it out of local materials?"

Perhaps the lack of sleep was getting to me, but I was having trouble understanding her questions. "What else, then?"

She waggled her beard at me. "You could use the transit machine, of course."

That made no sense. "You mean send to the Horch and ask them to give us a few dozen of the things? Do you really think they would do that?"

"Certainly they would not, Dannerman, but there is no need. I am not sure," she went on meditatively, "if either Wrahrrgherfoozh or Mrrranthoghrow is skilled enough to simply make a copy of the implant without making a copy of you as well, but

that is not necessary. We can simply remove the module from
your head—I can do that quite easily and without harm to you.
Then we put the device in the transit machine and make as many
copies as we like. Then, if you wish, I will put one back on you
so that you can continue to talk to us yourself."

I blinked at her. "Make copies?"

"Of course. You have seen that the transit machines have
made a number of copies of you, have they not? This one can
make copies of the device as well."

That was when the linguists woke up to the fact that there
was a lot that I hadn't been putting into English and demanded
to know what was going on.

I lied to them. I said, knowing it was going to screw up their
recorded comparisons, that she had been telling me at length that
Beert had to, absolutely had to, have better food. And then I told
Pirraghiz that we would have to continue that discussion at some
later time, because right then they wanted us to get on with our
work.

I didn't forget about what she said. I just put it aside to ripen
at the back of my mind, because it definitely sounded like something I would like to do, sometime. Some other time than now.

Rosaleen hadn't been around the
last couple of times I'd been translating Mrrranthoghrow's explanations of his drawings. I had wondered if at last she was following doctor's orders to take a little time off for rest.

She wasn't. Next time I went to the research lab the Docs
were late in arriving, but Rosaleen was there already, sitting
straight and perky in her wheelchair as she studied some fragment
of a Scarecrow gadget under a crystal hood. She looked up and
smiled at me. "Oh," she said when I asked about her absence, "it
is just some personal business of my own. I've been visiting the
Observatory to ask some questions. And oh, yes, Dan, before I

forget, just as I was leaving Patrice gave me something to give you."

To my surprise, she reached up and pulled my head down to plant a kiss on my cheek. It was more grandmotherly than sensual, but I found that I appreciated the thought. "Hum," I said, pleased and a little embarrassed. "Thanks." Then I cleared my throat and got back to the subject. "What kind of questions?" I asked.

She looked a little embarrassed, too. "It is simply a notion of mine. Perhaps it is no more than an old woman's foolishness, but still—" She paused to look around for the Docs. They still weren't in sight. "If you are interested, Dan, since we have a moment, let me show you something."

She spun her chair around and rolled briskly to another workbench. Under a different sort of crystal hood were two objects, one the shape and almost the size of a doughnut, the other looking like a miniature dark brown peppercorn. "The big one," Rosaleen said, "we took from the wreckage of Starlab's matter transporter, the other from a bug. Look here."

She leaned forward and lifted the hood, taking out the bigger gadget. At the same time she rummaged in her pockets and found a magnifying glass, and handed them both to me.

The doughnut was faintly warm, and it made my fingertips tingle. Without the glass it looked faintly spongy, with pits on its surface. Magnified a little, the pits turned out also to be pitted. "It is a fractal object," Rosaleen told me. "Do you know what that is? It means that no matter how much we magnify it, we see the same surface structure repeated, over and over. As far as we can do so, that is."

I hefted it for a moment, then put it back on the bench. I didn't like the feel of the thing. "And you don't know what it's for?"

Rosaleen looked surprised. "Oh, did I not tell you? They are the power source for their Scarecrow machines."

"Like batteries?"

She sighed. "I thought that at first, but Meow—Mrrran-thoghrow—says they are not. Or if they are, they are batteries of a kind which never needs to be recharged. Then I thought they might be receivers for some sort of broadcast power, but that means there would have to be some sort of transmitter some-where. Mrrranthoghrow says—if I understand him—there is not."

"Then what?"

She shook her head moodily. "That is what I have been asking the quantum people at the Observatory. You see, there is this thing called 'vacuum energy,' about which I know little more than the name. When I ask Kit Papathanassiou he tells me that, yes, it is all about us, everywhere, all the time. Virtual particles spring into being and disappear, vast quantities of them. We cannot detect them, but quantum theory says they are there. They are gone almost as soon as they occur—usually—but some scientists think they do not always disappear. They even think that it is such a 'vacuum fluctuation' that caused the Big Bang long ago, and thus created our whole universe."

"I never heard of any of that," I admitted.

"No. I had heard not much more. But when I ask Papathan-assiou he says certainly this vacuum energy exists, the theory is quite complete in this respect, but it cannot be tapped for any useful purpose. He is very positive about that. Yet these little things do tap into something, and I wish I knew what that was."

Thoughtfully she replaced the cover over the objects, then looked up. "Ah, here come our Docs."

So we got started late, but we made up for lost time: questions pouring out of the techs, Pirraghiz struggling valiantly to make sense of the answers from Mrrran-thoghrow and Wrahrrgherfoozh, me translating both ways. I didn't have much time to think about Rosaleen's worries.

But they did stick in my mind, and there was something else that was bothering me, too. When we had finished the session and I saw Hilda's great white box rolling toward us to take me to my next date, I asked Rosaleen about it. "Isn't that sort of, well, low priority?"

"My interest in how the Scarecrows get their power? But it is of great potential, Dan."

I waved a hand at her. "In the future, sure. But right now the Scarecrows are maybe going to kill us all, and shouldn't we be concentrating on doing something about that? I don't just mean you, Rosaleen. It's everybody. They don't seem to be worried."

She looked a touch offended, but then she put her hand on my arm and smiled. "You are right, Dan. Have you ever read the story by Mr. Edgar Allan Poe called 'The Masque of the Red Death'? It is about the time of one of the great old plagues. All over the city people are dying, but in this one place there is a ball and the people there are dancing and drinking and pretending nothing is amiss—although it is only a matter of time before the plague will come to them and they, too, will die. It is denial, Dan. What you cannot face, you deny. Perhaps it is better to do that than simply to dissipate your energies in useless worrying."

"Well," I said obstinately, "I do worry."

And Hilda, rolling up just in time to catch the end of the conversation, said irritably, "You sure as hell do, Danno, and you make me nervous. How about if you quit worrying and get on with your job?"

Well, she was right, too. But that didn't stop me from worrying. The human race was experiencing some sort of reprieve, sure, but I didn't think it could last.

And, of course, it didn't.

CHAPTER FORTY-NINE

Actually, it was that same night that things began to go sour.

When I got through with the 1730–1930 debriefing Hilda was waiting for me as usual, but she didn't hustle me off at once. "Listen, Danno," she said, sounding either embarrassed or annoyed, I couldn't tell which. "Do you think you can take yourself to dinner without me?"

"Well, sure," I said, startled. "Does that mean you trust me to go off on my own?"

"It means I'm a little tired tonight, Danno," she said, sounding irritable. "No argument, just go do it. And listen, I might be going to bed early tonight, so I'll see you in the morning."

I guess I was in my prisoner state of mind again, and any break in the routine made me uneasy. But when I got to their apartment Pat and Dan M. were unsurprised. "Actually," Dan M. said, "she called me a while ago, asked me to escort you to the rest of your dates if she wasn't up to it."

"She's about ready for dialysis again," Pat told me.

It was the first I'd heard of dialysis; Hilda had never said a word. "So she's sick?" I asked, trying to imagine Hilda Morrisey allowing herself to be sick.

Pat looked reproving. "She's always sick, Dan. That Tepp woman did a good job on her. Do you have any idea what she has to go through every night?"

I didn't, so Pat explained it to me while we were waiting for our dinners to arrive. It pretty nearly spoiled my appetite.

I knew that this religious fanatic named Tepp had killed a

Doc and shot Hilda before she offed herself as well. I didn't know quite how shot up Hilda actually was. There wasn't much left of some of her organs—thus the dialysis every couple of weeks—and even less of her whole autonomous metabolism. Every night, Dan said, when she rolled herself into her private little clinic, the medics extracted what was left of her body from the life-support box—as gently as they could, but never without pain. Then they did all the undignified things that had to be done for a body that had lost the skills of doing them for itself. Check the Foley catheter, empty the urine bags. Roll her over for the daily high colonic. Patiently massage every last muscle and tendon, kneading hard to keep them from wasting away entirely. Bathe her. Feed her the extra nutrients that weren't included in her permanent glucose drip. Lift her onto the air-cushion bed that hissed and grumbled at her all night long, but saved her vulnerably fragile skin from bedsores, and, yes, brush her teeth for her, too.

It sounded like a hell of a life.

"But," Dan said, "better than no life at all. At least she can work." Then he grinned at me. Let's talk about something else. Pat, did you tell him the news?"

Pat looked coy. "Oh," she said, "well, it's just that Pat Five is going stir-crazy, stuck in the house with the three babies. She wants to get back to work in the Observatory. So they're setting up a little nursery there—had to kick Pete Schneyman out of his office to make the space, and he's really mad about it, too."

"Yes?" I said, with only moderate interest.

But then she said, "So that means Patrice might have a little free time. She's talking about coming down here again for a visit."

I stopped eating, with a forkful of lukewarm Bureau mashed potatoes on the way to my mouth. "That—would be nice," I said.

Pat was grinning at me. "Just nice? Who do you think she's coming to see, Dan?"

"And listen," Dan M. said sternly, "don't blow it this time. Take my word for it, this is what you want. When a Dan Dannerman and a Pat Adcock get together, it's a match made in Heaven."

Well, I didn't doubt that. I didn't even mind this other me telling me so, either.

I don't mean that there were not some residual male-primate flashes of jealousy still floating around in my head. How could there not be? Jealousy is in the genes. No previous male primate had ever had to deal with this particular sort of situation before. My genes weren't up to the subtleties. They were still loudly complaining that this man had taken this woman away from me, and what was I going to do about it? Settle, for instance, for second best?

It was an unworthy thought. Patrice wasn't second-best anything. I knew that, but my genes weren't sure, and I was too busy refereeing the debate between reason and instinct that was going on in my mind to be very good company at the rest of the meal. And then the news came that took my mind off the pointless interior debate.

Dan M. stretched and yawned, pushed aside the rest of his uneaten soggy apple pie, glanced at his watch and said, "Well, about time to hit the road for your nineteen-thirty, Dan." But as we were standing up there was a call for him on his private screen. He took it in the other room, and when he came back he wasn't cheerful anymore. "Shit," he said. "There's been a leak. Let's see if I can call it up."

Pat said, "What do you mean, a leak?" But he waved her off while he tinkered with the wall screen. It took him only a moment before he got a bare frame with the legend:

National Bureau of Investigation
Excerpt from "Maxwell at Night" program
Recorded at 1850 local time

The legend disappeared and we were looking at the face of the TV newscaster known as Robin Maxwell. I knew who the man was. Everybody in the Bureau did. Maxwell had been on the Bureau's watch list for a long time because he seemed to have contacts in some dubious places.

It looked like he had found himself a new contact now. "The spooks are at it again," he was telling his audience. "You know what they've got at the NBI now? They've squirreled away a Scarecrow submarine and a live Horch, would you believe it? Take a look." The face disappeared and we saw a picture of the sub, with Beert standing on top of it. "They don't want you to know about it, but hey, that's what Maxwell's for, telling you the things the big guys don't want told . . ."

He kept on talking, but there wasn't any point in listening anymore. The thing that mattered had been said, and said on broadcast television which the Scarecrows were no doubt monitoring. So the secret was out.

CHAPTER FIFTY

I never did get to my 1930. All Camp Smolley's schedules were disrupted for sure, because inside of an hour there were a hundred reporters battering at the gates of Camp Smolley, demanding to know everything there was to know about this Scarecrow submarine and actual living Horch that we were hiding from them, and why hadn't they been told about them before?

The reporters didn't get in, of course. They didn't even get any answers. What they got was Daisy Fennell, sent out to face them down and tell them that: a, there was no truth at all to the rumor; b, those alleged pictures were obviously morphed fakes; and c, if any of Maxwell's story had been true, it would be an act of treason to the human race to report it, because the Scarecrows would hear. While inside the camp the deputy director was raging through the hallways, demanding that every living soul in the installation take a PET lie-detector test to find the criminal who had broken security.

Whether any of the reporters believed Fennell, I couldn't guess. The funny thing was that part of what she said was true. The photos Maxwell showed weren't photos, they were morphs, probably made from descriptions he got from someone who had seen Beert and the sub but hadn't taken their pictures. Beert looked more like the hideous cartoon of a Horch the Scarecrows had showed us than his living self, and the alleged photo of the submarine got the handling machinery at its bow all wrong.

It made a nice little no-win situation for the Bureau; they could easily prove Maxwell's pictures were fakes, but only by admitting that the sense of his story was true.

So the media carried Daisy Fennell's denials, but that didn't solve the problem. Wrong as it was in detail, Maxwell's pictures clearly showed what the Scarecrows would instantly recognize as their missing sub.

The question on everybody's mind was: what were they going to do about it?

As far as anybody could tell, nothing. At least, not right away. Pirraghiz reported no special traffic to or among the Scarecrow submarine fleet.

All the same, there was a lot of worrying going on around Camp Smelly. Even Hilda was snappish, and the deputy director was hemorrhaging wrath, blame and worry all over the installation. He had his own way of dealing with worry, and it took the form of starting a one hundred percent interrogation of everybody in sight, thirsty for the blood of the despicable traitor who had broken security. By "interrogation" I don't just mean questioning; he had four PET-scan machines flown in from Arlington for lie-detector tests.

I didn't expect much from that. Position emission tomography is pretty good at sorting out facts from fantasy, because those two files seem to be stored in different parts of the brain, but it takes three or four hours to test a single subject. Marcus had not only the couple hundred people at Camp Smolley to test but all the ones at Hampton Roads as well. The good part of that was that it kept him out of my hair.

And then even Hilda left me alone. When I finished my breakfast it was Dan M. who was waiting for me outside my room. "I'm your new shepherd, Dan," he told me wryly. "Hope that's all right with you. Hilda couldn't put her dialysis off any longer, so she's out of commission for the rest of the day."

"Fine," I said, more or less meaning it. I still wasn't entirely easy in the company of this other myself, but as the day went on it got better. He wasn't just someone to talk to, he was that nearly ideal person for a conversation who was nearly ideal because he had the advantage of thinking exactly the way I did. As we moved from one appointment to another we chatted about what was going on around us, and if nothing new came out of any of the chat, at least it was useful to be able to talk, but then the world obtruded itself on us.

We were just entering the chamber where the techs waited when every screen in the area turned itself on at once, and when we saw what was on all those screens it took our minds right off the planned questions.

The Scarecrows were talking to us again.

CHAPTER FIFTY-ONE

At least the Scarecrows were no longer going to the trouble of faking the face of a human being to deliver their little homilies. The creature displayed on the screen was unquestionably a Dopey. He was squatting comfortably on a gold-colored cushion, his little hands busy in his belly bag. Behind his head was a pretty background landscape, distant hills and fleecy white clouds in a blue, blue and very Earthly sky. All faked, no doubt. The Dopey was doing his best to look amiable and trustworthy, not an easy job for a Dopey. When he spoke his voice had the cajoling quality of a late-night, golden-oldie disk jockey.

"You know who I am," he said, the little cat eyes gleaming, his fan spread in glorious iridescence. "I have spoken to you before, bearing the generous messages of our Beloved Leaders, who know what is best for all of us and whose patience is great—but not without limit."

His plume darkened and his voice became sorrowful. "But you are a willful species," he scolded. "You have betrayed the trust of the Beloved Leaders. You have wickedly stolen a vehicle which is their property. You have begun the construction of armed spacecraft. And you have done even worse. You have brought to your planet a representative of the despicable Horch.

"The Beloved Leaders cannot permit this to go on.

"Therefore they command you to take two steps. Within the next four days you must broadcast an invitation for representatives of the Beloved Leaders to come to your planet. And, as a token of good faith, you must rid yourself of this evil monster, the Horch. Kill him. Do so in a public place. Broadcast his execution. And when he is dead amputate all of his limbs and head. Let it be seen that this is done, so there can be no question of the sort of trickery you have shown yourself capable of." '

He raised himself on his little legs and peered sternly into the camera. "Four days!" he said sternly. "If you have not complied by that time, at that hour you and your entire race will die."

He stood silent for a moment, then sank back on his cushion. The colors of his peacock tail brightened into soft pastels and his tone became wheedling.

"You must understand," he said, "that the Beloved Leaders seek no personal gain from you. It is for your own good—indeed, if you force them to put an end to your lives, even that is for your good, since it will speed your way to the Eschaton.

"The Beloved Leaders know that, in your present primitive state, this is frightening to you, for it is what you call 'death.' But death is only an incident. It will come sooner or later to each of you—the temporary death, which all organisms experience. It is not to be feared. It is only the way which we must all pass, in order to reach that great eternity of the Eschaton.

"Yet the Beloved Leaders do not wish to take this step unless you force them to it. It would be tragic if your entire species went prematurely to the Eschaton. You are a young race. You have not attained full development. You cannot ever achieve that on your own. That can only happen to you under the wise and benevolent guidance of the Beloved Leaders. That generous proposal is still open to you, but you must act now. Destroy that vile Horch. Invite our people to come to you. Accept the great gift that is offered you.

"Remember, four days! And if you have not done as instructed, at the very moment of the end of that time you and all your species will immediately perish."

And the Dopey curled his lipless little mouth into what he might have thought of as a friendly smile, and his image faded from the screen.

*   *   *

Next to me Dan M. was wearing the strangest expression I'd ever seen on his face, part anger, a lot confusion; mostly he looked as though he were either going to laugh or cry. "But, Dan," he complained, "*how?* The Pats guarantee that there's absolutely nothing in orbit that can get here in four days! Do you think he's bluffing?"

I was staring at the blank screen, hardly hearing him. "No," I said, "I think it's worse than that. I think maybe we've been worrying about the wrong thing. I'd better talk to Hilda right away."

CHAPTER FIFTY-TWO

When I got to Hilda's room she was there, all right, but the medics didn't want to let me in. "She was sleeping," the doctor in charge told me. "We woke her up after we saw the message from the Scarecrows. She's watching a replay now, but she doesn't want any visitors while she's undergoing dialysis . . ."

I didn't argue with the man. I just pushed him out of the way. As I opened her door I called, "Hilda? Sorry to break in on you, but—"

And then I stopped, because I saw why Hilda Morrisey didn't want any visitors.

I had never seen Hilda like that before. It was bad enough trying to get used to her white-enameled box. This was worse. She was out of her steel-enamel shell, but she still didn't look anything like the Hilda I used to know. She was lying flat on an airbed, with tubes going into her in a dozen places and a sort of steel corset surrounding her upper body. The thing pulsed rhythmically, because it was doing Hilda's breathing for her. Apart from that, all she was wearing was one of those inadequate hospital shifts, and she looked smaller, older and more defenseless than I had ever imagined her before. The sheet that had been thrown over her didn't hide the fact that there wasn't much left of Hilda Morrisey.

But she spoke right up as soon as she saw me. "It isn't going to be a comet, is it, Danno?" she demanded. "It's something to do with the subs, isn't it?"

She had put her finger right on it; it was what I had picked up on as soon as I heard the Dopey speak.

The fact that Hilda was ahead of me again didn't surprise

me; she often was, which was what made her bearable as a boss. Her voice did surprise me, though. It was the voice of the authentic Hilda Morrisey. I guess most of the toxins must have been dialyzed out of her blood by then. She still looked terrible, but not pathetic anymore. I said, "I think so, yes. But I want to get something settled first." I hesitated, then got to the point. "We aren't going to kill Beert for them, Hilda. No matter what. I won't let that happen, and that's definite."

She gave me a Hilda Morrisey stare. "Are you giving me orders, Danno?"

"I'm telling you that we can't afford to. He can help us figure out just what the Scarecrows are up to. And," I added, "we'll need that robot of his; it has a lot of information Beert doesn't. So get it flown in from Arlington right away, will you?"

She made a face. "Christ. Marcus will have a fit. All right. I'll give that order, and then I'll tell Marcus about it."

I didn't want to let it go at that, so I insisted. "And you'll tell him not to get any ideas about stalling the Scarecrows by wasting Beert in front of the cameras."

She gave me an opaque look. "Not right away, anyway. Now get the hell out of here so they can take all this crap off me."

Then it got crazy.

While Hilda was getting a team together I took a quick run to the sub. There was only one Doc on listening duty, and it was Foozh. He was jabbering at the duty guard as I came through the hatch, and mewed and whined at me twice as fast as soon as he saw me. Of course I couldn't understand a word, but I could hear the meows and growls that were coming from the speaker. Lots of them. They were busy out there, and when Pirraghiz and Mrranthoghrow got there she began translating at once.

The subs were doing something, all right. They weren't traveling very far; they were pausing at discrete points along the various continental shelves, then moving no more than a kilometer or two and pausing again. Pirraghiz said it sounded like they were depositing things on the sea bottom. What things? She had no idea; the orders from the scout ship never said. For what purpose? She didn't know that, either.

But I had no doubt that it was bad news.

An hour later we had a kind of a task force gathered—me and Beert and his Christmas tree, plus eight or nine Bureau specialists. Hilda was there, back in her box, and so was the deputy director; he had taken time out from his witch hunt to bring the robot in person—and also to let me know that this was all my fault, because if I had let him hide Beert away in Arlington, the way he wanted to, nobody would have known he was there.

He was wrong about that, of course—whoever leaked the story would have known about the sub, anyway, with or without Beert. I didn't argue. I spoke to Beert, ignoring everybody else. "Something the Greatmother said has been nagging at me, something about the Others killing off rebellious races by poison gas. Do you remember what it was?"

"Of course, Dan," he said promptly. "It is part of our history. What do you wish to know?"

"What kind of gas? How do they get it to the planet?"

He waggled his neck at me. "It isn't necessary to do that, Dan. On most planets like your own, such poisons are already there in the oceans. They need only to be released."

And when I translated all that, the yelling began. There was no poison gas in the oceans, the experts insisted. There certainly was, Beert said stoutly, because the Greatmother of the Greatmother had said so. All right, snapped the experts, what poison are you talking about?

Naturally, Beert's words meant nothing when he answered. Nor did the robot's, when asked, but the robot had a better way of communicating. It drew pictures for us. A big dot with a little dot near it. A cluster of a dozen big dots, some filled in, some just circles, with six little dots near it.

It was the Bureau's chemical-warfare specialist who figured it out: "They're diagrams of elements! Hydrogen and carbon!" And when the robot said there were four of the second diagram for every one of the first in this poison, the chemist blinked and smote her forehead with her hand and said, "Of course!"

It was the first time I had heard the word "methane."

PART ELEVEN

Methane

All right, I admit it. I should have thought of it before. Call it fatigue, call it too much going on—no, just call it that I screwed up. That's certainly what Hilda told me. It was what the deputy director told me, too, but he didn't waste any time. Two hours later he and Hilda and I, pumped up with the Bureau's wake-up pills, were watching the sun rise on the landing pad, where an oceanologist was tumbling off a VTOL from New Jersey. His name was Samuel Schiel, and he came from the Lamont-Doherty Institute—well, actually he came from his bed, because the deputy director's summons had come in the middle of the night— and he barely had time to catch his breath before Marcus Pell had whisked him into a conference room and the questioning had begun.

Pell didn't even sit down. He stood behind the big chair at the head of the table and turned on the man. "You, what's your name, Schiel? Is this methane thing possible?"

Schiel was unfazed. He took a seat halfway down the long table, next to me, across from Hilda, looking around the room with interest. "Possible?" he repeated ruminatively. "Yes, in principle, Mr. Pell. Methane is a very common compound. It's the first member of the alkane hydrocarbons, a very simple molecule, and there's a great deal of it around in the form of clathrates, at least ten to the fifteenth cubic meters—Pardon? Oh." He moved his lips for a moment, doing arithmetic. "At least ten thousand million million cubic meters of the stuff, that is. Probably more. Much of it's locked up in permafrost in Asia and North America, but there's a tremendous amount on the sea bottoms. If you'd care to look—I asked my staff to transmit a map of the main deposits to me on the plane—"

He did something to the control for the screens at each place. While we were looking at them he investigated the coffee jug at his place, found it was full, poured himself a cup and waited for us to see what he was talking about.

I swallowed when I saw where the main deposits were: some of the biggest along the Atlantic Coast of the Americas, along the Pacific shore of Panama, the Bering Strait—I knew those areas well. "That's exactly where the subs are concentrating," I said.

Pell gave me a shut-up look; he had obviously figured that out for himself. "How come you know all this?" he demanded, looking at Schiel.

Schiel put down his coffee cup. "Why, the methane beds have been investigated quite thoroughly; there was some hope of tapping them as a replacement for petroleum resources. Methane is a very good, clean-burning fuel, but some of the best deposits are a kilometer deep or more, and they're not easy to exploit. Perhaps I should explain their physical nature?"

Pell sighed, reconciling himself to being lectured at by an expert but seeing no way out of it. "Perhaps you goddam should," he grumbled.

Schiel nodded briskly and went on. "The methane content of the clathrates is hydrated," he said. "That means that each methane molecule is surrounded by a sort of cage of water molecules, in the form of ice under pressure. If the temperature rises or the pressure decreases, the clathrate disintegrates. When samples are trawled up from the sea bottom they begin to bubble and sizzle and fall apart even before they reach the surface, often quite explosively. Worse, there is some evidence that any attempt to exploit these resources for fuel may be quite dangerous. You see, under the clathrate beds there are trapped bodies of gaseous methane. When the crust is broken through, the methane gas can escape. In great volume, Mr. Pell. In which case it appears capable of turning the ocean itself into a sort of froth which is no longer dense enough to float a vessel. A Soviet drilling ship which was mysteriously lost many years ago is thought to have sunk when that happened, and there have been conjectures that such events, off the coast of the Carolinas, may have been responsible for some of the alleged disappearances in the so-called Bermuda Triangle." He looked around the room. "Is that what you wanted to know, Mr. Pell?"

The deputy director was frowning at the map. He stabbed at the Carolina coast. "Those submarines," he said. "Could they be used to blow a hole in this clathrate cap thing?"

Schiel shrugged. "I know nothing of the Scarecrow submarines," he said, "but if they could plant some very large mines, yes, I think so. That might not be necessary, though. If they simply disturbed the clathrates sufficiently, they could start a release, which might then sufficiently lower the pressure to cause a greater release, entraining more and more clathrates as they rise to the surface. Once started, it could be a runaway effect, increasing exponentially as long as the methane held out."

Pell thought that over. "That would be a pain in the ass," he said at last, "but it doesn't sound fatal. All right, they can turn some coastal waters into club soda for a while. We might lose some shipping, but so what? It wouldn't destroy the world."

"Oh, Mr. Pell," Schiel said forgivingly, "but it quite well might. Once a large-scale release began—Well, similar events have already happened here on Earth, you know. For example, it is believed that one such might have ended the Ice Age."

The deputy director blinked at him. "What?"

Schiel nodded. "That was twenty-two thousand years ago," he said. "Geologists have determined that there was a huge landslip in the western Mediterranean at that time. That was when the Ice Age was in full force; worldwide ocean levels were the lowest ever, the amount of ice the highest. This caused some sea bottom to be exposed in the Mediterranean basin around Sardinia. There were deposits of icy methane-containing hydrates there, as there are in many shallow seas. When the sea level dropped, the pressure on them fell, as I discussed. They began to release their methane; the methane lubricated the slide; the slide released more methane—we think about half a billion tons altogether, nearly doubling the amount of methane in the atmosphere at the time. And the world warmed up and the Ice Age ended. Methane is dangerous stuff, you see. And that was just one local release. Actually," he said, sounding almost pleased to be able to tell us about it, "there is some evidence that one of the great extinctions of the geologic past took place as the result of a larger event. It was when all the present continents were joined together in one great land mass, called Gondwanaland—"

"Screw Gondwanaland," Pell snarled. "What happened?"

"Why, as you may know, methane is a very powerful greenhouse gas. There would have been wide-scale warming—"

"Warming?" Pell looked almost reassured. "We could stand some warming, couldn't we?"

But Schiel was shaking his head. "We wouldn't live long enough to see it. I don't think I've made clear just how much methane we're talking about, Mr. Pell. Released, it could form a layer of gas thirty meters deep, covering the entire world. Because it is denser than either oxygen or nitrogen, it would tend to concentrate near the surface. We can't breathe methane."

Pell's expression was icy now. "And the Scarecrow subs could make this happen?"

Schiel looked stubborn. "Given the application of enough heat or physical intervention on a wide enough scale, given the likelihood that it could become a self-sustaining reaction—"

"Yes or no, damn it!"

"Well, yes," the scientist said.

* * *

The word hung there for a while. Then the deputy director stirred himself. "Will you excuse us for a moment, Mr. Schiel? If you'll just wait outside . . ."

He drummed his finger until the scientist was gone, taking his coffee with him. "All right," he said then. "What are our options? Hilda?"

She spoke right up. "We only have one immediate option, Marcus. It's out of our hands now. We have to tell the President."

"Negative," he said crisply. "You don't seem to understand. We've screwed up. We're the ones who're supposed to provide intelligence ahead of time, and we didn't do it. I'm not telling the President anything until I can tell him what we can do to fix it! We're going to sit right here until we have a plan." He gave me a look. "You, Dannerman; you know what the subs are like. What's wrong with sending out antisubmarine ships with depth charges to take every one of them out?"

He took me by surprise, and I gave him a knee-jerk response. "No! Those things are full of innocent people! It's the Scarecrows on the scout ship that *make* them run the subs!"

He overrode me. "Screw the innocent freaks! I'm not going to jeopardize the world's safety for a bunch of space weirdos! Hilda! Get me the Combined Chiefs right now, conference call. Wake them up if you have to."

"Hey," I said. "Wait a minute."

Marcus Pell was as tired as I was, and probably even more frazzled. It was not a good time to be getting in his hair. Staring at me in a way that promised no kindness, he took a deep breath before he spoke. "I understand your concern for these animals on the subs. I don't want to hear about it again."

"Then listen to some common sense," I said. "It can't be done. You can't locate the subs except in general terms, from what the board in our sub shows, and there are twenty-five of them. If you're lucky enough to hit one, what do you think the other twenty-four will be doing?"

"Ah," he said. "I see." He thought for a moment. Then, "You successfully invaded one sub. Could we use that transit machine thing to do the same with the others?"

Hilda answered for me. "Same problem, Marcus. There are twenty-five of them. If we were real lucky, we might get two or three before the others fired off their whatever it is they fire. No, Marcus. We can't take them out one at a time. We have to go after the scout ship."

The deputy director suddenly came to life. "Hell, yes!" he cried, excited for the first time. "That could work! A couple of those armed spacecraft are pretty close to ready. We send them off to the scout ship, blow it out of space—"

"Marcus," Hilda said, "when the Scarecrows see those ships coming at them, what do you think they would do?"

"Oh," he said. "Hell. Then we send a commando through that transit machine, same as you did for the sub. Tough men, heavily armed, they come out of that thing shooting. When you strike at the snake's head you don't have to worry about the rest of the animal. Right, Dannerman?"

I hated to pour cold water on him, but I didn't have a choice. "I don't think it would work," I said. "When we hit the one sub we had four Horch fighting machines, and we were only up against two Scarecrow warriors and a couple of Docs—and even so, they put up a hell of a fight. I'd guess there'd be more in the scout ship, and they'd probably be watching the transit machines pretty closely."

"Expecting us to attack?"

"More likely expecting the Horch, but it'd come out to the same thing."

Hilda spoke up then. "There is one alternative," she said. "Instead of sending them a raiding party, what would happen if we send a bomb?"

*   *   *

The deputy director was frowning. "But that leaves all the subs still in place. Wouldn't they just push their buttons and start the methane release?"

He was looking at me. "Maybe not," I said cautiously. "If the scout ship was destroyed, the crews wouldn't be controlled anymore—except for the Dopeys. But we could get Pirraghiz on the horn to talk to them all, and they'd deal with their Dopeys. The others all hate the Scarecrows too, you know."

"So that's it," Hilda said. "We bomb the scout ship."

I found myself instinctively arguing against that one, too. "I don't think so, Hilda. We don't know how big the scout ship is, or how well bulkheaded. And there's a limit to the amount of mass the transit machine can handle at one time. A few hundred kilograms, maybe. And—"

I stopped. Hilda wasn't listening to me. As far as I could tell, her eyes were on the deputy director.

Who was looking at her with a considering expression I hadn't seen before. "You aren't thinking of chemical explosives, are you, Brigadier Morrisey?" he said.

That startled me. "Come on, Hilda," I said, "what're you talking about? Nukes? But they've been outlawed all over the world, ever since some of the terrorists got their hands on a couple."

She said reasonably, "Shut up, Danno." She waited for a moment to see if the deputy director was going to say anything else. When he didn't, she went on. "I've been hearing these rumors for years, Marcus. Latrine gossip. About how some nations have been cheating on the nuclear disarmament treaties, maybe stashed away a few little backpack-sized ones, just in case. Have you heard those stories, too?"

He stared at her tight-faced. Then he sighed. "Shit," he said.

"You don't have any idea how much trouble this is going to make."

"More trouble than being exterminated, Marcus?" she asked politely.

He passed a hand over his face. "All right," he said. "Let me go talk to the President."

CHAPTER FIFTY-FOUR

Things went fast then. I don't know who the President gave orders to, or what the orders were, but by the time I was back in the sub, telling Pirraghiz what she would have to do about talking to the other sub crews, the word came. A special jet from some installation in Amarillo, Texas, would be arriving in two hours with "the matériel that was requisitioned." Nothing more specific than that, but I knew what that matériel was going to be.

While the Docs were left to rerig the sub's comm systems so Pirraghiz would be able to talk to the crews when the time came, Hilda and I went into Beert's room. He was making himself as comfortable as possible on the cot that had never been designed for Horch anatomy. He lifted his head languidly toward me. "Hello, Dan," he said, his voice mournful. "I was sleeping. When I came back here I found myself thinking about our friend, the Wet One whom we sent to try to liberate his people—or, more likely, to his death. Do you suppose they have killed him yet?"

It was a good question. It reminded me, a little guiltily, that I hadn't given the amphibian a thought since we got back to Earth, had never even learned his name. But when I was translating what Beert had said for Hilda, she broke in. "Screw your noble hippopotamus friend, Danno. Tell the Horch what we're going to do."

So I did. "We need your help," I finished. "Also your robot, to operate the transit machine and find the right channels."

He waved his neck around thoughtfully for a moment. "Do I have a choice about helping you?" he asked.

I shrugged. "Do you want one?"

He considered that. Then he said, "Oh, perhaps not. Of all

the things I have done for you that the Greatmother might not approve, I think blowing up a ship of the Others would be about the least. Very well. Let us get the robot, and I will instruct him in what you want done."

The little Scarecrow submarine was more crowded than it had ever been intended to be, and it still stank. I had forgotten about the persistent scorched-fish smell of the sub. For the two surprisingly elderly men from Amarillo, sweating in their white laboratory coats, it was something they had never experienced before. They didn't like it. They muttered to each other as they took the hatch plates off the "requisitioned matériel" and began to set their fuses. There were four of the chrome-plated beachballs, and I only hoped that the stink wasn't making the men careless in their settings.

Marcus Pell insisted on being present, though he stayed by my side, as far away from the nukes as we could get. It wasn't very far, and of course that kind of distance wouldn't have helped a bit if they had accidentally triggered one of the damn things. At the transit machine Beert's Christmas tree was methodically sorting out channels to the scout ship, with Foozh talking to it and Pirraghiz translating. "What are they saying?" Pell demanded. His collar was loose, and he looked nervous.

"The robot says there are evidently five transit machines on the scout ship."

"Hell!" Pell groaned. "We only have four bombs."

I didn't respond to that. If four nukes couldn't do the job, we were out of luck anyway. Beert drifted over, his neck pointed toward the bomb technicians. "Why are those persons so old?" he asked.

I told him, "I've been wondering the same thing. I guess there haven't been any additions to the nuclear weapons staff in a while." Which made the deputy director demand a translation of that, too.

Then the older of the techs stood up. "We're ready. Give us the word when you want to start the operation."

"You're sure these things will still work?" Pell barked.

The man shrugged. "Sure as we can be," he said. "Everything checks optimal. How about you, Deputy Director? Are you sure this machine will get them out of here right away? Because we've got sixty-second timers on them. It'll take about half that to activate the fuse, pop the hatch back and set the first bomb in the machine. If they're still here thirty seconds later, we aren't going to know it."

Pell swallowed and turned inquiringly to me. "Ask that thing," he ordered, pointing to Beert.

There wasn't any point in asking Beert again what he had already told us ten times, so I just observed to him that it was crowded in here, and when he agreed I reported to Pell: "He guarantees it."

The man from Amarillo sighed. He glanced at his partner, then said: "All right. We'll start arming the first device."

In the event, the men from Amarillo didn't take any thirty seconds. I guess they were worried about the time pressure; anyway, they closed up the first beachball pretty quickly and the two of them together rolled it on its little wheeled pallet over to the transit machine. By the time the door was closed and the Doc activated the transmission, less than twenty seconds had passed.

And when the Doc opened the door again, the chamber was empty.

So far, so good. "Reset for the second machine," I ordered the robot. It didn't move. All it did was extend a couple of twiglets questioningly toward Beert.

Who sighed. "You will obey this person," he ordered, and it did. When it reported the setting was complete I told the technicians to ready the second bomb; which went as expeditiously as the first.

But when it came to getting ready for the third, the Christmas tree fiddled for a while, then spoke up. "No additional transit machines are in operation at the target. It appears destruction is complete."

"Thank you," I said absently, thinking. Beert could not have known what I was thinking about, but it was clear that he knew something was going on in my head.

"What is it, Dan?" he asked worriedly, just as Pell ran out of patience: "What the hell, Dannerman? Are we going to send the third bomb or not?"

I gave Pell a shake of the head and turned to Pirraghiz. "Get on the horn to the subs!" I ordered. "Tell them to take their Dopeys into custody!"

And then, as she excitedly began meowing into the microphone, I faced Beert. "Do you want to go home?" I asked.

That shook him up. His head darted to within centimeters of my face, his jaw dropped. "Dan," he whispered pleadingly, "what are you saying?"

I couldn't meet his eyes. "Just answer the question," I said.

His long neck was trembling with excitement. "Go home, Dan? My belly yearns for it! Would you allow this?"

Marcus Pell was turning from Pirraghiz to me, his expression angry. "What's she jabbering about? What's going on?" he demanded.

I ignored Pell, speaking to the Christmas tree. "Can you transmit Djabeertapritch to the machines in the nest of the Eight Plus Threes?" And when it confirmed that it could, I ordered, "Set the machine up for transmission." And then at last I turned to the nearly apoplectic deputy director.

"I just wanted to make absolutely sure," I said apologetically.

"The job's done. The survey ship is destroyed; there's nothing left to transmit to."

He made me repeat it two or three times, alternately blinking at me and at Pirraghiz as she meowed urgently into the ship-to-ship microphone. I jerked a thumb at the two remaining bombs. "Don't you think you should get the hoists back so we can get these things out of here?" I suggested.

That took him by surprise. "Right," he said, as glad as I thought he would be of the excuse to get away from them. And when he was out of the hatch to find the hoist operators, I said, "Good-by, Beert. Don't linger. If he comes back, he'll try to stop you."

Horch don't cry, but Beert's hard little nose was running as he wrapped those reptilian arms around me for a moment, then leaped into the chamber. The men from Amarillo were goggling at what was going on, but they didn't have any authority to prevent it.

I had one other thing to say to Beert. I held the door from closing for a moment, making him dart his head at me inquiringly. "Tell them for me, Beert," I said. "Tell them we will fight the Others in every way we can. We won't let them conquer us. But if we have to, we will fight the Horch as well. Tell them that."

"I will tell them, Dan," he said as I closed the door. And when it opened again the chamber was empty.

PART TWELVE

Victory

By the time Beert was gone the deputy director was already scrambling back down the ladder, shouting my name in a very unfriendly way. I didn't look at him. For that matter, I didn't stop to rejoice, or even take a deep breath; I had more important things to take care of.

First priority was giving Pirraghiz the orders to pass on to the sub crews: "Tell them all to turn off their transit machines and *keep them off.* Make sure they do that! Then," I added as an afterthought, "tell them all to head out to deep water and stay there." I didn't want any of them where somebody could try a depth bomb.

When I was sure she was passing the word on I turned back to the deputy director, interrupting his tirade. "I'm sorry, Marcus," I said, reasonably politely, "but I'm too busy to talk to you now."

That was nowhere near the kind of deference he was used to, and it made him yell even louder. "The hell you say! You've got a lot of explaining to do, Dannerman!"

I sighed, and put it less politely. "Shut the hell up," I ordered.

Amazingly, he did. Or else had a heart attack. He turned a peculiar color and sat down heavily on the nearest flat surface. Whatever he was doing, I let him do it and went back to Pirraghiz. "Have they all done what I said?" I demanded. She raised one of her lesser arms to fend the question off while she was meowing into the microphone and listening to the yowls that came back.

Then at last she turned that great pale face toward me and said, "They are doing it, Dannerman, but not without much trouble and fighting."

"Doing it isn't good enough! Make sure it really gets done, by every last one!"

"Yes, Dannerman," she sighed, and began polling the subs one by one. When it occurred to me to turn around again, Pell wasn't there anymore. He had evidently gone out of the sub again—probably, I thought, to line up a firing squad for me.

At that moment I didn't take much interest in what Pell might be up to. I was tired and cranky and not all that sure in my mind that I had done the right thing by letting Beert go. But it was done. Whatever the consequences might be, I had no way to deflect them.

Of those consequences there turned out to be plenty, though it took me a while to find out what they all were.

The deputy director didn't come back that day, but Lieutenant Colonel Makalanos did. He gave me another of those unfriendly looks, but he didn't say anything. He just sat down, silently watching my every move and occasionally stealing glances at the news screen he had brought with him. I wasn't ready to talk to him, so I did my best to pretend he wasn't there. It wasn't that hard. There was plenty of back-and-forth talk with the subs to keep me busy.

They had followed my orders. Every one of them had turned off its transit machine, and they were all slipping quietly away from the shallow coastal waters. None reported any human attempt to bother them.

It was time to start asking them questions. I did—at length—and the answers came back the same way. After nearly an hour of that I sighed and turned around to face Makalanos. "All right," I said. "I'd better tell you what they say the subs were doing so you can pass it on to the deputy director."

He leaned back and scratched his chin. "I was hoping you might," he said.

I let that go. "The freed crews, the Docs and the warriors,

are all in control now. There was a lot of fighting. In the Sixteen Plus Eight and One—I mean in sub twenty-five—their Dopey tried to activate the methane release manually. They had to kill him. Four or five of the other Dopeys got killed too, but only one warrior died—his Dopey happened to have a weapon at the wrong time, so that was a close one. And," I added, "we were right about the methane, I think, although none of the controlled crews were ever told what was going on and the Dopeys, the ones that survived, aren't talking. Starting a couple of days ago the crews began receiving objects through their transit machines. They were tapered metal cylinders that they'd never seen before, and their orders were to push the things out through the disposal hatch. The crews weren't told what the objects were supposed to do. Dr. Schiel's idea was that they might use incendiaries, or maybe just high explosives, to blow up and release the trapped methane. It looks like he was right. I would guess," I said, striking off on my own, "that the bombs were meant to be triggered from the scout ship, but I don't think they were all in place yet. The sub crews were still busy emplacing the things when we blew the main ship up."

I stopped there. Makalanos was staring at me. "Jesus," he said. "And they're still out there, those live bombs?"

It was a dumb question, but it was one I hadn't thought of. "Shit," I said. "I guess somebody's going to have to pick them up and disarm them before we're through. Anyway, get the word out. The D. D.'s going to want to know all this."

"Oh," he said, gesturing to one of the cameras, "the word's out, all right, though whether anyone is paying attention right now, I don't know. They've got other things on their minds." And he turned his news screen around so I could see what was on it.

CHAPTER FIFTY-SIX

Things weren't going exactly the way I had expected. I had always understood that when you won a war it was a big event, so big that you stopped everything else to celebrate it. *Extensively*, with dancing in the streets, bands playing, maybe a ticker-tape parade down Broadway for the returning heroes with everybody laughing and drinking and hugging the handiest stranger.

There was no trace of any of that. When I looked at the screen what I saw was a free-for-all scramble for loot. The President had had nearly two hundred ambassadors all trying to make urgent diplomatic representations at once—plus every major executive in his own administration, plus Congress, plus every news medium and just about every single individual in the world who happened to know the telephone number of the White House. That was bad news for the deputy director's probable desire to have me shot. He would need the President's permission for that, and the President looked to be a lot too busy to give my personal future much of a thought.

See, that was the other thing that was different about winning this war.

As I understand it, the way it was usually done was that the victors took what they wanted that had formerly belonged to the losers—it was what they called the "spoils of war"—and everybody was happy (well, everybody except the losers).

This time it couldn't work out that way. The victors were everybody in the human race. But there were spoils of war, all right, mostly comprising those twenty-five free-ranging Scarecrow submarines. Each one of those subs was packed with so much priceless Scarecrow technology that every last nation on Earth was demanding to have one for its very own, and there just weren't anywhere near enough of the things to go around.

It was Pirraghiz who shook me loose from the news screen. "Are you all right, Dannerman?" she asked worriedly, touching my forehead with one lesser arm, like any human mother. "You appear to be near clinical exhaustion."

"I'm fine," I said, although it wasn't true. She peered incuriously at the screen, but didn't ask me what was going on and I didn't volunteer. "What's happening with the subs?"

She was looking worried. "The submarines are quite intact, but there is a problem," she said. "The crews no longer have functioning transit machines."

I was too tired to take her meaning right away. "Damn straight they don't! They're going to keep them that way, too."

She gave me one of those six-armed shrugs. "That is the problem," she said. "The crews will be getting hungry."

Well, I couldn't have thought of *everything*. It simply had not occurred to me that the transit machines were what kept the sub crews supplied with food and water. I swore a little bit, and then said reluctantly, "I guess we could make more food for them with the machine here, but maybe we're going to have to let them surrender themselves so we can get it to them."

"Perhaps not, Dannerman," she offered. "Wrranthoghrow says it is possible for the crews to rework the machines so that there can be no incoming, but they can be used to make copies from stored data. Is that all right?"

"If he's sure," I said reluctantly.

She looked at me with reproof. "Of course he is sure. I will tell him to give the order." And all the time she was talking she had begun touching me all over in the way I had become used to while I was recovering in the compound. "You require much more rest," she informed me, motherly and stern. "You cannot continue with this work without sleep indefinitely. Is it now an appropriate time to copy your translation module so that one may be inserted in some of your conspecifics?"

I blinked at her. I hadn't been thinking about that possibility. When she brought it back to my mind it seemed like the best idea I'd ever heard. Sharing the translation work with two or three of the linguists would delight them, and let me get a little time off—not to mention a little time to think about such personal matters as what I wanted to do about Patrice. On the other hand—

On the other hand, I had got pretty used to being the most important man in the world. I temporized. "We'll see about that when we get all this straightened out. How long will it take the crews to rejigger their machines?"

When she told me it seemed a reasonable time, so we began checking the subs, one by one, to make sure they could handle the job. And while we were doing that I felt Colonel Makalanos tap me on the shoulder. "It's Brigadier Morrisey," he said. "She's outside the sub and she wants to talk to you right away."

I thought about telling Hilda what I had told the deputy director. Still, getting out of the sub for a few minutes sounded pretty good to me, and besides, Hilda wasn't the deputy director. She was always thorny and sometimes she was just damned brutal, but she was my friend.

So I climbed the ladder up to the hatch and clambered down the one on the other side, breathing deeply of the cleaner air. Hilda was waiting for me at the foot of the ladder. "Well, Hilda," I said, "what's it going to be? Are you going to discipline me?"

Her box stirred slightly on its wheels. She said, "Not me, no. The President might, though. He wants to see you."

That wasn't good news. I stared at her vision plate that didn't look back. "Have a heart, Hilda! I can't leave here to go traipsing off to the White House."

"Who said White House? The President's got the idea that you're a VIP, Danno. Important enough for him to come to you. Right now his plane should be about touching down on the landing strip. Pop another wake-up pill and get over there. He'll be waiting for you."

CHAPTER FIFTY-SEVEN

The President hadn't tried to bring his big Air Force One to Camp Smolley. He had come in his VTOL, which was still an incongruously big ship to be perched on the camp's little landing strip. It was snow white with the lettering *THE UNITED STATES OF AMERICA* luminously emblazoned on its side.

At the plane's ramp an army of American Marines were guarding the VTOL under the eyes of an army of blue-beret United Nations troops. That was as far as Hilda was going to go. She stood motionless at the foot of the ramp while a couple of Marine officers body-searched me, their hands in all my pockets, their sniffers all over my body, poking into every fold of my clothes. At least they didn't bother with body cavities before they allowed me to enter. "Hurry up," the female colonel ordered me as she led the way to the President's cabin. "The President doesn't have much time."

Apparently he didn't. He didn't keep me waiting. When the colonel shoved me into his office the President was sitting at his desk, looking up from his array of miniscreens to regard me. There was no one else in the room, just the President and me, though I had no doubt there were eyes and recording gadgets in the walls—and maybe even, behind some panel, a Marine sharp-shooter with his weapon aimed at my heart, just in case. When the President had finished looking me over, he said, "Sit down. Talk to me."

So I did.

I had never been alone with the President before. He looked a lot older than his pictures: suntanned face, mop of curly white hair, the powerful shoulders of the Harvard oarsman he had once been. He was a lot better listener than I had expected. He didn't interrupt. He didn't speak at all. A couple of times, when he wasn't quite catching everything I had to say, he cocked one of those bushy white eyebrows at me. Which I interpreted as a request to clarify, so I clarified. When I got to the part about letting Beert go home he didn't start throwing the book at me. He looked, if anything, amused. He didn't speak then, either, or even push any buttons that I saw, but a moment later the office door opened and a pair of good-looking girls in Marine uniform pushed in a dolly with white linen, a silver coffeepot and two cups. "Help yourself, Agent Dannerman," the President said, speaking at last. "So you took it upon yourself to order the Scarecrow subs away from the coast.

There didn't seem to be any point in trying to explain my reasons, so I just said, "Yes, sir."

He nodded. "Maybe that was the smart thing to do. Or," he corrected himself, "the wise thing, anyway. It's not hard to be smart in politics. It's a lot tougher to be wise. Of course, that doesn't solve the long-range problem of what to do with the aliens on board."

"No, sir."

The President sipped his coffee meditatively for a moment, and then he sighed and began to talk. "Ever since you got here, Agent James Daniel Dannerman Number Three," he said, "your friend Marcus Pell has been on my ass. He likes you even less now. He says letting a known enemy of America go free—he's talking about your Horch friend—is something pretty close to, his word, treason."

That made me start to open my mouth, but he gave me the kind of look that made me close it again. "See," he said, "I don't agree with him. I'll tell you what I think. I think you were protecting a friend, and you've way exceeded your authority to do it. Don't say yes or no to that, Dannerman. It's not an accusation.

It's what I might be doing myself, if I were in your shoes, and anyway it's done, so we just have to live with it. But it does make a problem."

He paused long enough to refill his coffee cup, motioning me to do the same to mine. He didn't seem to be in nearly as much of a hurry as I had thought, and then he began to get reminiscent.

don't know if you paid any attention to my election," he said. "Sixty-seven percent of the voters evidently didn't, because they didn't bother to go to the polls at all. I won with fifty-four percent of the thirty-three percent who voted. That wasn't much of a mandate, actually—though that's not what I say to the Congress. I campaigned on two main issues: Stop inflation, stop terrorism. So I'm batting five hundred right about now. I haven't been able to do a thing about the inflation rate, but terrorism is down all over the world. Did I do that? No. It happened on my watch, so I take the credit, but what did it was the Scarecrows. It has now become pretty clear to most people that someday we're all going to find ourselves in a shooting war worse than any we've ever known before, and if we don't hang together, like the fellow says, we're sure to hang separately.

"So, for the first time in the history of the world, the human race is starting to act as though there are more important things than what some part of us wants to do to some other part.

"I'm not talking about the various nations. They've all got their own superpatriots—I won't name any names, but you can probably think of a couple right here—and they're all getting grabby. But we can deal with that, as long as the terrorists don't screw everything up. They aren't doing that, Dannerman. The IRA, the Tamil Tigers, the militants in our own country, the Sons of Palestine, even the Lenni-Lenape Ghost Dancers— they've all been turning in their weapons caches, and even the ones that haven't gone that far are mostly laying low. For that matter, the Floridians are beginning to talk as though they were part of the United States again. I can see it happening myself— do you know that nobody's tried to assassinate me for nearly three months? And it's not just here. Why, a couple of Sundays ago the President of the Russian Republic took his grandchildren for a walk in Gorky Park without a single bodyguard, and nobody roughed them up.

"I like that. It makes my job a lot easier. And I don't want it to stop."

He finished his coffee, looking into space for a moment, as though he were coming to an important decision.

As a matter of fact, he was. "So, two things," he said. "As long as you're exceeding your authority, exceed it one more time. Don't let any of those subs contact any human forces until, and how, I tell you. I don't want them landing anywhere until we've sorted this out a little better. All right?"

I said, "Yes, sir." At that point I would have said, "Yes, sir," to just about anything the man said.

"Good," he said. "The other thing doesn't affect you directly, but I think you ought to know. Today I'm going to push all the chips into the middle of the table. I've asked our UN ambassador to call an emergency session of the General Assembly, and I'm heading up there as soon as I've finished with you. I'm going to admit that to attack the Scarecrow ship we used a few nukes that we'd stashed away—well, I don't have much choice about admitting that. Pell wanted me to claim we'd used only conventional chemical bombs, but the astronomers have already detected gamma radiation from where the Scarecrow ship used to be, so that's that. And I'm going to tell the General Assembly exactly how many nukes we still have, and exactly where they're hidden, and I'm going to invite UN troops to come in to safeguard them. And I'm going to release every last bit of data we have on the Scarecrows and the Horch, including all your translations and all the secret work we've done at the NBI place in Arlington. And I'm going to tell them that, using my powers as President, I am pledging to accept whatever decisions the UN makes as to where the submarines at sea should go, and what should be done with them.

"And then I'm going to come back here and face up to the Congress. God knows what they'll do to me.

"But that's not your problem, is it? So you go back to work, Agent Dannerman Number Three, and—Now what? Is something bothering you?"

I said, "Sort of. I mean yes, definitely. I was hoping to get out of this job pretty soon."

The President looked surprised. He opened his mouth to speak to me, but someone somewhere cleared his throat. So instead the President said testily to the air, "What is it, Hewitt?"

The air sounded apologetic. "It's your appointment with the ambassador, sir. If you want to meet with him before you go to the General Assembly, we're cutting it pretty close."

"We'll cut it a little closer. Call him to say we'll be late." Then, to me, "What did you have in mind?"

So I told him about my hope of fitting some others with language implants, and what Pirraghiz had said about my needing more rest, not to mention my wanting to get on with some of my personal concerns. And then—because he seemed to own the most sympathetic ear I was likely to have for a while—I went on to tell him what some of those personal concerns were, such as Patrice Adcock.

When I ran down he took another meditative sip of coffee, and then he looked up at me and grinned.

"I love solving other people's problems," he said, "because they're always so easy. You've got yourself tangled up in a problem that doesn't exist, Agent Dannerman. I've met your Patrice, you know, briefing me on Threat Watch now and then. Seems like a very nice woman to me. Why do you think she isn't the real one?"

I frowned. "Because she's a copy, naturally."

"Naturally she is," he agreed, "but so are you, aren't you?

And how 'real' do you think you are? Shit, man! Marry the girl, if she'll have you. Only," he said apologetically, "don't count on any long honeymoons, because I've got to say no to making any more translators just now. See, you're all I've got."

I can't say I didn't hear the last part of what he said. It was on a sort of delay circuit, though, shunted aside while I considered what he had said about me and Patrice. As the man said, other people's problems were the easiest to solve, especially when—as he said—the problem didn't exist, but was only something I had put into my own head.

Then I woke up to his last remarks. I said. "What?"

He was patient with me. "The thing is, as long as you're the one and only person who can talk to these, ah, persons from other planets, everybody has to be reasonable. I'll make damn sure this job is made as easy as possible for you, Dannerman, I give you my word. But until further notice, I'm afraid you're stuck. If that's all right with you?" he added, just as though I had a choice.

I said glumly, "I guess."

He grinned and stood up, shaking my hand to show that the interview was over. He didn't let go of it right away, though. He said, "I know what you're thinking, Dannerman. You're saying to yourself, 'Cripes, I just got these guys out of the worst trouble they've ever been in, so doesn't that settle it?' Only it doesn't, Dan. It never does. You solve one problem and another one comes up and starts biting you on the ass before you have a chance to catch your breath. Welcome to the real world, where the only final solutions come when you die. And," he added, dexterously turning me toward the door as he let go of my hand, "if these people are right, maybe not even then."

A multiple Hugo and Nebula Award–winning author, Frederik Pohl has done just about everything one can do in the science fiction field. His most famous work is undoubtedly the novel *Gateway,* which won the Hugo, Nebula, and John W. Campbell Memorial awards for Best SF novel. *Man Plus* won the Nebula Award. His mature work is marked by a serious intellectual agenda and strongly held sociopolitical beliefs, without sacrificing narrative drive. In addition to his successful solo fiction, Pohl has collaborated successfully with a variety of writers, including C. M. Kornbluth and Jack Williamson. The Pohl/Kornbluth collaboration, *The Space Merchants,* is a longtime classic of satiric science fiction. *The Starchild Trilogy* with Williamson is one of the more notable collaborations in the field. Pohl has been a magazine editor in the field since he was very young, piloting *Worlds of If* to three successive Hugos for Best Magazine. He also has edited original-story anthologies, including the early and notable *Star* series of the early 1950s. He has at various times been a literary agent, an editor of lines of science fiction books, and a president of the Science Fiction Writers of America. For a number of years he has been active in the World SF movement. He and his wife, Elizabeth Anne Hull, a prominent academic active in the Science Fiction Research Association, live outside Chicago, Illinois.